HELL FOR THE HOLIDAYS

TALK OF THE TOWN
BOOK 2

RACHAEL OGLE

This one is for anyone with almond parents and toxic families. Simply because they're your blood doesn't mean they're your family. Your REAL family will cherish and love you exactly as you are. Find them.
Found family is still family.

CONTENTS

AUTHOR'S NOTE

Dear Reader,

Please know that when I set out to write *Hell for the Holidays*, I had every intention of it being this fun enemies-to-lovers romcom between a sassy, fat FMC (Augusta) and her best friend's broody—and smoking hot—brother (Graham). Images of all sorts of—spicy—holiday shenanigans played through my mind when I thought about all the trouble two people who hate each other can get into when they're trapped together over the holidays. Especially when there's only one bed.

I will freely admit that I'm a pantser; I can't plot to save my life! While I may have a general idea of how I want a plot to develop when I begin writing any given story, my characters always end up driving the bus. Most of the time, I simply feel as though I'm an historian, capturing the lives of these amazing people who take up space in my brain and heart. So while I wanted to write a fun holiday romp, Augusta and Graham had other plans.

Turns out, they decided to pry open my psyche and drag out every bit of my trauma stemming from growing up in late

1990s/early 2000s diet culture and my parents—whom I love dearly, but at various times in my life have been almond parents—as well as my own self-loathing due to my lifelong struggle with my weight.

Thankfully, my home life has never been anywhere nearly as extreme as the one Augusta endures in this story. I know some people aren't as fortunate.

All of that is to say that while there are moments of levity in *Hell for the Holidays*, there are also serious themes and situations detailed throughout this story that may be triggering for some readers. Please take care of yourself. No book is worth your peace or mental health. Not even mine.

Themes and situations include:

- Death of a parent (historical, off-page)
- External fatphobia
- Toxic family dynamics
- Domestic/sibling violence (not between the MCs)
- Cheating (not between the MCs)
- Pregnancy
- Miscarriage
- Alcoholism

I'm not sure I'll ever get over the joy I feel bringing these characters to life and watching them get their happily ever afters. Augusta holds an even more special place to me because she is who I strive to be. She loves herself exactly as she is and knows her worth. May we all be so fortunate.

Much love,
Rach

CHAPTER ONE

AUGUSTA

This. Cannot. Be. Happening.

I reread Gemma's text to be sure I'm not misunderstanding her words.

> Gemma: I'm in labor, so I can't come get you from the airport. Obviously, Brew can't either. I'm so sorry! And I apologize in advance for who will be there to pick you up. Graham was already headed that way since he's coming up from Atlanta for Christmas. Remember, I'm about to give birth to your goddaughter and I've had to deal with them calling my pregnancy "geriatric" because I'm 35. You can't hate me.

Graham. Graham Hopkins. Gemma's brother. My—. Nope. He's nothing. Not anymore. Never again. No fucking way I can survive the three hours to Loudon with him. Not a fucking chance. Another text comes through and I'm hoping it's Gemma telling me it was all a big joke.

Alas, I'm nowhere near that lucky.

> Graham: I'm guessing you know? I'll be there in twenty. Don't keep me waiting.

Blowing out a breath, I tap out a response as I head toward the exit of the airport.

> Augusta: Yes, I know. I'll be waiting. Don't be an asshole.

There. At least I got the last word. My phone buzzes in my hand and I curse under my breath, already knowing who it'll be.

> Graham: Last I checked, asking someone who is perpetually tardy to be punctual isn't being an asshole. How about don't be ungrateful?

Yep, definitely not going to survive the car ride with him. Not if we're both supposed to arrive alive and unharmed. I take a few deep breaths in an attempt to quell my rage. I am a grown-up. I can do grown-up things. Like, ride in a car for three hours with someone who has the world's largest stick rammed so far up his ass, he probably tastes bark every time he burps. I mean, if Graham even burps. He probably makes his paralegal or assistant do it for him. God knows Graham Hopkins would never do something so undignified as to belch.

Hoisting my pack higher on my shoulder, I tell myself that I'm too pretty for prison and killing my best friend's brother—satisfying as it might be in the moment—is probably bad form.

Surely, this is some sort of punishment for something I did in a past life, right? It's bad enough Creed broke up with me two days before Christmas when he was supposed to visit my family with me. And that was *after* I endured a long weekend with his chain-smoking mother and her jello salad that I'm not sure I'll ever be able to untaste.

Sorry, doll, I just don't think you're the type of person I can see myself sharing the rest of my life journey with.

Life journey? I'm as boho and free-spirited as they come and that was a little out there, even for me. I guess I should've known when he used more essential oils than I do.

Now I get to show up to yet another family Christmas without a partner. I hadn't even been able to tell Mom and David that Creed and I broke up. Hell, I hadn't even told them his name. When I texted to say that I was bringing someone home for the holidays, I offered only the vaguest of details. Now, though, I'll have the distinct pleasure of telling them he's not with me.

Just fucking great.

I've barely made it through the exit doors when I hear my name called and I snap my head to the right, where Graham stands beside his shimmery black Mercedes C-Class. As usual, despite the perpetual scowl he wears whenever he's in my presence, he's hotter than any man who's this big an asshole has a right to be.

That's the thing about Graham Hopkins. He's fucking gorgeous and he knows it; never lets you forget how good-looking he is. Like now. He's dressed in an immaculate three-piece charcoal gray suit—Tom Ford, if I were guessing—that costs more than double my rent. His shirt is a crisp white and he's paired it with a black silk tie and black leather loafers. Italian, if I had to bet. The suit perfectly hugs his stocky six-four frame. With his olive complexion, wavy, dark brown hair, stubbled jaw, and dark-brown eyes, he looks more like some kind of sexy Italian mobster than the successful lawyer he is.

Even though he's completely buttoned up and covered from neck to toes, I know exactly how solid his chest, arms, and thighs feel. I know exactly what the coarse, dark hairs that cover his chest and abdomen look like when they're matted with sweat. I remember with achingly vivid clarity what he looks like all disheveled and sleepy and I—.

Stop torturing yourself, Augusta.

"Took you long enough. I want to get ahead of the weather," he says as he pops the trunk. He glares up at the sky as if daring the forecast to disobey him.

I fight the urge to kick him in the shin as I drop my worn, second-hand North Face pack in beside his fancy Louis Vuitton suitcase. "Well, hello to you, too. You said twenty minutes; it's only been ten. So I'm actually early, Ham."

His jaw clenches. "Don't call me that."

"But it's so much fun," I retort with a scowl of my own.

Rolling his eyes, he gestures to the passenger door. "Can we just go, please?"

"One second. Damn. I just need to get my purse from my pack."

He heaves an inconvenienced sigh before walking around to the driver's door and sliding behind the wheel to start the engine. Blowing out my own annoyed breath, I pull my purse from the top of my bag before closing the trunk and getting in the car. I've barely shut the door when Graham guns the engine and pulls out into traffic. Horns blare from the cars he's cut off in his attempt to flee and I nearly scream with the shock. Fumbling for the seatbelt, I glare at him. "Jesus, Graham. Are you trying to kill us before we even get on the interstate?"

He wordlessly weaves between slower cars and ignores my question, as well as how tightly I'm gripping the "oh shit" handle. "Listen, I'm not super thrilled to be stuck with you, either, but I don't have a fucking death wish."

I don't know what to make of his driving, but it's been five years since I was last in a car with him, so I guess he's more reckless now? Still ignoring my comments, he shifts gears and speeds up even faster as he merges onto the interstate.

Gritting my teeth, I pull out my phone and shoot Gemma a text.

> Augusta: You owe me so big. If I make it home, that is. Pretty sure your brother has no interest in me arriving alive.

When he cuts off a semi truck ten minutes later, after he still hasn't said a word to me, I send her another.

> Augusta: Who gave him his driver's license? Ricky Bobby? That baby better be really, really cute.

And yet again, when I'm sure my life is about to flash before my eyes, I shoot off one more.

> Augusta: I swear, if I survive this, I'm going to kill him.

Trying to distract myself, I turn on the radio, only for him to turn it off when I've finally found a decent holiday station. Glaring at him, I reach for the touch screen again just in time for his phone to ring through the car's bluetooth.

Seeing that it's Gemma's husband, Brewster, I expect him to answer it. Instead, he lifts his hand to his left ear and starts speaking. That's when I realize he must also be wearing an earbud. Hoping he'll be distracted by his conversation with Brewster, I reach for the radio again and he smacks my hand away. My mouth falls open in shock. "What the hell?"

He ignores my outrage and continues talking to Brewster. "I don't know what you're talking about. I'm just doing as I was told; not even *asked*, by the way. I was voluntold that I'd have a passenger with me for three hours, so tell Gemma to cool her jets...I know she's in labor, Brewster. Otherwise, I wouldn't be doing this."

Folding my arms, I look out the window and try to ignore Graham's conversation.

"Jesus, I'm not going that fast. It's a brand new C-Class; I might as well put her through the paces...Ugh, fine. Can't even drive my damn car how I want." Much to my surprise, he actually slows considerably and moves out of the left lane. I glance at him, but his expression is still that same scowl. "Okay. See you in a few hours. Bye."

He reaches up to touch his ear again before glaring at me for a beat. "You ratted me out to Gemma? She doesn't need you bothering her while she's in labor, and I sure as hell don't need her husband up my ass about her being upset."

I'm not sure Brewster would fit up his ass with that giant stick he's got rammed up there.

Narrowing my eyes at him even though he's not looking, my reply comes out a lot calmer than I actually feel. "Well, maybe if you were driving like a human person with some actual sense and not a Nascar wannabe, I wouldn't have had to involve your sister. I'm so happy you have this fancy death machine, but some of us want to arrive at our destination with minimal damage. Regardless of if we actually want to be there or not, intact is preferable to roadkill."

I clamp my mouth shut because I didn't mean to say the last sentence and now I'm pissed at myself for not just keeping my thoughts to myself. I *so* should've taken that edible before I landed in Atlanta. At least I would've been too spaced to notice we were flying down the interstate.

"All you had to do was ask, Gus."

"Don't call me that. My sister calls me that and I hate it. And what part of 'I don't have a death wish' says 'keep attempting to break the land-speed record'?"

"You're so dramatic. I wasn't even going that fast."

"Yeah, well, you're an asshole."

And apparently, I'm a twelve-year-old if that's the best retort I could come up with.

His jaw clenches and his perfect—damn him—nostrils flare with an exhale. "Don't call me Ham and I won't call you Gus; how about that?"

"But asshole, you're okay with?"

"Never claimed I wasn't one."

"It's Christmas, though. You don't have to be a total Scrooge at Christmas. Gemma and Brewster are getting ready to have another baby; doesn't that at least spark a little holiday spirit for you? If this kid's half as cute as Collier, she's going to take over the world."

"Collier had a big head," is his only response.

I scoff. "Damn. You don't even cut babies slack? And you're wrong. Collier's head was perfect, it was his shoulders that were huge. Between the Hopkins and Lincoln genes, it's a wonder Gemma was even able to have him vaginally."

He grimaces. "Don't talk about my sister's ability to give birth or in what manner. I prefer not to be scarred for life, thanks."

I roll my eyes. "It's an entirely natural process, Graham. She's getting ready to do it all over again. I bet Collier is excited, but he's only three, so maybe it's not that big a deal to him. You were five when Gemma was born; were you excited about becoming a big brother?"

"I wasn't informed until a few weeks before she was born, so I didn't have a lot of time to consider the implications of the impending loss of my only-child status or decide how I felt about it."

Finding his wording strange, I frown. "But once she was born, were you cool with it?"

"She cried a lot."

I huff a laugh. "Yeah, babies do that."

His jaw clenches. "If you're still so jazzed about babies, how come you haven't found some schmuck to put a ring on it and help you pop out a few kittens?"

Seriously, such an asshole.

No way I'm discussing babies with this man. No thank you.

"I swear, Graham. You vacillate between talking like a lawyer and a frat boy."

"Comes with the territory. I am a lawyer."

"And a forty-year-old frat boy?"

"Sometimes. You didn't answer the question."

"Neither did you."

He drums his fingers on the steering wheel. "Yeah, it was alright. Gemma was never annoying, so I guess that's good." I reach into my purse to pull out my water bottle and take a long drink. After I recap and tuck it back in my bag, I look out the window.

"So, you're not going to answer my question?" he adds after a beat, his tone more than a little smug.

I fold my arms and give him my full attention. "What, the very insensitive and invasive question about my current relationship and fertility statuses? Just a word of advice, you should never ask a woman or couple when they're going to have kids. It could trigger someone who's infertile or has suffered losses. Not me; but others. I have no problem talking about my desire to have children someday."

Even if I probably never will.

He's quiet for a moment and the slightest bit of pink fills his cheeks, but as he usually does when he's uncomfortable or he wants to avoid emotions, he lobs a snappy one liner. Today is no exception. "Wow, I didn't realize I was going to get a lecture."

He's still afraid to be real. Nice.

"Just spreading knowledge. You never know what someone's going through, so it's best not to assume."

"Pretty sure you should've been a lawyer. We both know you love to argue."

I let out a derisive huff. "Please, and have to wear a stuffy suit every day? No thanks."

"Suits aren't stuffy; they're classy."

I roll my eyes. "You think anything money can buy is classy. I bet since you became a big shot litigator, you haven't bought anything secondhand."

"That's not true. My cufflinks are antiques. I got them at an estate sale."

"I would also bet they're Tiffany or something, aren't they?"

"Cartier, actually."

Shaking my head, I breathe a soft laugh. "You're still proving my point. You don't have anything that doesn't have a label. I bet even your underwear is some high-fashion, uber-expensive brand."

"Ralph Lauren, actually. So, there; not ultra-pricey."

"Just the stuff people can see, right? That's what you spend all your money on?"

"You have a problem with money? Need I remind you, you accepted the ride in my car. I have yet to hear you complain about anything except my driving. And last I checked, you also like eating at nice restaurants and sleeping on high thread count sheets."

"I don't have a problem with money, per se, but people who flash it around like it's their entire personality are just obnoxious. And *last you checked* was a long time ago, so don't pretend you know me anymore."

He smirks, ignoring my pointed comment. "So let me see if I have my insults correct. I'm an asshole, I'm a terrible driver, I'm a label whore, and I'm obnoxious. Did I miss anything?"

"Don't forget Scrooge," I deadpan.

"Oh, right. Scrooge. You've just got me pegged, don't you?"

"You make it pretty easy."

"And yet, I'm not the one deflecting nearly every single question I've been asked."

CHAPTER TWO

GRAHAM

Augusta stiffens slightly when I call her out for her evasiveness. I shouldn't be surprised that she'll ask questions, but never answer them directly. She's been that way ever since she and Gemma first became friends their freshman year of college. Does she even know I know that about her?

I mean, I guess she might now, but oh, well. A long time ago, I thought she might eventually get past doing it with me, but she never did. Not that I've ever been Mister Feelings or anything, but I do typically answer direct questions. I'm pretty sure one of Augusta's superpowers is deflection.

Among other things.

Nope. I will not think about things Augusta Parsons is good at. Not for a single second.

When Gemma called to inform me I'd be bringing Augusta along with me—I wasn't lying, I was *voluntold* by my bossy baby sister—I nearly opted to delay leaving Atlanta for another day simply so I could avoid having to drive her. She's a terrible passenger. She complains and backseat drives and picks the worst radio station. And with our past, being stuck in a car for three hours with her is possibly the worst form of torture anyone could devise for me.

But knowing that aside from Brewster, Augusta is Gemma's favorite person, and since Gemma's producing a human and all, I couldn't tell her no.

One might ask why I would prefer to avoid Augusta. To them, I'd say don't ask questions. Simply trust that I have my reasons. Are they rational? Not in the least. Does that matter? Not in the least. So, because of *reasons*, I'm an asshole to her. At this point, I'm not sure I know how to stop.

As I steal glances at her following her initial reaction to my statement, she does exactly as she always does when she's uncomfortable. It's a whole process at this point and I've seen her do it so many times, I have it memorized. First, she pushes her sandy blonde hair—currently cut in a bob that falls just below her chin and is styled in loose waves—behind her ear. After that, she fiddles with the links in the wristband of her watch—an ancient Timex that she's had for as long as I've known her. Finally, she scrapes her top teeth over that full bottom lip until it pops free. Today, though, she also fidgets with her septum ring.

I've never understood why she doesn't just answer questions. Does she do that with Gemma, too? Surely my sister isn't that oblivious. I take that back; she actually might be. She and Brewster worked together for ten years and were best friends. Everyone on the planet knew they were in love with each other years before either of them actually figured it out. It took them waking up together in Vegas, married to each other, before they realized it. But that's a whole other story.

I would imagine Augusta is more honest with Gemma, though. They've been friends for seventeen years. Surely she's open with her. I decide to go ahead and ask.

"Do you do that to Gemma?"

"Do what?" she asks, annoyance flashing in her big green eyes as she folds her arms over her chest and crosses her legs. Even in this small coupe, it's not a chore for her since her legs aren't super long. She's maybe five-five and what my mom likes to call "voluptuous". I've always just thought of her as *damn*. Read: great tits, ass, hips, and thighs. She's definitely not someone likely to get blown away by a stiff breeze. Yeah, I'll totally admit it; she's hot. Like, break-your-neck-turning-to-watch-her-walk-past-you-because-surely-no-one-is-that-gorgeous hot. Especially because, once upon a time, I knew exactly what all those lush curves looked and felt and tasted like. I knew exactly what she—.

No. Fuck no. Don't even think about it.

Compared to my carefully curated wardrobe of—yes, designer—suits and classically styled pieces, Augusta's style is more edgy-boho. She tends to favor thrifted flowy skirts and jeans, along with tank tops and oversized, chunky sweaters or cardigans. Usually, she wears either an ancient pair of Dr. Martens boots or Chaco sandals, depending on the weather.

Today, though, she wears a dark red, knee-length, cotton dress and dark green tights with a thin, black cardigan and her Docs. Something about her ensemble irks me, because aside from the boots, it doesn't really feel like her, even though she still looks great. As usual, she's barefaced, except for a bit of eyeliner and swipe of mascara.

"Do you evade with Gemma? Answer questions with non-answers? Gotta admit, you're great at it. Most people probably wouldn't even notice."

Again, she fidgets with her watch band before folding her hands in her lap. "I don't know what you're talking about."

I huff a laugh out of my nose. "Yeah, you totally should be a lawyer. Evasiveness is a good quality. And yes, you do know what I'm talking about. Case in point, the question about you getting married or having kids. Instead of actually answering the question, you explained why that type of question is insensitive. I'll admit, I've never thought about that before, so I appreciate you bringing it to my attention. I'll try to remember that in the future. But then, you go on to say how you're an open book and still, you don't answer the question. Like I said, evasive."

She's quiet for a beat before sighing and focusing her attention on the road. "I was seeing someone for a few months. We broke up. He was supposed to come with me and ended things right before we were about to get on the plane in Fort Worth. I thought it was serious. Apparently, I wasn't someone he could see as part of his 'life journey.'"

She puts the last words in air quotes, and I blink. "*Life journey?* What kind of crunchy-granola bullshit is that? And two days before Christmas? That's why you were scrambling for a ride? Because some tool dumped you?"

"Pretty much," she says, still keeping her gaze fixed ahead.

"Did you have to fly back with him?"

"Yeah and to top it off, he offered the flight attendant a palm reading as she was serving drinks and totally got her number while I was sitting right there."

"Damn. And you *chose* to be with him for months? It wasn't, like, some Stockholm syndrome kind of situation?"

"What can I say? I was in love. People do stupid things and overlook red flags when they're in love."

Her words, spoken in a resigned tone with pointed intent, hit their mark somewhere deep down, but I feign dismissiveness. "Pretty sure you were in delusion." Even without seeing her eyes, I know she rolls them. "So, why were you in Fort Worth?"

"Visiting his mother for Christmas."

My mouth falls open in shock. "Let me see if I have all

the facts. You went to visit his mother and did all his family Christmas shit only to have the asshole dump you right before you got on the return flight. As if that weren't bad enough, he then forced you to watch him flirt with a flight attendant the whole time? Sounds to me like he did you a favor."

"I guess."

"That's why you should never spend Christmas with a significant other's family until you've known them for at least two years."

Her head snaps my direction. "Two years? That's ridiculous. Do you not think by two years in, things would be serious enough that there'd at least be an engagement ring, if not a wedding band by then?"

She smacks her forehead as if remembering something. "Silly me. This is *you* we're talking about. Mister No-Strings. Mister Never-Settle-Down. Mister One-Night-Only. Tell me, Graham, aren't those college girls you gravitate toward starting to feel a little young? You have books older than some of them. I mean, can you actually converse with them, or do you have to have a translator?"

I open my mouth to speak, and a bark of bitter laughter works its way up her throat. "Oh, who am I kidding? Of course you don't need a translator. 'Get on your knees' can be understood by any generation. All you have to verify are their ages, right?"

I grip the steering wheel tighter so I don't explode, but this is Augusta. God knows I've never been good at not rising to her jabs at how I've chosen to live my life in the years preceding and following...*that time.*

"At least I'm not caught up in some fantasy about what my life is going to be like. At least I'm not willing to settle for just anyone simply because they feed me some bullshit about love and romance and soulmates just to have a consistent lay and someone to nag me about picking up my dirty socks.

"Let's get something straight. I might enjoy taking a different woman home every night, but there's no question as to why either of us is there. There aren't rosy promises or broken hearts. At least I'm not some sad sack who's dreaming about his glory days with all the college girls he used to bag while he gets his weekly roll in the hay with the wife."

She nods, resigned, and I instantly hate myself for everything that's just come out of my mouth. Not that I'd ever admit it to her.

"Spoken like an emotionally immature man-baby who wouldn't know genuine love or intimacy if it smacked him in the face."

"Says the sappy romantic who thinks that falling in love will fix all her problems and life will be all rainbows and butterflies."

"Better a hopeless romantic than a bitter and lonely cynic," Augusta mutters. She looks out the window, where fat snow flakes have begun to drift down from the smoky-gray sky.

Unable to not have the last word, I reply, my tone carefree, "Trust me, I'm never lonely, Gus."

She sighs, turning her face back toward me, her expression sad. "Just because you're not alone doesn't mean you aren't lonely, Ham."

Well, fuck me.

Not wanting to contemplate her statement, I turn on the radio, hoping if it's on, we won't talk and I'll survive this trip without one or both of us killing each other. Augusta's back straightens when music begins to stream through the speakers. She glances at me, but then returns her gaze out the window. She sings along quietly with "Last Christmas" and drums her fingers on the tops of her thighs.

If I weren't such an asshole, I'd ask her to sing louder. She's got a great voice and I know from gatherings over the many years I've known her, she can also play guitar. If I weren't an asshole, I might ask her what she's been playing lately and if she plays when she goes to her parents' house. But I *am* an asshole, so I don't ask her any of that. I simply keep driving.

By the time we get to Cleveland, the snow has started falling in earnest. My experience as a native Tennesseean—even if I no longer live here—has taught me that the falling white stuff equals chaos and pandemonium. By the time there's about a half-inch on the ground, traffic on the interstate has slowed considerably and I'm just hoping I can get Augusta to her parents' house and that I can get up to Knoxville to be with my own family before it gets much worse.

"Been a long time since we had snow at Christmas," Augusta says after we've made it to Sweetwater, another twenty-five minutes closer to our destination of Loudon.

"Yeah; a few years at least. Of course, it'll probably be gone by Christmas morning."

"That would be a shame. Collier would have so much fun playing in it. It'd be this great core memory for him. That, and the birth of his baby sister, but I think he'd remember the snow more."

"Probably. I'm just hoping we make it without any of the other drivers giving into snow-induced panic. You know people can't drive in this stuff."

"Like Atlanta's any better."

I shake my head. "No, it's definitely not, but I'm not in Atlanta right now; I'm in Tennessee. And most of these Tennessee drivers forget themselves when it snows or gets icy. I predict there will be at least two wrecks before we even get to your parents' house."

"Possibly," she says with finality and returns her gaze to her window, effectively giving me the cold shoulder.

Fine with me. I should probably focus on the road anyway. Judging by the twinge in my gut, I also probably shouldn't have had that drive-thru burger before I picked Augusta up. I always regret them a few hours later, and today is no exception. Damn fast food.

As the snow continues to come down harder, I'm simply praying at this point to make it to Augusta's parents' before I shit my pants. The bubble guts tell me I'm going to be cutting it close since we're still a good half hour out.

Hoping to distract myself, I ask, "Have they sent any updates about Gemma or the baby?"

She doesn't move for a moment, as if contemplating if she'd prefer to pretend she didn't hear me, before pulling her phone out to glance at the screen. "Not yet." A beat later, she makes an almost inaudible pained noise in the back of her throat as she sighs, shoving her phone back into her purse.

"What?"

Looking out the window again, she leans back against the headrest. "Nothing."

Knowing Augusta, I know if she's not feeling like talking, she won't. So I don't even try. Another alarming, stronger cramp low in my abdomen makes me inhale and grit my teeth. Sweat pops on my brow and I blow out a breath. Fifteen minutes.

Her head rolls toward me and she sits up straighter. "What's wrong with you?"

"Nothing."

"Then why are you sweating?" Another cramp grips my stomach and I wince. "Are you sick?"

"No." I tighten my hold on the steering wheel so hard my knuckles turn white.

"What did you eat?"

Surprised, I blink. "What?"

She yanks her purse out of the floor and begins to rummage through it. "What are your symptoms? Do you think it might be a virus or food poisoning or what?"

I shake my head. "Like I said, I'm fine."

"What you are, is a stubborn ass. If I was going to guess, you stopped to get a burger and now you're rethinking all of your life choices." She extends something to me, along with her bottle of water. "Take this."

"You know I don't do those oils and stuff."

"It's not an oil; it's Pepto with gas relief. Try to get ahead of it."

I frown. "Since when to you take anything that's manufactured by evil, corporate Big Pharma?"

"Jesus, Graham, just take the damn meds. I'm not trying to poison you. You're never going to be my favorite person, but murder is a stretch where you're concerned, even for me."

I sigh, holding out my palm. She drops two pink tablets into it and opens her water, wordlessly extending it in my direction. I down the pills and water and pray for superior sphincter control as I hand the bottle back. "How did you know it was a burger?" I ask as I signal to exit the interstate.

"Because you love fast-food burgers, but they don't love you. You always regret eating them. You really should lay off them. That stuff barely qualifies as meat to begin with."

Not wanting to feel touched or any kind of warm emotions about the fact that she knows this about me, I quip, "What are you, my mother now?"

Rolling her eyes, she drains the last of her water. "Hell no. Your mom is a lot nicer than I am." Changing the subject, she asks, "Do you remember how to get to my parents' house?"

"Yeah. I think so. I haven't been there since that time I came to bring you and Gemma home that weekend during college. We had to make a quick stop to grab something there, but I think I remember." I remember a lot of things about that weekend. Mostly about how my little sister's new roommate was *stacked*. I spent almost the entire weekend trying and failing to study because I kept getting distracted by Augusta's ass. But there's no need to dwell on that.

"Great. Then I'll leave you to it." She unlaces her boots. Then, from the compartment of her purse that now seems like more of a tote bag, she pulls out a pair of black flats and slips them on.

"What are you doing? And since when do you carry enough stuff in your purse that you could be mistaken for Mary Poppins?"

"Eyes on the road; this weather's getting really bad." She still doesn't answer my question as she fishes out a small zipper pouch from her bag and begins to apply makeup. This isn't just a touchup of her eyeliner and mascara. She brushes on foundation and completes an entire face of makeup heavier than I've ever seen on her, with the exception of Gemma and Brewster's reception.

I quickly steer my thoughts away from that night. Nope, not thinking about that.

Finishing her look with a swipe of dark red lipstick, she tucks her items back in her bag and retrieves yet another small pouch. She plucks out a set of pearls that has my mouth falling open as she puts on the necklace and earrings. Then she replaces her septum ring with some sort of retainer that looks almost invisible. "I'm sorry, did you get body-snatched or something?"

"Stop looking at me and drive. The turn off is up ahead, and it's getting icy. They haven't salted the roads and there has to be a good three inches on the ground already. The temperature's dropped, and with the sun going down, this road's going to get bad. Don't need you wrecking your precious death trap." Her tone turns snarky at the end as she fusses with her hair in the visor mirror.

"Seriously, why do you look like this?"

"Don't worry about it. I'll be out of your hair in a few minutes."

CHAPTER THREE

AUGUSTA

Graham looks as though he wants to continue to question why I'm dressed and made up like the exact opposite of myself. But thankfully, he doesn't and a moment later, he switches on his blinker for the road leading to my parents' house. As the sports car makes the turn, he hits a patch of black ice and the vehicle fishtails. I close my eyes, gripping the door handle as Graham curses under his breath while he attempts to regain control.

"Like I said, it's getting bad. Watch out for that bend about a half-mile up; it's pretty sharp." Even in the muted light under the blanket of slate-gray clouds, I don't miss the way his jaw clenches. I narrow my eyes. "Fine. I'll just keep my mouth shut and let you run us off this road. Not like I've been driving it for twenty years or anything."

His grip tightens on the wheel. "It's not that."

"Then what?"

"My stomach. I think I'm going to have to borrow your bathroom."

"Oh," is all I can say, most of my ire fading. "Of course."

"I hadn't had a burger in months and thought it wouldn't be

a problem," he supplies as he takes the turn onto the winding gravel drive leading to my parents' house. "Guess I was wrong."

"You should know better."

"What, you never eat or do anything you know you'll regret later simply because you enjoy it in the moment?"

I fold my arms and look out the window. *Not touching that question with a ten-foot pole.* Thankfully, I don't have to answer since the house comes into view a beat later. Anxiety and—yep, that's all—fills me as we draw nearer to the two-story brick house. As usual, Clark Griswald has nothing on my parents in the decorations department.

The entire roof of the house is covered in colorful string lights, as well as the frames of all the windows. The porch, which spans the entire length of the house, has garland and lights wrapped perfectly around every banister and post. The large cedar trees that line the driveway are all decorated to within an inch of their lives with large silver, red, and bright green ornaments. Simple evergreen wreaths with festive red bows hang over every window and a larger, more ornate one adorns the front door.

Graham rolls to a stop, leaning down to peer through the windshield as he puts the car in park. "Wow."

"I know. Pop the trunk?"

He blinks. "Oh. Right." Shutting off the engine, he does exactly that before climbing out of the car. I lift the trunk lid and shove my ancient and comfy Docs inside my bag before pulling it out.

"Come on. You should be able to get in and out without anyone asking a ton of questions."

"Works for me." He mops his brow and I know his stomach must really be killing him if he doesn't have some sort of witty retort about wanting to stick around and watch me be tortured.

Jogging up the porch steps, I ignore the large topiaries

shaped like snowmen that flank the door and, after digging out my keys, I unlock the front door. Graham is right on my heels as I step through it, bracing myself for all the Harvey-Parsons family fun. Not hearing voices or clicking of paws or loud, electronic toys, I breathe a sigh of relief and point to a door just inside the hall on our right. "Bathroom's there."

"Thanks." He practically runs and a second later, the door slams behind him.

Setting my bag down under the console table to the left of the front door, I shuck my purse and lay it on top before taking in the space. It's exactly the same as it was last year. Light blue walls with white trim, medium-warm laminate flooring throughout the space. Area rug under the furniture in the living room. Beige, microfiber sofa and recliner. Older, but serviceable, wooden end tables and entertainment center. Large flatscreen TV. Huge Douglas fir in front of the large picture window in the living room.

As always, the house is clean, but still in dire need of updating to incorporate more modern and energy efficient elements. I've mentioned this to Mom on several occasions, to no avail. And so, all the floors, walls, cabinets, and fixtures are original to the house, along with the appliances. When you walk into this house, you feel like you've stepped right into the late 1980s. But I no longer live here, so I guess I should be content to feel nostalgic when I come home.

Home. Yeah, right.

Walking over to the kitchen bar, I notice some important papers that I already know Mom or David will want me to look at, so I flip the switch to turn on the overhead light, only for it to blow.

Groaning inwardly, I glance at the hall and wonder if I should tell Graham I have to run out to the garage to get a new bulb. Knowing it'll only take me a minute and I really don't want to disturb him, I hurry out the side door and into the garage. It takes me a moment to locate the bulbs since they're never put in the same place twice. Finally, I pull down the box of old-school, warm-white incandescent bulbs and make a mental note to remind Mom and David to switch to LEDs the next time they go to the store.

Walking back into the room, I freeze when I see Graham standing by the front door; especially because he's not alone. My younger sister, Carrie, stands only about a foot away from him. Perfect, taller, thinner, blonder, smilier, everything-er Carrie. Carrie, with the successful job as the executive vice president of her sales firm and a happy, shiny family.

Even if I know the last part is bullshit, she oozes sophisticated perfection.

As is her custom, she's dressed like she's ready to walk a runway at any moment—even in a snowstorm—and her platinum blonde hair hangs to the middle of her back in soft curls. Her black sweater dress clings flawlessly to her size-two frame and goes great with the black, knee-high stiletto boots she wears. Her four-caret Tiffany engagement ring—because really, who needs a band with that honker—sparkles where she has her hand planted on her hip. Remembering what I've chosen to wear, heat climbs up my neck as I suddenly feel frumpy and sloppy.

I hate that coming here makes me question every piece of clothing, hairstyle, and even the words I choose to use. Even knowing this isn't my real life—only my yearly visit to hell—doesn't help during the moment. Thank God I already have my next therapy session booked.

Neither of them see me, but Graham looks as though he's feeling better. I'm about to step forward to tell him goodbye when Carrie says, "When Gus said she was bringing a boyfriend, I expected it to be some sort of loser, since that's typically the type she goes for. You definitely don't look like a loser. Is that your C-Class outside? What am I saying; of course it's yours. Gus would never own anything like that, even if she could afford it."

She tilts her head and even though I can't see her face, I can picture the snide smirk on it. She lowers her voice, but I still hear her. "Blink twice if this is some sort of joke. No way my *big* sister could ever pull someone like you. Did she bribe you to come so my parents wouldn't think she's a total loser?"

To his credit, Graham blanches with her words and I slump against the wall, mortification washing over me. The last person on the entire planet I want witnessing this is *him*. But I guess I won't even be spared *this* humiliation. After closing my eyes and giving myself a mental five count, I blink back my tears of embarrassment and stiffen my spine, pasting a smile on my face. When I stand up straight again, Graham's gaze is on me. My heart lurches, my mouth going dry as my anxiety spikes.

"There you are," he says, his tone affectionate, a warm smile aimed at me. My steps falter for a beat in my surprise— hell, I hadn't even realized I'd begun walking toward them. I'm even more shocked when he steps around my sister and comes to stand beside me, his expression still friendly.

"Oh, uh, yeah. Sorry. Had to go get a lightbulb from the garage."

Carrie spins around, her own smile is big and wide. And totally fake. "Gus, there you are. So glad you made it in before the weather got bad. Mom and Daddy are down in the woods with the kids and Mason. I was just getting acquainted with your...*friend*." She closes the distance between us and wraps her birdlike arms around my shoulders for a quick hug. I swallow back the bile that rises up my throat knowing how much of a monster my sister is.

"Well, he was just—."

"I was just going back out to the car to get my bag," Graham cuts in. "Too much coffee before we hit the road and with the weather, I didn't want to stop. Babe, did you get all your stuff out of the trunk?" He stares down at me, his expression still warm. His brows tick up, and I'm not sure anyone would notice if they weren't as familiar with his face as I am. "Or, do you want to come make sure so you don't have to go back out later?"

I swallow around the lump in my throat, honestly terrified of what might happen if I follow him out to the car. Maybe he's going to feign some sort of emergency and he'll have an easy out. Surely that's got to be it. He's feeling sorry for me after what Carrie said and, for some reason, feels compelled to help me save face. Clearing my throat, I nod. "Yeah, I should probably do one more check."

He smiles, mirroring my nod, before taking my hand in his. "Okay." I let him practically drag me out the front door and down the steps as I shiver almost immediately with the cold. I say his name and he shushes me.

"Don't shush me," I hiss.

In an almost identical tone and volume, he whispers over his shoulder, "Not yet. Shut up."

He pulls the key fob from his pocket and clicks open the trunk before tugging me behind the car so we're out of sight of the window I'm sure Carrie is spying through. I yank my hand from his. "What the hell was that? 'Getting my bags?' What are you thinking, Graham? If this is some sort of ploy to wait until the worst possible moment to humiliate me, I'll have to pass. It's bad enough she truly thinks the only way I could get a guy like you is if I bribed you."

He lifts his suitcase out of the trunk, carelessly dropping it on the ground as whips his head in my direction. "Do you honestly believe I'd humiliate you like that?" He looks almost pained, and I take an involuntary step back in surprise. Big, fat snowflakes continue to fall and several land in his hair and on his still-pristine suit.

I quickly shake my head. "No. Not on purpose."

He closes the distance between us and reaches to take my hand, but thinks better of it, dragging it through his hair to dislodge the snow. "I will freely admit I'm an asshole. Especially to you. But only because you can give it back to me. I'd like to think I'm not needlessly or purposely cruel, though. And hearing your sister talk about you like you *couldn't* get a guy like me unless something was in it for him? If she were a man, I would've knocked her fucking teeth out, Augusta. Is she always like that to you?"

I swallow thickly, my cheeks heating with embarrassment. Honestly, what do I have to lose by telling him the truth? "Our whole lives. At least, when it's just us. Of course, when our parents are around, she's still condescending, but mostly harmless."

He nods. "Well, that explains why you don't look like you."

I frown. "What do you mean?"

He scoffs. "What do you mean, *what do I mean*? You're wearing dressy flats and a shit ton of makeup and fucking pearls. You even took out your septum ring. None of this is you." He blows out a breath. "Listen, I know I'm not your favorite person, but in all honesty, I don't know if my car will make it back out to the road. In just the twenty minutes we've been here, it's already snowed at least another inch. And part of me really wants to show up your sister. It's not like we don't know each other, so it would be easy to pretend and be convincing. When the weather clears, I'll do something publicly douchey so you can break up with me and I'll leave."

"You want to be my *pretend* boyfriend?" I sputter, folding my arms even as my teeth begin to chatter. "I don't need your pity, Graham. I've survived every Christmas up to this point and I'll survive this one, too. I don't need you to do me any favors. You can stay because of the weather, but you don't have to put on a show to do it."

"So you're just fine with your sister saying all that stuff about you? You have no desire to make her eat her words? I can't believe that; not coming from you."

"I'm just here to put in face time and get out. I don't need you for that." I blow into my hands to generate warmth.

Graham rolls his eyes and pinches the bridge of his nose. In annoyance or frustration, I can't tell. "Augusta, there's no ploy, and it's not a favor. I sincerely want to annihilate your sister. I throw down with people twice as bad as her on a daily basis. No one gets to treat you like garbage when I'm around."

"No one except you, right?" I retort.

He squares his shoulders. "I've never talked down to you like that, nor would I, and you know it. Giving you endless amounts of shit is different than treating you like shit. Like I said, I'm an asshole, but I'm *your* asshole. No one else can talk to you like that because I know when I do it, you're not afraid to call me out on it and give it right back to me. It's what we do. The minute you stop standing up to me, we're going to have major issues. I'm not sure why you can't call your sister out the same way you do me, but I want to help you put her in her place."

I'm your *asshole.*

His words hit a soft place I don't want to feel because it feels too much like a Graham who's not this Graham and THAT Graham is dangerous for me.

"It's a bad idea. We fight all the time."

"We're just passionate, babe," he says with a wink. After a beat, he rubs his hands together. "I promise that after this, you won't have to talk to me again until one of the family get togethers or the kids' parties or something. We can pretend it never happened and go back to antagonizing each other."

He shivers. "Can we at least discuss this further in the house where I won't be likely to freeze off my dick? I'm sure you'd love to see it lying on the ground all shriveled and frostbitten, but I'd like to keep it around."

I sigh, and even though I'll probably regret it, I nod. "Just until the weather clears."

"Deal." I turn to go back in the house and he grabs my hand, yanking me into his chest. He wraps his arms around me and I nearly gasp when his warm breath ghosts over my ear and down the side of my neck.

"You and I both know exactly how easy it is for you to get a guy like me. And not just a guy like me. *Me.* Your sister could never; not even with guys *like* me. Her kind of ugly shows straight through." He rests his forehead against my temple and I should pull away because alarm bells are clanging somewhere dangerously close to my heart. "I know you hate me, but I promise not to let you down this time."

I do step back then, tears burning my eyes. "Don't do that. I'll do this, but when we're alone, we're still us. Don't be nice to me, Graham. I don't know what to do with it."

Sighing, he nods, picking up his bag as he shuts the trunk. "You've got it."

CHAPTER FOUR

GRAHAM

Fuck. Fucking fuckers who fuck. Guess I figured out how to stop being an asshole to Augusta, huh? Find one who's an even bigger asshole to her than me and take them down. Except Carrie isn't just an asshole, she's cruel and petty. I don't understand it at all or why Augusta would let her talk about her like that. She would punch me in the face if I ever said half of what Carrie did. Not that I ever would. Jesus.

I'm not sure I even have a heart anymore, but seeing the resigned acceptance on Augusta's face when I caught sight of her over her sister's shoulder nearly made me keel over in both rage and sadness. To watch that sassy indignation she's always had just fall away, only to be replaced by a meek shell of herself? I won't stand for it.

And no, I can't guarantee I'm being rational. In fact, I can about guaran-damn-tee I'm not. She's right. This is probably a terrible idea. But I also don't have anywhere to go, so I might as well roll with it, right?

I don't reach for her hand again as we return to the house and when we walk in the door, the atmosphere is a lot louder than when we left. But after I shut the door behind me, you can almost hear a pin drop. Not even the kids, whose toys are still making an awful racket, are speaking. Everyone is looking from Augusta to me and back to her and then me again. It's like something out of a fucking tennis match.

I step up behind Augusta, putting my hand on the small of her back as I lean in. "So, I'm guessing this is a big deal?"

She instantly straightens her spine. "I told you guys I was bringing a guy for Christmas. Look, he's real and everything." I can tell she's trying to keep her tone light, but there's an edge of that resignation again and I want to tell her she's coming home with me. Because even as her family all stand around completely gobsmacked, this is never a reaction my family would have and Augusta knows it.

Her mother seems to snap out of her trance first and walks over to shake my hand. She's taller than Augusta and rail thin like Carrie, but her hair is darker than both her daughters' and swept back in a sleek updo. She's dressed in slim black slacks and a forest green sweater to which she's pinned a festive Santa brooch high on the right side of her chest. Augusta looks almost nothing like her mother, save the green eyes.

I know her father is actually her stepfather, so I rack my brain trying to remember what her last name is. As if sensing my dilemma, Augusta intervenes. "Mom, this is Graham Hopkins. Graham, this is my mother, April Harvey."

"Mrs. Harvey, it's great to finally meet you. Augusta has told me a lot about all of you. Thank you so much for having me in your home."

She shakes my hand limply, her eyes taking in my entire form as she nods. "You as well, Graham. I just wish we'd heard more about you over these past few months. But please, make yourself at home while you're here." She steps over to Augusta to give her a brief hug and perfunctory kiss on the cheek before backing away. "Well, I won't keep you; I'm going to get started on supper."

"Yes, ma'am."

"Guess we better make the rounds," Augusta mutters under her breath once her mom is out of earshot. I gesture for her to lead the way and set my bag down next to hers before joining her in the living room.

A white man in his early seventies dressed in khakis and a navy sweater sits in a recliner but stands as we approach. He, too, is tall—probably around six feet—and slim with thinning salt-and-pepper hair. "This is David Harvey, my stepfather. David, this is Graham."

The older man extends his hand and I grip it firmly. "Mr. Harvey, so nice to meet you."

He nods and smiles, and for the first time since I arrived, it feels warm compared to Carrie and April's greetings. "Good to have you here, Graham. I hope you're being good to our Augusta. She's one of the rare ones."

Augusta makes a dismissive noise in the back of her throat, but I ignore her. "No worries, sir. She's perfectly capable of putting me in my place when I get out of line."

He chuckles. "I like to hear that. Like April said, make yourself at home." Glancing out the window, he winces. "I hope y'all aren't trying to make a break for it anytime soon. Especially in that little thing you've got out there. According to the forecast, we're really in for it this year. You may get to know us better than you'd like. Your folks expecting you and Augusta in the next few days?"

"I'm sure they'll be understanding if we're unable to put in an appearance. They'll have their hands full with my sister's new baby anyway, so I'm not worried."

"Well, stay as long as you like. If we run out of food, we can always eat the dog."

"Grandpa!", a very blonde little girl who appears to be about eight, scolds David.

He waves her off and points to a huge golden retriever mix I hadn't noticed when we came in. "Look at that lump over there. You think there'd actually be any usable meat on him? He's all fur and fat. Butterball is safe, Amelia."

Augusta gestures to the kids on the floor. "That's Amelia, she's nine. Wade is six and Wesley is four."

I wave to all of them before turning to the sofa where Carrie sits with a man in his mid-to-late thirties. He has blonde hair the color of straw and the start of a beer belly. He's dressed casually in a pair of dark jeans, a flannel shirt, a puffy vest, and thick socks. He hauls himself off the couch and as he pulls himself to his full height, I feel a bit of satisfaction knowing he's at least half a foot shorter than me and aside from the paunch, is as slim as the rest of the people in this family.

What the hell? These people don't eat?

"Graham, this is Mason. Mason, Graham."

"Good to meet you," I say and shake his hand.

"You, too. That your C-Class out there?"

I nod. "Sure is. Got her about six months ago."

"Damn. She's beautiful. What do you do to afford something like that?"

"I'm an attorney. Tort law, specifically."

He blinks. "Like, class-action suits?"

"Usually. Some pro bono family law, too, since that's where I started."

"Damn. Is it true the lawyers take a big cut on those class-action suits?"

"Yes, but our clients get theirs too. And if it doesn't pan out, we don't get anything, so we take the gamble. What do you do? I can't remember if Augusta mentioned it."

"I'm a stay-at-home dad, actually. Carrie brings home all the bacon and I fry it up," he says good-naturedly.

"That's great you get to devote so much time to your family." I gesture to the TV, where *Miracle on 34th Street* is playing. "Well, we'll let you guys get back to your movie. I think I'd like to freshen up before supper."

"Sure." He turns his gaze to Augusta. "I hope you don't mind, but we stuck some things in your closet. We ran out of room."

Her nostrils flare, but it's almost imperceptible. If I didn't know her as well as I do, I would've missed it. "No problem. Thanks for the heads up."

We fetch our bags from beside the door and I follow Augusta up a set of stairs with worn, clean carpet. The entire house is spotless, if a bit rundown and in need of some updates. As Augusta leads me down a hallway lined with family photos, I stop to look. I spot several from April and David's wedding, along with many of a very blonde baby and toddler that I know must be Carrie, since her eyes are bright blue. Family photos with April, David, and Carrie. Carrie and Mason's family photos through the years. Several of both Augusta and Carrie throughout their school years, as well as photos of the family of four in later years. What I don't see are any of Augusta when she was any younger than about six years old.

"Graham, we're in here." I blink, still frowning at the wall of photos when I catch up with Augusta in what I assume is her room. She shuts the door behind me and slumps against it as she closes her eyes. "No judgement that I still have my Green Day and Dropkick Murphys posters up. I don't come here enough that it matters what's on the walls."

Taking in the room, I'm surprised to see that the walls are a dark gray and while the same carpet that's on the stairs and in the hall is in here, there's a deep red rug under the black metal, queen-size bed. It's flanked by black nightstands topped with lamps, and a matching black dresser with a mirror sits on a far wall next to the closet. Between the two windows stands a bookshelf with only a few poetry books and some small framed photos. A red upholstered chair sits in the corner next to one window. The bedding is a lighter gray with red and black decorative pillows. Although if you changed some elements, it would feel very masculine, it only feels like Augusta to me.

"Can't argue with good music. You'll hear no complaints from me. To be honest, I would've expected more System of a Down or Rage Against the Machine."

"That was college. I listened to my Rage albums so much I thought Gem would string me up by my toes. She hates that kind of stuff."

"Yeah, she's always been a bit more pop." I dig my phone out. "Speaking of Gemma, we should probably check in with them. I need to let Mom and Dad know I won't make it in for Christmas."

Augusta stands up straighter, opening her eyes. "I'm really sorry, Graham. I'm sure you had a lot better plans for your holiday than this."

I can't get over how defeated she appears to be and I instantly hate this place and what it seems to reduce her to. I'm guessing her sister is a huge reason she's obviously miserable here, but what I don't get is why her parents seem oblivious to her misery.

"I told you, I'm fine. Nothing I love more than a good old-fashioned takedown. Your brother-in-law seems really nice. Why is he with your sister?"

"Because she can bend him to her will," she says matter-of-factly. "She cheats on him at least a few times a year and he looks the other way."

I blink, shocked at what she's saying. "What? Why?"

She sighs. "Because Carrie would take the kids. Even though she doesn't care about them, she'd take them just to spite him. He's a good dad and seems to be a decent guy. Carrie is all about appearances. What looks better than a devoted husband and beautiful kids? In public, they're all apple pie and picket fences."

I shake my head as I look down at my phone. Opening a message from Brewster, I can't help but smile. "Looks like there's a baby. Eight pounds, six ounces, headful of dark hair. Julie Augusta Lincoln."

Augusta drops her bag, her head snapping up. "What?" Her voice comes out thin and breathy as she blinks back tears, a soft smile on her face.

"You didn't know they were going to name her after you?"

She shakes her head. "No. I didn't know at all. They were keeping her name under wraps."

"Well, it's official; you have a namesake. Congrats. That oughta make your Christmas."

She nods. "It does. You've got a pretty good sister."

"She's alright." A thought hits me. "Does your family not know Gemma? They didn't react to my last name. Like, at all."

"No. She's been here once, maybe. It was our freshman year of college and we were on our way home from school for spring break. My car was acting up, so I put it in the shop before we left. Since it was on her way, she offered to drop me at home.

"Since it was so late when we finally got into town, I convinced her to just spend the night. Carrie had some friends over from high school and because your sister is amazing and fun, Carrie's friends gravitated to her and asked her—and by extension, me—to hang out. They pumped us for information about college guys and frat parties and all that stuff. I thought we had a good time"

Her jaw clenches. "I was wrong. After that, I stayed on campus unless I couldn't. And during summers, I worked a lot and if you recall, crashed at your parents' a lot simply to avoid being here."

I think back. "Wasn't that the year you shaved your head?"

She sighs. "No, that was the year that Carrie put Nair in my shampoo and conditioner after her friends left and most of my hair fell out by the time I got back to campus. I had no choice but to buzz it off."

My mouth falls open. "She did what?"

"It was a long time ago. I always make sure to guard my toiletries now."

"Why haven't you beat the shit out of her? Is that the only time she's ever assaulted you?"

She sighs again. "I don't want to talk about this. I'm fine. I have to pee. The bathroom is across the hall; I'll be back in a minute."

I want to object and be outraged on her behalf for what happened to her, but if she doesn't want to talk about it, what can I do? Blowing out a breath, I call my parents to let them know what's going on and although they're bummed, they get it. I also respond to Brewster's text with a quick "congratulations" as I pull a pair of jeans from my bag, along with a long-sleeved henley and casual socks.

Slipping off my loafers, I tuck them inside their designated bag in my suitcase. Then, I go through the routine of pulling off my belt, emptying my pockets, and taking off my cufflinks to stash in their case. Not wanting my suit to be super wrinkled by the time I leave, I walk across the room to the closet. When I open the door, I'm filled with indignation. The entire space is full of wrapped boxes from floor to ceiling. They've even gone through the trouble of taking the hangers off the rack and laying them on the upholstered chair in the corner.

I shed my clothes with probably more fervor than is necessary, and I'm down to my boxer briefs when Augusta walks in. When she sees me, she pivots to face the wall. "Sorry, I didn't know you'd be half-naked."

Rolling my eyes, I huff a laugh. "Nothing you haven't seen before." I take a moment to get my suit sorted on a hanger and ask, "Does this look like 'some things' to you?"

"What do you mean?"

"In the closet. Is this their definition of 'some'?"

She turns, walking over to the closet to peer inside, not bothering to spare me a glance. "Pretty much."

"So, where are you supposed to hang your stuff?"

"I don't," she replies, as if it's the most obvious answer in the world. "Actually, I take that back. The night before, I'll hang what I want to wear on the closet door and spray it with wrinkle spray."

"So it's like this every year?"

"Graham, I'm used to this. You don't have to get all indignant on my behalf. Why do you think I don't come home much? I'm out of here the day after Christmas and I won't be back until next year."

"But why are you used to this? This is your space; it deserves to be respected. This isn't respect."

"Carrie doesn't respect me. She'd have to see me as a person for that to happen. And she doesn't, so just drop it." She retrieves her large backpack off the floor and rummages through a pocket, smiling once she finds what she's looking for. "Just do what I do," she says, opening a zip-top bag and popping what looks like a gummy bear into her mouth. "If you stay stoned, you don't care."

She extends the bag to me and I shake my head. "Drugs? Seriously, Augusta?"

Shrugging, she tucks the bag back in her pack. "They're

just Delta-8. Completely legal. But my family is dry and if I'm going to survive this dinner, I'm going to need to be medicated."

I frown. "They don't drink?"

"No. David's on the wagon, so it's a respect thing. I have a bottle of wine in my bag, but I won't bring it out when I'm with them. Thus, the edible."

"Do I need to worry about you?"

Augusta plants her hands on her wide hips. "No. I'm a big girl. You do, however, need to put on some pants."

Glancing down, I realize that, yes, I am indeed still in only my boxer briefs. I drag on my jeans and shirt, followed by my socks, and finish with sliding on my belt before returning my items to my pockets.

CHAPTER FIVE

AUGUSTA

I don't bother unpacking, because what's the point? While I wait for Mom or David to call up the stairs to say that supper's done, I lie on my bed with my legs dangling off the side, anticipating the numbness of the edible washing over me. "Can I join you?" Graham asks from the edge of the bed.

I don't bother looking at him. "I'm not getting up to stop you."

"Good enough for me." He lies down beside me, leaving a few inches between our shoulders. We're both quiet for a long moment and I will him not to ask questions about everything here. I honestly don't have the energy to reopen old wounds and dredge up trauma simply so he'll understand. "So, you've really never brought anyone home?"

"Nope," is all I say.

"Is that because you're afraid to expose someone to them or that you're worried the person would see you differently if you did? They'd see how—."

"Stop, Graham. You're going to kill my buzz if you keep

asking questions. And believe me, I need as much of it as I can get to make it through dinner."

"You shouldn't have to be stoned to survive a dinner with your family."

"And yet, I will be."

"Gus, dinner," Amelia calls from the bottom of the stairs and I shut my eyes, willing myself not to care that even Carrie's kids call me that awful nickname.

I haul myself off the bed with a grunt. Once I'm upright, I roll my shoulders and blow out a breath. "I guess it's showtime."

Rising to his feet, Graham runs his fingers through his hair. "Guess so. Anything I need to be aware of?"

"The food will be terrible. Thus, the Pepto pills. Don't worry, I also have snacks in my bag we can eat after and I'll cook tomorrow morning, so that'll at least be edible."

He frowns. "Really? After I lost everything I ate for the last month, I was kinda looking forward to good food. You can cook; I figured you learned from your mom."

"And you would be wrong. Like I said, I have snacks. Just follow my lead. There's a reason Butterball is so fat," I say with a chuckle.

He sighs, gesturing to the door. "I'm going to wash up and I'll be down in a minute. Will you be okay, or do you want to wait for me and we can go down together?"

"I don't need a buffer; I'll see you down there."

He looks like he wants to say something, but only nods. "Alright."

He walks across the hall and as I always do before I head down the steps, I remind myself that this isn't my real life. I just have to make it through a few days and I'll be back home. Thankfully, the sharp edges are beginning to blur and I paste on a smile as I head downstairs.

Even though they called me down for supper, I expect the table to not be set yet, since I'm usually the one who does it. To my surprise, everyone is seated around the long rectangular table. "About time you got down here. We're starving," Mom says, annoyed. Looking past me, she frowns. "Where's your friend?"

It's only a few days. It's not my real life. I will survive.

"Graham will be down in a minute."

"I hope tea's okay. I already poured you both a glass."

I hate tea. Always have. But even if I did like it, my mother steeps hers too long and it's dreadfully bitter and unsweet. "Thanks, but I can't do caffeine this late in the day. I'll just get us some waters." Hurrying to the kitchen, I pull down two glasses and fill them with ice and water before heading back to the dining room.

Hearing footsteps on the stairs, I turn to see Graham walking down. Damn him and his handsomeness. Don't get me wrong, he looks good in a suit. But in casual jeans slung low on his hips and in that fitted gray long-sleeved henley with a couple of buttons undone that he's wearing now? Just go ahead and kill me. And the way he's smiling at me, I could almost forget this is all for show.

"One of those for me?" he asks as he comes up beside me.

"No, I'm just extra thirsty," I retort.

He chuckles, leaning in close to whisper in my ear. "Yeah, but you're high, so that might actually be true."

I roll my eyes. "Take the water, Graham."

"With pleasure." He reaches for it and plants a kiss on the side of my head. It takes me by surprise, so I nearly flinch. Even more shocking, he puts his arm around me and walks me to the table; like this type of behavior is completely normal for us. Like this isn't my best friend's big brother with whom I have an extremely complicated history. Like I can survive him touching

me or showing me any sort of kindness; even as a way to perpet-
uate this lie to my family.

I continue to reel from both the tiny peck to my scalp and
his arm ever so casually draped around my waist as we take our
seats. I down about half my glass of water in a few long gulps
before setting it down and pulling my napkin into my lap.

On the table lies serving dishes of dry pork chops, bland
green beans, mashed potatoes I know for a fact have neither
butter nor salt, and steamed broccoli that has been cooked so
long that it's lost every bit of its normal green color and is
verging on brown. I pull just enough food onto my plate to
appear as if I could be on a diet and not simply disgusted by my
mother's cooking.

It wasn't until I got to college that I even learned people
used more than simply salt and pepper for seasoning. I'm pretty
sure that was the first time I had actual butter, too. Even the
college cafeteria food was a huge improvement on the food I
had growing up.

Graham seems to follow my lead with his serving sizes and
even compliments my mom on her pork chops. After taking two
minutes to chew and swallow the one bite he took, that is. At
least he's a good actor.

For the first five minutes, I'm completely ignored. This is
nothing out of the ordinary and I honestly prefer it to being
offered backhanded compliments or questions that sound
inane, but in reality, are barbed. Everyone ravenously devours
their food and I'm still only two bites into my pork chop when
Mason asks, "So, any big news from the locker room,
Augusta?"

While I have no issues with my brother-in-law—he's great,
even—having the spotlight put on me for any of my accomplishments for more than thirty seconds is not likely to end well, so I
deflect as usual. "Not much going on right now with the break

and all. How's the remodel going? What is it now, the sunroom?"

He opens his mouth to answer, but Carrie puts her hand on his arm. My heart rate immediately kicks up since I don't know what's coming. Although knowing her, it'll be something I won't like. She smiles, and it appears genuine, but there's a gleam in her eye that makes me nervous.

"Yes, how are things in the locker room? Graham, I don't know how you'd be okay with her working so closely with all those tall and strapping college athletes. Rubbing them down and all that. Don't you get jealous of her putting her hands all over other men and women all the time?"

Graham dabs his mouth with his napkin and takes a sip of his water. All the while, he casually takes my hand under the table and gives it a squeeze, shooting me a smile before turning his gaze on my sister. "I don't know; I like to think I'm pretty tall and strapping myself. But I don't worry about Augusta, actually. Not for a second. She's great at her job, and the university is lucky to have her as one of the best athletic trainers on their staff. She's also one of the most loyal people I know." His smile turns a bit smug. "Plus, she knows what she's got at home."

Carrie examines him. "And how did y'all meet? I don't remember Gus mentioning it."

I pick up my glass of water and wish for the ability to transform it into wine or vodka or anything that will numb me further. "His sister, actually," I offer.

She smiles, but it's not real; it's never real. The thing is, I know my sister and one thing she's never offered me is any kind of genuine smile. Not sure I'd know what to do if she did. "Nothing wrong with needing a little help to find a man. Good on you for using the connections you have."

Her words sound sincere, but the implication is clear: I

couldn't find a man without help. I'm about to open my mouth to change the subject when Graham says, "Gemma introduced us, but that's not how we got together. I've known Augusta since she was in college. If anything, it was me using my connections to get her. Pretty sure she didn't know I existed." He offers her a lopsided grin. "I finally wore her down enough that she'd give me the time of day."

Carrie blinks as if she's unsure what to do with this information. Truth is, I've always known who Graham was; where he was in proximity to me when we were in the same space. For almost twenty years, I've been acutely aware of this man. I just wish that awareness would go away.

David pipes up as he fishes out another pork chop. "I spoke with Walt and Jan. They're still planning on having the party tomorrow night. Of course, it'll just be the neighborhood, so I hope you brought your heavy coats for the walk over."

Graham turns to me. "Party?"

I nod. "The neighbors throw a big Christmas Eve party every year. Play Bingo, karaoke, dancing, the works. There's a hot chocolate station, s'mores, and a bonfire."

His eyes light up. "Karaoke? Are you going to sing?" If I'm not mistaken, he almost sounds hopeful, and I'm surprised. It's short-lived when Carrie snorts a laugh from across the table.

"Gus? Sing? I'd rather not draw all the feral cats in a two-mile radius, thanks."

Anger flashes in Graham's eyes and I squeeze his hand. "It's fine," I mutter. His jaw clenches and his nostrils flare, but he gives me a subtle nod before returning his attention to his food.

As is my custom, I push my food around on my plate for the rest of supper and I'm the first one up and gathering dishes once everyone backs away from the table. Mom calls over her shoulder as she and David head to the living room, "You've got the dishes, right?"

I nod. "Yeah, Mom. I've got 'em. Thanks for supper."

She smiles, lowering herself to the sofa as I ferry dishes and serving platters into the kitchen. For the first trip, Graham simply stays seated at the table, his elbows planted on the tabletop as he stares at some fixed point off in the distance, lost in thought. By the second trip, he jumps up and gathers the remaining plates to follow me into the kitchen.

I scrape the uneaten food into the garbage because my family doesn't do leftovers. Of course, that could be because this food is almost inedible the first time around, so there's no telling how bad it would be for a repeat performance. He pitches in and opens his mouth to speak, but I shoot him a glare. "Don't."

"Augusta," he objects in a whisper, his tone indignant.

I drop the plate I've just scraped into the sink and keep my voice low. "I said don't, Graham. I told you I didn't need a buffer and I still don't. Let me do what I do. If I'm in here and busy, I don't have to avoid them."

"You realize this is bullshit, right? Your parents just let her be awful to you?" I open my mouth and he presses forward. "And yeah, I get that none of what she said was in-your-face hateful, but I don't even know her and I could feel it. Why do you let her run roughshod over you?"

"I already told you; this is my life. I'm fine." I blow out a breath. "You don't have to help with this. You can go hang out or whatever."

His brows inch up his forehead as his face transforms into a horrified grimace. "You think, for one second, I want to be alone with those people? Jesus. I wish I'd taken you up on your offer of the edible. Damn."

"I tried to warn you."

"That you did," he agrees. "Can I ask you something?"

"No. I'm too tired and stoned. I need all of my mental faculties to wash these dishes."

"Then why don't you go on upstairs and I'll finish them," he offers. "You can go take a shower and wash your face and put on your comfy clothes and read. You know, things that you actually enjoy doing."

"I'm good. I've got some papers I need to look at for Mom before I go up."

"What papers?" he asks as he steps around me to start the dishwater.

"Some insurance stuff. She likes me to look over all her EOBs to ensure their insurance hasn't screwed them over for the year."

"All of them? That would be a lot, wouldn't it?"

"Yeah."

He frowns. "Why do you agree to do it? You're supposed to be relaxing with your family."

I lift a brow and level him with a gaze. "What part of anything that you've witnessed thus far could ever be considered relaxing? It's just part of it. Let's just get these dishes done, okay?"

He inhales a deep breath and finally nods. "If that's what you want."

"It is."

"Okay."

CHAPTER SIX

GRAHAM

After the dishes, I offered to help go through the insurance papers with Augusta, but she declined. And because I know no amount of arguing will change her mind, I slip into the living room. I notice that with Carrie, Mason, and April seated on the sofa and with David in the recliner, there aren't any other seats readily available. The kids are all spread out on the floor, engaged in various activities involving loud games on cell phones. The TV is turned up to an almost deafening level to compensate and I'm suddenly exhausted and on the verge of being overstimulated.

As no one seems to even notice or acknowledge my presence, I head on upstairs and into Augusta's room. I want to explode with how angry I am on her behalf. So angry, I'm almost in tears. Even though I know my sister has just given birth, I need to get her input, since she knows Augusta better than anyone else.

Checking my watch and seeing that it's not even eight, I pull up Brewster's name in my contacts, clicking it to connect the call. No need waking her if she's asleep, so I'll try him first.

"Graham, hey. Y'all make it into town okay? The weather's pretty gnarly."

"Yeah, tell me about it. How's Gemma feeling?"

"Great. Julie's already nursing like a champ and is currently passed out. Did you get my text?"

I smile as I remember Augusta's face when she found out they named the baby after her. "I did. Did Mom and Dad tell you I wouldn't make it in for Christmas? I'm snowed in with Augusta and her family."

"And you're still alive? Wow. I would've thought the three-hour drive would be enough for y'all to kill each other."

"Right? At any rate, the reason I called was actually to talk to Gemma, but I didn't want to bother her if she wasn't up to it or she's asleep. I know she just gave birth, but I have something I need to bounce off her."

"She's here and she's awake." He sounds far away for a second, but then comes back. "Here you go, Graham. Thanks for checking in on her, man."

"Graham?" Gemma's voice comes on the line a beat later and I breathe a sigh of relief.

"Hey, sis. How you feeling?"

She huffs a laugh. "Exactly how you'd expect I'd feel after pushing a human out of me. What's up? Brew said you needed to talk to me. And you're stuck at Augusta's parents'?"

"Yeah." Unsure how to actually begin, I open my mouth and close it again.

"I know. It's bad." It's not a question and a whoosh of air leaves my lungs.

"Who even are these people, Gemma? They're awful to her. And that sister of hers? Jesus."

"Yeah. Is she okay?"

"She says she's fine, but she's not. I want to see her get mad and tell them off. She's not Augusta."

"It's complicated, Graham. Are you at least being nice to her? I know you all are probably never going to be on the best of terms, but you're not adding to her stress, are you?"

"No, of course not." I relay the events of us deciding to pretend to be in a relationship, and Gemma chokes out a surprised laugh. "Yeah, I know. I just couldn't let her sister think Augusta could only get a decent guy if she bribed him. What is that woman's damage? She's a—."

"Cunt," Gemma finishes.

"I mean, I don't know that I would've said that, but yeah."

"So what's Augusta doing now?"

"Something with her parents' insurance papers. I offered to help, but she wouldn't let me. She barely even let me help wash the dishes. And that's another thing; after supper, it was like it was a given that Augusta was going to be the one doing the dishes. The rest of the family just got up and walked away from the table. There was no discussion or anything; she just starts gathering up plates and taking them to the kitchen. I couldn't believe it. Is it always like that?"

She sighs. "Yeah."

"And she just puts up with it? I don't understand it."

"Like I said, it's complicated, Graham. I've spent our entire friendship trying to understand it. I still don't. Just take care of her while you're there? She's never had anyone there in her corner. I've offered to come home with her in the past and she wouldn't let me. Not after—."

"That spring break?" I ask.

"Oh, she told you about that? Yeah. That was pretty rough."

"So rough that she had to shave her head because Carrie put fucking Nair in her shampoo? Out of spite?"

"Yeah. I wanted to drive back to Loudon and knock her

block off, but she was only sixteen and I would've gotten arrested, so Augusta hid my keys."

"Did she even tell her parents?"

"I'm not sure. Although I don't know if it would've mattered, honestly." Her tone is resigned, and I pinch the bridge of my nose.

"Probably not," I agree. "I guess I now get why she's never really talked about her family much over the years. Jesus. By the way, great name."

"Did Augusta see the text? It only shows mine to her as delivered, but not read, so I wasn't sure."

"Yeah, she saw. Pretty sure it made her year. First time I've seen her smile the whole time we've been here."

"Good. Well, I'm going to go. Try not to kill anyone while you're there. I know you're a good lawyer and all, but there are too many witnesses for you to get away with it."

I huff a laugh. "Thanks for the reminder. Take care, sis."

"You, too."

She disconnects the call and I lie back on the mattress, feeling no better after the call than I did before it.

I must've dozed off for a bit, but as soon as the bedroom door opens, I sit bolt upright. Augusta holds up her hands. "It's just me."

Checking my watch, my mouth falls open when I see it's nearly midnight. "Four hours?"

She shrugs. "Sorry I was gone so long. I didn't mean to wake you. I'm just going to take a shower and turn in."

"Four hours?" I repeat. "You worked on that insurance stuff for *four hours*? By yourself? Why didn't you come get me? I offered to help you. And why did you have to do it in the first place? I don't understand why you were the only one who could go through that stuff. Your parents are capable, aren't they?"

She sighs, hauling her bag off the floor to set it on the bed. "Graham, I'm tired. My brain is fried, and I just want to shower and go to bed."

"So, I'm just supposed to sit here and let you get steamrolled the entire time we're here? I'm just supposed to watch you get treated like shit and do absolutely nothing about it? If this was an actual relationship, what man in his right mind would let his girlfriend's family treat her the way you're expecting me to let them treat you? Make it make sense, Augusta."

She pulls a packing cube and toiletry bag from her backpack and glowers at me. "First of all, you don't *let* me do anything. Secondly, I never asked you to do this for me. So, you want to talk about steamrolling, you oughta look in the mirror. How is you jumping in to come to my perceived rescue any different? I told you I didn't need you like that. I still don't." Without another word, she pivots, heading back out of the room.

I guess I should just be glad she's still willing to stand up to me because at least that means she's not broken. But I still don't have to like that she allows her family to treat her like a second-class citizen.

I'm still stewing twenty minutes later when Augusta returns to the bedroom dressed for bed. Her face is bare, her hair is damp, and she wears an adorable nightgown with a gnomish holiday print. It's the most like herself she's looked since I picked her up at the airport. "Bathroom's free if you need to brush your teeth."

"Sure." I gather my supplies and pad across the hall. Since it's still steamy from Augusta's shower, I leave the door cracked and tug my shirt over my head before grabbing a washcloth and hand towel from the linen closet. While the water heats, I brush and floss my teeth. After, I wash my face and moisturize before running my electric razor over my stubble. Satisfied with my job, I rinse and wipe down the sink. Once I'm done packing up my supplies, I don't bother putting my shirt back on since I'm just going to bed. I reach for the door, only for it to open, Carrie on the other side, dressed in a skimpy satin nightgown.

She feigns surprise at seeing me, but I'm honestly not all that surprised to see her, considering the way she acted when we first met. "Oh, my. I didn't realize anyone was in here."

"I'm sure," I deadpan. "With the lights and running water and electric razor noises, I can see how it would appear the room was unoccupied."

She leans against the doorframe, folding her arms under her breasts, making them nearly fall out of the top of her nightgown. I don't even give her the satisfaction of a glance. Even if I weren't supposed to be in a relationship with Augusta, Carrie isn't someone to whom I'd ever give the time of day. I attempt to squeeze by her, but she shifts to stand in the middle of the doorway. "Something I can help you with?" I ask and toss my shirt over my shoulder, annoyed.

Although I'm not willing to look at her, she makes no attempt to hide the hunger in her own gaze as it drags down my body. "This has got to be some sort of joke, right? No way Gus even knows what to do with someone like you. You can tell me if she's got something over on you that would make you have to pretend to like her." She slowly drags her fingertips down her chest and raises a brow. "If you need a distraction from Gus's incessant sniveling, I'm happy to provide you with one."

"Not that I need to dignify any of what you've just accused me of, but all it does is speak to your own insecurity, Carrie. As does all the petty shit you say and do where Augusta is concerned." She reaches out to touch my chest and I bat her hand away. "Let's get one thing real clear. Even if I weren't about to go get in bed with your sister—one of the most amazing people I know—I'd never get in bed with you. Not even on your best day could you ever make anyone half as happy as she does. And the thing is, she doesn't even have to try. Look at you; throwing yourself at your sister's boyfriend when you've got a good husband right down the hall. I'm sure it's not the first time you've been jealous of her, but on the first night? Talk about desperate," I say with a chuckle. "Do us both a favor and stay the hell away from me."

Indignation flashes in her eyes. "You'd really turn all this down?" she asks, sweeping her hand down her body. "For that?" She points toward Augusta's room with a sneer on her face.

"Without a second thought. And *that*, as you put it, is someone very dear to me and you'll either treat her with respect in my presence or keep your fucking mouth shut."

I shove past her, striding back across the hall. Expecting Augusta to already be asleep, I'm shocked to find her sitting up with her knees drawn up to her chest, her gaze fixed on the windows on the other side of the room. "You're still awake?"

Shrugging, she sighs, her posture defeated. I close and lock the door, lest Carrie get any wild ideas about sneaking in to continue her attempt at seduction. Tossing my shirt toward my suitcase, I take a moment to shuck my jeans and fish out my phone charger and plug it up before dropping onto the bed next to Augusta. I'm about to pull the covers up when I think better of it. "Do you want me to sleep on the floor? We didn't even talk about that. I can. I locked the door, so it's not like anyone would know."

She shakes her head. "It's fine." Her voice sounds so anguished and a pang of sadness mixed with rage hits me square in the chest. I reach up to tuck her hair behind her ear, but she leans out of my reach and lies down, rolling away from me. She turns off the lamp, plunging the room into darkness, and I want to scream.

Instead, I lie down, one arm folded behind my head. For what seems like hours, I stare into the darkness and think over my entire past with Augusta. It's messy and complicated and she hates me now—she has every right to. Given what I now know about her *family*—and I mean that in the loosest sense of the word—I feel even worse than I ever did for everything that went down between us. For how I treated her and how I hurt someone who's already been hurt more by people who, biologically, should be predisposed to love her and still, they don't seem to.

Yet, despite all that, Augusta is a hopeless romantic. She dreams about marriage and kids and love. I get it now. I get why she'd want that for herself; to have a family of her own. She sure as hell doesn't get it here. She probably never has.

I'm brought out of my thoughts when Augusta's side of the bed shifts and she sniffles. Inching toward her, I don't even have to touch her to feel her body shaking with what must be silent sobs. My throat tightens with emotion, knowing she won't even let herself cry properly because she doesn't want me to know.

To hell with that.

Rolling toward her, I wrap my arm around her and she startles. "No, Graham." Her voice is thick with her tears, and her body still shakes.

"Yes, Augusta."

"Stop. I don't need you." She shoves my arm away and I try not to take the rejection or the fact that she won't even let me offer her comfort personally.

"I just want to help."

"You can't. Just go to sleep."

Sighing, I return to my back and continue to lie in the dark until hours later when sleep finally finds me.

When I wake, I'm alone and Augusta's side of the bed is neatly made. A glance at my watch tells me it's barely seven and I don't hear any voices down the hall or streaming up from downstairs. Stretching, I rise from the bed and pull the blankets up to mirror the other side. Peering out the window, I grimace when I see over six inches of snow on everything. Checking the forecast is even more depressing, considering there's another winter storm scheduled to move in sometime this afternoon. Any hopes of getting myself—and Augusta, because I'll be damned if she stays here with these people—out of here soon are dashed.

Still tired and now annoyed at the weather, I gather up some items to grab a quick shower and head across the hall. This time, I make sure the door is locked as I get ready for the day.

By the time I make it downstairs, I'm greeted with the smell of smoked meat cooking and coffee brewing. I let my feet take me to the kitchen, where I find Augusta standing at the counter in front of a mixing bowl. She's dressed much the same way she was yesterday, except today's dress and tights are both black and her cardigan is red. She still wears those damn pearls and her hair is styled much the same way it was yesterday, her face heavily made up.

Today, though, I recognize why she's dressed a certain way. She has no desire to draw attention to herself. She's adjusted her personality and appearance to what she thinks her family will approve of. Because she thinks if she's the real her, they'd deem it unacceptable. The thought alone makes me want to rage, but I bite it all back and close the distance between us.

I don't bother asking her how she slept or anything close to checking on her because I know she wouldn't tell me the truth and I don't feel like watching her try to fake it with me. So I simply ask in a hushed voice, "Is the coffee safe?"

CHAPTER SEVEN

AUGUSTA

I almost work up a chuckle at his question, but I'm too tired. "Yeah. I made it. You're stuck with skim milk, though. Sorry."

He glances around as he pours himself a cup of coffee. "Okay, can I ask about the lack of basic seasoning?" he questions in a whisper. "This is Christmas. If there were ever a time to drag out the butter and heavy cream and all the yummy, heavy foods, it's now."

"Can't do that; might get fat," I quip.

Graham rolls his eyes. "Such horseshit. Please tell me you're sneaking me actual food for breakfast? I don't know if I can do another meal like last night. I'm legit wasting away here."

"Turkey bacon, flaxseed muffins, and fruit. Lots of healthy protein and good fiber." I lower my voice to a conspiratorial whisper. "But I did sneak some contraband cinnamon into the muffin batter. Try not to rat me out."

He tries to smile, but it turns into a grimace. "Dear sweet baby Jesus, what kind of fatphobic, white people hell have I stumbled into? Next year, you just come to Mom and Dad's.

This sort of treatment has to violate something in the Geneva Convention." I snort a laugh and he smiles. "Well, good to know you can still laugh."

"When it's at your expense, always. And your parents are white, too, so climb on down off your high horse."

He sips his coffee. "Nope, you must've forgotten. Mom is half-Italian, so you know full well Nonna taught that woman how to season." He examines my face. "I meant what I said, you know."

Returning my attention to the batter so I can scoop it into the muffin tin, I ask, "About what?"

He takes another step closer and I stiffen. He sighs, and I know it's because he's seen me do it, but I don't know how to *be* with him so close. Just like last night when he somehow knew I was crying and tried to hold me. I don't know how to accept that kindness. Not from Graham. Not anymore.

Setting his mug down, he reaches to grip my chin to turn my face to look at him. I make myself not react to his touch and neutralize my features. His eyes roam over my face and his own expression looks a bit sad. "About you coming to Mom and Dad's next year. You're as much a part of our family as Brewster; probably more. You should at least be with people who love you."

His words hit that soft place I'm trying desperately not to expose while I'm here. I yank my chin from his grasp and blink rapidly as I turn my focus on the muffins.

"Aug—."

"Don't, Graham."

Planting his hands on the counter, he hangs his head. "I didn't mean—."

"I know. It's fine. It'll be a while before anyone gets up. Why don't you go watch the news or scroll through social media? It's likely to be loud again once everyone starts streaming downstairs and you'll get overstimulated. Enjoy the quiet while you can."

"You need any help in here?"

"No," I answer immediately. "Nothing to do once I get the muffins in. Go enjoy your coffee." I don't look at him again and he makes no move to touch me. He watches me for another moment before heaving a sigh, raking his fingers through his hair, and leaving the room. Thankfully, he doesn't see the stray tear that falls into the muffin batter.

Try as I might, I can't get his words out of my mind.

You should at least be with people who love you.

I don't think he was saying my parents don't love me; even if it's only obligatory familial love. I know he wasn't saying that he loves me. He only meant that his family loves me. I know they do; they're wonderful people. His words just hit too close to that soft place. And that soft place has no place here.

Breakfast is blessedly uneventful. Carrie has never been a morning person, so her vitriol is rarely very sharp this early in the day. But as I rise to gather up the dishes, Graham snatches my hand before I lift a plate. I frown at him and he shoots me a quick smile. "You ready to go on that walk through the woods you promised me last night, babe? Carrie, you and Mason have cleanup this morning, right? Augusta and I got it last night. Teamwork and fair play and all that, you know?"

My heart rate kicks up as Carrie chokes on her coffee. "Yeah, no. I just had my nails done. Gus always does the dishes; she doesn't mind."

I open my mouth to say that it's fine, but when I glance at him, he's got his lawyer face on. The one he gets when he interrogates a witness during a deposition and I sigh, knowing he's not going to give up on this. At this point, after overhearing Carrie and Graham's conversation last night, I have a feeling none of this is even about me anymore.

"While I'm sure, in days past, she was happy to contribute so you could spend time with Mason and the kids, maybe you'd be willing to return the favor so she can also spend time with her guest? She came to bed so late last night, I've already missed out on a lot of quality time with her. I hope you can understand where I'm coming from."

Mason downs his coffee. "Sure, guys. I've got it. Enjoy your walk."

Graham nods. "Thanks, Mason." He gives my hand a tug. "Come on, babe, let's go put on some warmer clothes." I don't even have to look at Carrie to know that she's seething and I should probably watch my back for the next two days. I let him pull me up the stairs and into my room, shutting the door behind us.

Even though this should feel like some sort of victory, it doesn't. Not when I have no clue what Carrie will do to retaliate. I simply stand beside the door and after Graham starts pawing through his suitcase, looking for his boots, he glances up at me. "Put your Docs on. You'll freeze if you try to wear those other shoes."

"You were serious about a walk?"

He huffs a laugh. "Well, I'm not letting you stay in this house to get roped into doing other shit that your parents or Carrie are perfectly capable of. So, yes." When I open my mouth to say okay, he holds up his hand. "And I didn't mean 'let' like I *let* you do things. I know no one lets you do anything. I just meant—."

"I wasn't going to argue. It's a good plan."

He blinks, surprised. "Oh. Well, in that case, gear up."

I nod, hurrying to pull on a pair of leggings over my tights, along with a pair of thick socks, before shoving my feet into my Dr. Martens and lacing them up. Once I have them tied, it nearly feels like I'm me again and I breathe a sigh of relief.

"I heard that."

"Heard what?" I ask, standing to tug my jacket out of my pack, along with my hat, scarf, and gloves.

Graham grins. "That was a good sigh. It was nice."

"Well, sometimes, so are you."

His eyes widen dramatically. "Holy shit, did you just pay me a compliment? I'll go ahead and mark that off the bucket list."

I roll my eyes. "Don't be a smart ass. You did a good thing today. Don't let it go to your head or anything."

He tugs on a hoodie and hat and nods. "I'll try, but no promises."

After ensuring my pack is tucked away under the bed, we head back downstairs. Mom, David, Carrie, and the kids are all in the living room. My sister's eyes follow me as we walk through and her jaw clenches, almost imperceptibly. We're nearly to the front door and Graham stops, dropping my hand. "I forgot something upstairs; I'll be right back."

"Sure." I stand there with my arms folded as my mother and sister wear almost identical looks of dismay at the sight of my boots. I look down at my feet, suddenly feeling like I've done something wrong, as I fidget with my watch band and take some deep breaths.

"Did you do something different to those muffins this morning, Gus?" Carrie asks, her head tilted in curiosity.

I shrug. "No. Why?"

"They tasted off. You didn't put any of your kooky essential oils or anything in them, did you?"

"No. No essential oils."

"Well, whatever you did, don't do it again."

I splay my hands. "Like I said, I didn't do anything different."

Mom nods. "You know, now that you mention it, they did taste really spicy. You followed the recipe, right? You used applesauce in place of oil and banana in place of an egg?"

"Yes, Mom. Although, eggs aren't bad for you. They have a ton of protein. They're actually one of the most nutrient-dense foods you can have. And some oils are actually good fats."

I nearly breathe another sigh of relief when Graham starts down the steps. "You know we can't have eggs," Mom continues. "David's cholesterol is too high as it is."

"Like I said, no eggs were put in the muffin batter," I reply, resigned.

"Something was, though," Carrie starts. "What was—."

Graham cuts her off. "We'll see y'all later."

"Can I come?" Wade asks, jumping up off the floor. "You're going out into the snow, right?"

Graham stops in his tracks. "I'm good with it." He turns to me. "Augusta?"

My stomach instantly knots up with anxiety, but I finally say, "Ask your mom, honey."

He looks at his mother with a hopeful smile, but Carrie shakes her head. "No, you need to stay inside. Your dad's almost done with the dishes and we're all going to watch a movie and make a veggie plate for the party tonight. You guys can help put it all together."

He slumps, disappointed, and drops back to the floor. I feel bad, but what can I do? He's not my kid. Graham wastes no more time before he tugs me out the front door and down the porch steps. It's frigid, but not windy, so it probably won't be too bad. The sky is so pale, were it not for the trees, you might not know where the ground ends and the sky begins. It's also threatening snow again, according to the forecast.

"What was with your face when your nephew asked if he could go? You looked almost scared."

"Nothing," I respond, shoving my hands in my jacket pocket as I walk around the house and toward the woods.

"And what was all that shit about the muffins?"

"A witch hunt," is all I say. "Can we not talk about it?"

"Sure. So, what's this party going to be like?"

"Exactly like what I said last night. Cocoa, s'mores, dancing, lots of festive merriment."

He huffs a laugh. "You don't sound too festive. Didn't you also say karaoke? You could sing. You love to sing and you're great."

I keep my eyes straight ahead. "I don't sing in front of my family."

"Ever?"

"Not since I was about fifteen."

Even from the corner of my eye, I see him frown. "Do they even know you can play the guitar?"

"No. My family doesn't know me. I thought you would've figured that out by now."

Even in the half-foot of snow, the trail into the woods is relatively easy to find and I head that way. For a long time, the only sounds I hear are the crunching of the snow beneath our boots and our exhales. No animals or birds or even the normal sounds of traffic streaming from the highway a few miles away. It's almost like we're in some sort of snow globe, and if I weren't so on edge, I'd probably think it was beautiful. As it is, I only want to curse the snow for holding me hostage.

"What's the real answer for why you got nervous when Wade asked if he could come with us?"

I blow out a breath. "Because I knew she'd say no, and I didn't want to see the disappointment on his face. But for a split second, I thought she might say yes, and then somehow make it my fault when his boots or gloves or hat came back with snow on them. I should've known better, though. She doesn't let me watch her kids. I don't get invited to birthday parties or school plays or recitals or ball games. They don't even call me 'Aunt Augusta' or even fucking Augusta for that matter. I'm Gus. I don't even think I've ever been allowed in the same room alone with her kids. She wouldn't even let me hold them after they were born."

He stops, turning to face me, his eyes wide, his expression incredulous. "I'm sorry, what the fuck?"

I shake my head, regretting I've said anything at all. "Forget it. Forget I said anything. Let's just walk. I don't want to turn this into a bitch fest."

He grabs my arm when I step past him. "Augusta, stop."

I yank my arm away. "Like I said, I don't want to talk about it."

Graham steps in front of me, but doesn't touch me. "Why do you come here every year? You obviously hate it. They're terrible to you. Even if you didn't feel like you could come to my parents'—you know, if it's because I'm there—why not just stay home? Eat Chinese and watch *Die Hard*. Even that would be preferable to *them*. Why torture yourself year after year?"

"Because that's exactly what Carrie wants. At this point, I'm fueled by pure spite where she's concerned. I can't do more than survive this, but I do. Every fucking year. If I stop showing up, she wins. I refuse to let her have that. Not after everything she's put me through."

His jaw clenches and he opens his mouth and I shake my head, stopping him from saying whatever he's about to. "No. You don't get to ask. I'm done talking about this. I'm too tired and we still have two days—if not more, depending on the weather—so I need to conserve all my energy to simply withstand her, okay?" I close my eyes and take a deep breath. "I just can't, Graham. Please?" My voice comes out weaker than I want him to hear, so I clear my throat and open my eyes, injecting a strength I don't possess into my tone. "Please."

He searches my face as he heaves a resigned sigh. "What do you need? Right this minute, what do you need?"

I hang my head. "I have no fucking clue."

He nods. "Can I suggest something?"

"No, you can't see my boobs," I deadpan and level him with a gaze.

He barks out a laugh. "Trust me, I've got the memory of those locked tight up here," he says, tapping his temple. "That's not what I was going to suggest."

I roll my eyes. "Fine. What is it?"

"A hug?"

I stand up straighter. "You hate hugs."

He nods. "You're right; I do. But you love hugs and no one has hugged you the way you deserve to be hugged the whole time we've been here. Your family is supposed to give you the best, tightest hugs and yours doesn't."

Tears spring to my eyes and I instantly bat them away. "I already told you not to be nice to me, Graham."

He shrugs. "Sorry. Also, not sorry. But it's not right, babe."

"Don't call me that when we're not around other people."

"My bad. It slipped out. Is that a yes on the hug?"

"It's a bad idea."

It's a terrible fucking idea is what it is.

Nodding, he scratches his chin. "Probably. I'm offering to do it anyway."

We've been here for less than twenty-four hours and I'm already so tired. I'm tired of trying to be invisible and not make waves. I'm tired of being scrutinized at every turn. And were it not for my spite, I'd be tired of being here and I'd start walking home, regardless of how long it took me to get there. Because at least I wouldn't be here anymore.

"Okay," I finally say.

Graham wastes no time closing the distance between us as he wraps his arms around me, pulling me into his chest. Although I shouldn't, I loop my arms around his waist and rest my cheek on his chest, splaying my hands over his back. I've never understood how, with our substantial height difference, but his hugs are always perfect and he doesn't seem to have to bend to give them. I breathe him in and he smells familiar and definitely dangerous.

I used to be addicted to his scent. It's clean and earthy and I even bought a bottle of his cologne to spray on my pillow so I could smell him. It wasn't the same since it hadn't mixed with his body chemistry, but it was close enough. He still smells the same after five years. I haven't been this close to him in that long and it's exactly what I need, too much, and not enough, all at the same time.

I can't make myself stop. I can't bring myself to drop my arms or step back or do any of the things I know I should. Especially as he drags one of his hands up and down my back while the other cups the back of my skull.

"I've got you, okay?" He whispers the words over the top of my head and even through my knit cap, I feel his warm breath on my scalp. All I can do is cling tighter to him, even though I know I shouldn't.

CHAPTER EIGHT

GRAHAM

Don't ask me how long the hug lasts, because I couldn't say for sure. And Augusta's right; I hate hugs. Mainly because I'm not a touchy-feely kind of guy, and hugs equal touchy-feely. But Augusta loves hugs because she is all kinds of touchy-feely. It was obvious she needed one, so I offered. As soon as I pulled her into my arms, I realized my mistake, though. Memories and sensations of the last time I held her like this and everything that came after flood my entire system. An ache instantly spreads through my chest and God, I miss her.

Some might argue that for the amount of time we spent together, it's absurd to feel it with such acuteness five years later. It's not rational. I've already established that I am not a rational man.

I have no hope that she can ever forgive me for everything I did and said and was. I can't even be mad about it. But in this moment, I've never wanted anything more than for her to look at me with anything other than passive indifference or anger or sadness. I want her to look at me the way she did before I ruined everything. I want to be here for her for real. I want to be able to comfort her and hold her and just fucking love her again. I want permission to do that again.

But after seeing everything her family puts her through, can I even ask for her to attempt to give me a second chance? Is it even fair to her when I can't promise I won't hurt her again; no matter how hard I try not to? Is it worth it to even try? I mean, I know she's worth it. I never saw it then until it was too late. But would she think I am?

A voice in my head—a super loud, sounds like a clanging alarm bell voice—says to wait. To get her through these next couple of days and beg her to try again. Beg her to let me spend the next thousand years making up for my many, many mistakes. A few days. I can be patient, right? It's definitely not one of my strong suits, but for her, I can be patient.

When she drops her arms and retreats from my embrace, I don't hold on to her, even though I want to. She looks around and sighs. "I think I want to go take a nap before we have to go to the party. I got up really early and I'm tired already."

"Sure. You want company?"

For a solid thirty seconds, she searches my eyes and I nearly fidget under her scrutiny, but then she finally shrugs. "It's a free country."

By the time we make it back to the house, my toes are getting cold and I'm thankful for the heat that hits us as we walk in the door. We slip our boots off and carry them through the house and as we pass the dining room, Augusta stops abruptly. Everyone is sitting at the table, eating lunch. *Guess we were gone longer than we thought.*

David smiles over at us. "Y'all feel like joining us? It's just sandwiches, since we'll be eating pretty heavy tonight at the party."

Augusta pulls her phone out of her jacket pocket and taps the screen. No missed texts or anything to inform her they were eating. Anger on her behalf bubbles up in my chest and I'm about to ask why no one reached out to us when she says, "We were just headed up for a nap. We'll get something later. Y'all enjoy."

She doesn't wait for a response before heading up the stairs. I follow behind her and as I pass the wall of photos before I get to her room, I'm again struck by the fact that there are no earlier photos of her. I open my mouth to ask about it, but think better of it. She's adamant that she doesn't want to talk about her family. The photos probably fall under that category and for now, at least, I should steer clear. I simply tuck the information away for a later time.

She's shed her jacket, scarf, hat, and gloves, along with her cardigan by the time I get to the bedroom and she drapes everything over the back of the chair in the corner. After rubbing her scalp and fluffing her hair, she shucks her leggings and tights before pulling the leggings back on.

I take a moment to pull off my hoodie and run my fingers through my hair. Without warning, Augusta pulls her dress over her head and my mouth instantly goes dry, my eyes go wide, and my dick gets rock hard. Even with her in a bra and leggings, there's still a considerable amount of skin showing. Plus, the bra she's wearing is one I've seen before; one I've taken off of her before. Although, it's been five years, so maybe it's just a similar one? Even so, I nearly have to bite my fist to keep from groaning.

She doesn't seem to notice my agony as she lays her dress neatly over the arm of the chair and pulls my hoodie on. I want to take some sort of pleasure in the fact that she's done it without asking me if she can or seemingly without a second thought. She pulls down the covers, but then appears to remember something. Tugging her bag out from under the bed, she digs around and then smiles as she pulls out a bag of Gold-fish crackers and a bottle of wine.

"Wow. Cheese and wine. So fancy."

"They're organic, at least." Extending the bottle and a corkscrew in my direction, she asks, "Will you open this; my fingers are still a little numb. Last thing I need is to slip and stab my hand." I take it, making quick work of the cork, and hand it back. "You want some?"

I wave off the offer. "No, thanks."

She frowns. "But it's your favorite."

I drop onto the bed beside her. "I actually don't drink anymore."

Taking a sip straight from the bottle, she looks at me like I've grown three heads. "Since when?"

A few weeks after everything happened.

"A while."

"But you drink beer at the family get togethers. I've seen you."

"Non-alcoholic beer," I explain. "But you and I haven't really stood close enough in the last few years that you could tell."

She takes another sip and nods. "I guess that's true. Why, though?"

"It got to be where it was something I needed, not just something I enjoyed." Picking up the bag of crackers from her lap, I open it and pop a few in my mouth. "I will take some of these, though. Those super spicy muffins really did a number on me this morning," I say with a smirk.

She elbows me lightly in the arm. "Ha-ha. So you heard all that, huh?"

I swallow my current mouthful of crackers and clear my throat. "What I heard was your sister trying to stir shit and your mom feeding into it while David was entirely oblivious to the entire thing."

"Well, look at you. You've figured out the Harvey-Parsons dynamic and it only took you a day. Good job, smarty pants." She sighs, taking another long drink of her wine. "I don't even feel like going tonight."

"Then we don't have to."

"Yeah, we do," she replies, resigned.

"Why? We can say we want some alone time and make our hair look all messy and pretend we had really hot sex. They wouldn't even question it."

"For starters, you underestimate my family's ability to question things. Carrie probably still thinks I've somehow bribed you to be here, and she'd demand photographic evidence or it didn't happen. Because who would touch me? Oh, the horrors of fucking a fat girl."

"Don't do that, Augusta," I warn. "All it does is give her headspace she doesn't deserve. You and I both know what's true."

Another long drink has the bottle nearly half empty and I'm making a mental list of things she's going to need after her nap. The thing about Augusta is, she loves red wine, but it definitely doesn't love her. Even after one glass, she gets a massive headache. And with how little she's actually eaten since we got here, there's almost nothing on her stomach. *Water, Tylenol— that she'll probably refuse to take—carbs.* I'm brought out of my thoughts once I realize she's spoken and what she's just said.

"Except it's not true anymore."

I want to tell her it's not because I wouldn't want it to be. But I've already decided to be patient and wait until she's recovered from this time with her family. Instead of saying what I really want, I just nod. "Yeah, but it was at one time, and

I think we both know exactly how much and how often I touched you."

She looks over toward the window, her throat rolling as she practically guzzles the wine. "That was a long time ago."

"It was. They don't have to know that, though."

She shakes her head. "I have to show up at the party. Otherwise, it's not just her who thinks I'm hiding."

I frown. "What, some other awful sister I don't know about who lives to make your life hell going to put in an appearance?"

She sighs. "No. The couple throwing the party?" I nod, even though she's still not looking at me. "Their son is going to be there. I got a text while we were on the way here that he was in from Harvard where he's a professor. We have history and if I don't show up, then he and Carrie both think it's because I'm still hung up on shit that was almost twenty years ago. At least, she will. Because that's who she is. And it's just one more thing she'll think she's gotten over on me."

"What happened?"

I honestly don't think she'll tell me because she's been so tightlipped thus far about anything Carrie has done to her, so I'm shocked when she actually explains.

"Trey—their son—was my first boyfriend when I was seventeen. They moved into the neighborhood when I was sixteen and because he went to private school, Trey didn't know what a loser I was at my school." I open my mouth and she presses forward. "I know I wasn't a loser, but Carrie was popular and, as you can imagine, even though I'm two years older than her, she made high school hard for me. I was practically a pariah.

"Trey didn't know that, though. He was sweet and funny and actually treated me like a person. So like you do when you actually have something to call your own for the first time in your life, you keep it all to yourself; you hoard it. Especially when it's the only bright spot in your entire existence."

She sighs and takes another long drink then wipes her mouth, gone dark purple from the wine, with the back of her hand. "He ran cross country and would run through the woods and I liked to take walks and read. Anything to get out of the house, right? We ran into each other one day. Literally. I had my nose in a book of Emily Dickinson poems and he had on headphones, so neither of us were paying attention.

"Turns out, he liked poetry, too, and I thought he was cute. Then we started intentionally running into each other at the same time most days in the woods. Like I said, he was sweet. I was reading one of her poems out loud and he kissed me. I'd never been kissed before. For someone as hopelessly romantic as me, getting your first kiss while you read poetry is pretty up there in terms of experiences.

"After that, we'd meet at his house because I sure as hell wasn't bringing him to mine. We'd still read and stuff, but we'd fool around and I actually started to feel good about myself and was happy in longer than I could remember. I fell in love with him. Hard. I mean, how could I not? He was the first person to treat me like a human. So when we'd been together for about three months, we had sex. He wasn't a virgin, but he was gentle. It was a good experience."

She returns her gaze to the window, and it loses focus, as if she's remembering something. "The next week, Trey broke up with me. He said he'd met someone else. That I was a sweet girl, but it was time for him to move on. I was devastated, but you would've never known it. With all the shit Carrie pulled, I got so used to pretending to be indifferent. I wouldn't even cry in my room. I'd wait until I was in the shower.

"A few days after we broke up, Carrie announced at dinner that she had a new boyfriend and he was going to come over after school the next day. Honestly, this wasn't big news because Carrie had a lot of boyfriends. But the next day, when

I got off the bus—because Carrie had friends who drove her and I'd lost my car—Carrie was having sex on the couch with her boyfriend. I'll give you two guesses who her boyfriend was, but you'll probably only need one."

My chest grows tight with emotion for how bad that must've been for her. Not only the feeling of being dumped, but by her sister's betrayal and blatant disregard for her feelings. I want to wrap my arms around her, but I already know she won't let me comfort her, so I don't even try.

"Of course, Trey was sufficiently mortified and promised he didn't know she was my sister, but Carrie's face said that she knew who he was to me. She told him he could go and he just kinda looked at her like he didn't understand what was going on, but he got dressed and left.

"And I still didn't cry because that's exactly what she wanted. She said that it should serve as a reminder to me that anything I have is fair game for her because wastes of space don't deserve nice things. And where did I get the audacity to think that a guy like Trey could ever actually want me? That him breaking up with me for her was just proof of that.

"I still didn't cry. Not then. I think it just made her that much more angry because without my tears, how would she know how much she'd hurt me? Except for a couple of other times, she's never seen me cry."

She turns her gaze on me and her eyes are dry, even though mine aren't, and she swallows thickly. "So when I tell you I've survived mainly on spite for years, it's because I have. I know it will probably never matter that I've quietly withstood her endless torture for nearly thirty years, but it matters to me. And I will continue to show up and be an affront to her for as long as I live. Because I refuse to let her think she's broken me. Even if the reality is that she has many times over.

"When I go home, I will call my therapist and hash all this

shit out and I won't have to see her again for another year. I have that entire time to shore up my defenses and prepare myself for her barrage of hate. Because I have to believe that someday, it will have all been worth it and she will either see the error of her ways or she'll get hers. And if I'm not here, I can't see that. So that's why I show up. That's why I put up with this shit."

I blink back the tears threatening to spill down my cheeks and blow out a breath. "I'm sorry you went through that." I can't resist reaching up to take her face in my hands. Her reflexes must be a bit slow from the wine because she doesn't pull away. Although I'd love nothing more than to kiss her right now and remind her how much I care, I can't yet. I simply look into her eyes. "You are not a waste of space, Augusta Parsons."

She swallows, her eyes not leaving mine. "I know."

CHAPTER NINE

AUGUSTA

Graham drops his hands from my face, but not before leaning forward to press a soft kiss to my forehead. It's a testament to how buzzed I am that I don't recoil. Not because I wouldn't want him to touch or kiss me. Sweet Jesus, how I still dream about what those things are like.

At present, though, I have to pick my battles. On two different fronts, apparently.

The war with Carrie was a given; expected. I just never imagined I'd ever have to go to war with my heart at the same time.

I can only hope my defenses hold out long enough for me to get away with my sanity—and resolve—intact.

He pulls the bottle and bag of crackers from my hands and sets them on the nightstand. "Take a nap. You're already going to have a headache from that wine. No point in you being tired on top of it if we have to put in an appearance at that party."

Wordlessly, I lie down facing away from him as I pull the front of his hoodie up over the bottom half of my face so I can smell him as I drift off.

There's no law that says I can't want to breathe him in even if I'm still resolved to resist him.

Sometime later, Graham gently shakes me awake. "We have to leave in an hour. Sit up and drink some water. Also, eat some more crackers. I went down to make us both a sandwich, but all the bread was gone."

Sighing, I pull myself up to a sitting position and drag my hands down my face. "Figures. Did you get anything to eat?"

"Yeah. I found some crackers and peanut butter."

"God, I hate it here."

He sighs. "I know. And I know I said I would be douchey and you could break up with me, but I'd rather them think you're completely and utterly blissed out. So when I leave, you're coming with me."

I swallow against the tightness in my throat and nod. "Okay."

"Wow, no argument? You must be worn down."

"I am," I admit.

"I also tracked down some Tylenol in case you would actually take it." I shake my head and he nods. "I figured, but I wanted to be prepared anyway. At least drink the whole bottle of water."

I pick it up off the nightstand and after several large gulps, I blow out a breath. "What did you do while I napped?"

"Read, answered a few emails, looked at some stuff Gemma and Brewster posted about Julie and pictures of Collier getting to meet her. Gotta admit, it was pretty cute. I also checked the video cameras from when we were gone on our walk."

I blink. "What video cameras?"

He points to a book on my bookshelf that wasn't there previously, along with another on my dresser. "Those cameras."

"Why did you put up cameras?"

"Because I'm a lawyer and I don't trust your sister as far as I can throw her. I keep them in my suitcase since I travel a lot for work."

Still a bit caught off guard by this revelation, I frown. "Okay. And did you see anything?"

He gives me a slow smile. "Other than watching you get half naked about twenty times?" My mouth falls open and he laughs. "I erased it; don't worry. No, I didn't see anything. But I didn't want to take any chances. Like I said, I don't trust your sister."

I nod. "Me, neither. I guess I better get ready."

"Sure. Now, are we staying the whole time at this thing, or can we eat—and please tell me the food will actually be edible —mingle for a few, and then cut out?"

"The food will be good. It'll probably be catered. Although, maybe not with the weather; I'm not sure. They usually do, like, Mexican or ham and stuff. Whatever they do, it'll be good. It's always good."

"Sounds amazing. Do I need to wear my suit? Is it that kind of party?"

I huff a laugh. "No. What you have on is fine."

"Alright. Well, I'll let you get ready." He flashes me that great smile that used to be able to make me do just about anything. "I'm guessing there's no chance you'll let me stay in here and watch so I don't have to be around all those awful people downstairs, is there? It would definitely make my Christmas."

I roll my eyes. "Yeah, right. You apparently already got an eyeful on those cameras. I think a fair punishment would be for you to have to endure those awful people."

He feigns disappointment. "Fine. I will take my punishment and when you come down, I will act appropriately besotted."

I snort a laugh. "*Besotted?* What did you read while I was asleep, some regency romance?"

He bends over the side of the bed and comes back with exactly that and grins. "How did you know?"

A bark of shocked laughter falls from my mouth. "You don't read romance. What the hell is that?"

"It was on one of the bookshelves downstairs and I asked your mom if I could borrow it. I think she thought I was joking, but I wanted to look sensitive and in touch with my feelings and shit. Turns out, it's pretty good."

"Oh, God. Wow. Fine. Go down and when you act appropriately *besotted*, I will act as though your reaction is completely normal."

"It's a plan." He climbs off the bed to head toward the door. "See you soon, Tesoro."

My heart kicks over hearing the pet name he used to call me.

Tesoro.

Treasure.

He may only be a quarter Italian and knows next to none of the language, but I know his pronunciation is spot on. Chalk it up to all the time I've spent with his family over the years. Hearing him speak what little Italian he does know has never failed to light me up inside.

Even now, all this time later, it still does. But why did he toss it out like that? It almost seems cruel, considering he knows what I'm dealing with here. Surely it was simply some kind of slip, right? We've spent so much time together in the past two days, all this proximity is blurring the lines.

I can survive this. Taking some deep breaths, I steel myself for what lies ahead at this party and proceed to get ready.

———

Five minutes before we're all scheduled to walk over, I head down the stairs dressed in the same dress I had on earlier, just with a thicker cardigan, warmer tights, and my Docs. My makeup is still heavy, even though it feels smothering, and my hair is curlier than normal.

Ugh.

I also miss my septum ring.

Everyone is waiting by the front door, looking impatient, and I have a feeling that Graham must've said something about waiting for me. I don't want to feel warm things toward him, but it's growing increasingly difficult to not do exactly that.

He grins up at me as I descend the stairs. He steps forward to take my coat off my arm before pulling me toward him, brushing a kiss across my cheek as he whispers in my ear. "Although I prefer the real you, this isn't bad. I can't wait till we get back and I get to see the real you again once you scrub all the stuff off your face. I know it's your armor, but I'm happy to be your shield while we're here. Let's go make this party our bitch, Tesoro."

My breath catches with his words, because again, that stupid name. Except it's not stupid. It's lovely and I remember so many times when he'd say it with a sweet smile that honestly made me feel like a treasure. But that was *before*. And I have to remember that.

My sister clears her throat and Graham huffs a laugh before stepping back to help me into my jacket. After I get my scarf and gloves on, he intertwines his fingers with mine. "Now we're ready to go." His words are said to the group, but he doesn't take his eyes off mine.

"Thank God," Carrie quips. "All the good tables will be taken."

"Just be glad I wasn't on my timetable. I'd still be upstairs," I retort and clamp my mouth shut when I realize I've just mouthed off to my sister for the first time in longer than I can remember.

Graham shoots me a big grin, but it's short-lived when Carrie shoots back, "I'm sure you're just excited about all the food, right, Gus? Did you wear your stretchy pants so you can shovel it all in?"

My steps falter and Graham's expression turns murderous as his head whips in her direction. "What did you just say to her?"

"Come on now, let's not fuss before we've even had our hot chocolate," my mother says in an attempt to calm things down.

Inside, I deflate. I no longer want to go to the party, even though I know I will. I will paste on a smile and pretend Carrie's words and my mother's dismissal don't rip open a wound that's barely had time to heal in the year since I was last here.

"No, ma'am, I believe we are going to have a *fuss*," Graham replies, his tone seething. "What Carrie just said to Augusta was uncalled for, and she needs to apologize."

Color fills Mom's cheeks and she blinks, shocked that he's causing a stir. Carrie scoffs. "If the feedbag fits. It's not my fault she has no self-control. It's bad enough we all have to pretend that anyone, let alone *him*, would want her. I'm not going to act like she doesn't gorge herself when we go to this party every year. It's embarrassing. *She's* embarrassing."

One would think her words would sting and they do. Somewhere deep, deep down, they hit their mark, but outwardly, I keep my features neutral and pretend I'm unaffected, even as bile rises up my throat.

"Carrie, stop," Mason pleads. I know it's bad when even *Mason* is speaking up.

Even from the corner of my eye, I can see Graham's chest heaving. "Carrie, you have approximately five seconds to apologize to Augusta. I'm telling you right now, if you were a man, you'd be picking your teeth up off the floor and I'd smile for my mugshot."

Indignation flashes in my sister's eyes. I can't take another verbal assault right now and keep my composure. I drop Graham's hand and hold mine up defensively. "That's enough," I croak out. "Y'all go ahead. I've lost my appetite anyway. Tell Jan and Walt I said Marry Christmas."

Graham opens his mouth and I shoot him a warning glare. His jaw clenches, but he stays quiet as I turn to walk up the stairs. I make myself not sprint, but I don't miss hearing Carrie say, "See, we can go. She'll get over her little tantrum." A beat later, she huffs in frustration. "Now we really are late."

I don't look to see if Graham is following me; his footsteps thundering up the stairs are plenty of indication. As I get to my room, I don't even bother taking off my jacket or gloves as I drop onto the bed, even though I know I'll get hot.

When he enters the room, he slams the door. "What the fuck was that?"

I heave a resigned sigh. "What do you think it was? That was my normal, Graham. If I had just kept my mouth shut, none of that would've happened."

"None of it should've fucking happened. How do your parents think that's okay? Your mother practically condoned what she said."

"It doesn't matter. I'm tired. I don't want to talk about it.

I'm sorry about us not going over for dinner. I'm sure I can find something for us to eat."

"I don't give a shit about the food, Augusta; I give a shit about you. I'm done letting them all railroad you. I'm *this close* to needing bail money. How are you so calm? I've never once seen you unable to stand up for yourself until we get here. I understand—actually I don't. I don't understand any of it. I know you don't want to talk about it, but I'm at my wit's end and I need you to explain it to me.

"Why do your mother and sister treat you like they do? Why does David seem content to simply pretend to not see it? Why are there no photos of you from when you were a little girl? Why don't you beat the shit out of her? I know you know how; you and Gem take those kickboxing classes. So why do you let her treat you like you don't matter?"

Ignoring his questions, I stand, shucking my jacket and gloves and make to step past him. He grabs my arm and I attempt to yank it away, but he simply pulls me closer and wraps his arms around me, his face inches from mine. His eyes are pleading and earnest and prod that soft place he's always had access to. Honestly, I don't know if I even have the strength to extricate myself from his embrace anymore.

"Please. Talk to me. I just want to understand." He drops his forehead to mine, and I shut my eyes, needing to block him out. "I don't understand how the fiercest, most free-spirited, self-assured person I know can let herself be reduced to a meek, cowering shell of herself simply because these awful people treat you the way they do. That's not the woman I fell in love with, Augusta."

Unwilling to hear more, I shove him away. "Don't, Graham. You don't get to do that. You don't get to bring up shit from the past when you were the one who decided you didn't want it. That was *your* choice. And I don't have the energy to deal with them and you. It's too much. I'm barely hanging on by a thread as it is." My voice comes out thick with emotion and held back tears and I blink rapidly in an attempt to keep my eyes dry.

He nods, his expression apologetic. "I know. I'm sorry. I just hate seeing you like this. I hate seeing this diminished version of you. It's killing me. Gemma said it was complicated and I don't know what that means, but to me it's pretty fucking simple. These people are not any sort of family who deserve to have you in their lives. Simply because you share DNA with them doesn't give them the right to your mind or your heart or your spirt. It seems to me like they've taken enough of your peace.

"I get wanting to make a stand, but this pacifist approach isn't working, Augusta. You want me to make her life a living hell, I will. Just say the word. She is not your sister. *Gemma* is your sister. I'm not going to say I'm your brother, because that's just weird considering I've gotten you naked and all."

In spite of myself, I chuckle, and Graham seems to relax a bit. "But we are your family. I know the shit between you and me is complicated and messy and fucked up, and I wish it wasn't. I will forever take the blame for all of it and have so many regrets about everything that happened. But even our messy shit doesn't turn you into what five minutes with them does.

"At least, in spite of everything, we can still stand to be in the same room with each other. We're still able to show up for the people we love and give each other shit. That's what family does. I get the feeling if you never showed back up here, they wouldn't spare you a thought. People like that don't deserve you. I know what I lost. There's not a day that's passed in the five years since that night that I don't think about how differently everything should've gone. Do you think they consider any of the shit they've put you through?"

His eyes well with tears and my own burn as he closes the distance between us to take my face in his hands. "If I have to spend the entire night shoveling that fucking driveway or call in the National Guard to air lift us out of here, we're leaving tomorrow. I'm not spending another day in this place with those people and I refuse to continue to let them treat you worse than their fucking dog. If I have to carry you out of here kicking and screaming, I will."

He searches my eyes as color fills his cheeks. "And if you only knew how much self control it's taking for me to not kiss you right now, you'd be so proud."

I huff a laugh despite the ache that spreads through my chest with his words. The ache to let him kiss me. The ache to let myself think we could ever be what we were before everything happened. "I know. I am proud of you. I've always been proud. I'm especially proud of how much of that huge stick you've been able to dislodge from your colon in the past twenty-four hours."

He cracks up as he drops his forehead to mine again. "What can I say; wanting to take down your sister loosens me up, I guess."

I heave a sigh as my stomach growls. Because contrary to what Carrie said, I've barely eaten the entire time we've been here and I'm legitimately starving. Graham kisses my forehead and takes my hand in his. "Let's go find some food. Surely between the two of us, we'll find something."

CHAPTER TEN

GRAHAM

Even after calming considerably following my rant, I'm still so beyond enraged at Augusta's entire family. Not even cooking alongside her in the kitchen—an activity that reminds me of all the nights we spent in my kitchen or hers doing exactly the same thing—lightens my mood much.

We're able to cobble together a decent supper of homemade tomato soup and although we don't have bread, she makes some quick tortillas and finds a bag of shredded cheese in the back of a drawer. She insists her mother must've bought it in a weak moment since it's full fat. Oh, the horrors, right? Even though there's no butter, they're still some decent quesadillas.

Considering how fatphobic and food-controlling her family seems to be, Augusta's remarkably comfortable in her skin and has a healthy relationship with food. I'm sure coming here and enduring all the hateful and snide things her sister and mother spout isn't easy. But for as long as I've known her, she has always been confident in her self-image. It's always been one of the things I love most about her.

As we're washing up the supper dishes, I ask, "So, what do

y'all normally have for breakfast on Christmas morning? I'm almost scared to ask, but I'm morbidly curious."

She huffs a laugh as she dries a bowl. "Spinach and mushroom crustless quiche made with egg whites only, sugar-free blueberry muffins, and turkey sausage links."

"Jesus," I breathe. "Is it like that every year?"

"Yeah."

"And how, considering how you grew up, are you so good with food? Most people in your situation would probably struggle with major disordered eating."

Nodding, she stores the clean dishes in the cabinet. "I did. But freshman year in college, I took a nutrition class as an elective and the professor was a food-neutral dietitian. Pretty much my whole life, I'd been told that food had moral value. I know now it's bullshit. Food isn't good or bad."

She smirks. "Plus, when you actually taste good food, it makes more sense. Your mom's lasagna helped. Seeing Gemma have a healthy relationship with food helped. Learning how to cook helped."

She grows serious, turning her body to hop up onto the counter. "There were a lot of years when issues would crop up and getting into therapy helped even more. I learned that my mother and sister's opinions and their relationships with food and obsession with dress size don't determine *my* worth. I am the only one responsible for the way I feel about my body.

"It took me a long time to truly love it, but I do. I know how good I look and everything I've overcome to love it. Honestly, coming here and seeing how they react to me and my audacity to be bigger than a size two helps solidify my resolve to continue to love good food and my body."

I drape the dishrag in my hand over the middle of the sink and close the distance between us until I'm standing in front of her. In days past, she would've parted her knees and pulled me between her legs, wrapping them around my waist until there was no space between us. This usually led to us getting naked in my kitchen so often that I kept a stash of condoms in there.

That doesn't happen anymore, nor does it happen now. I do however, plant my hands on either side of her hips. My arms and torso are long enough that I can bend and not touch her at all, even though it's all I want to do. Despite what I told myself about waiting, seeing her like this and all the feelings it elicits are just too tempting.

She doesn't push me away or jump down, so I take it as a win. "You're certainly right about how good you look. And you're definitely not the only one who loves your body." I lean my face to within a few inches of hers and she drags in a deep inhale. "Seriously, Tesoro, I still can't take my eyes off you when we're in the same room."

Augusta swallows. "You're not supposed to be nice to me. Use of Italian pet names probably qualifies as nice."

I let my eyes trail down her face and body and almost smile when I see her hands are balled into fists around the fabric of her cardigan. "What can I say? I'm a nice guy."

"You're an asshole."

I nod. "Yeah, but like I said, I'm your asshole. Not sure I ever stopped being yours."

She hangs her head. "I can't do this, Graham."

"Do what? We're just talking."

She scoffs. "No. You're flirting. And we're alone. When we're alone, we're still supposed to be us. *This* isn't us. Not anymore."

"I like flirting with you. I'd like to think I'm pretty good at it. I'd like to think I'm pretty good at a lot of things where you're concerned."

"Graham, I can't do this," she repeats, pleading.

I lean in until my mouth is closer to her ear, but I still don't touch her. "What if I told you that you didn't have to *do* anything? You can let me do everything. I know it's been a while, but surely you haven't blocked out how good it was. I know I still think about it. Frequently." She balls her fists tighter into her cardigan as she drags in another deep breath. "God, I miss you."

She plants her hands on my chest, and I pull back. The look in her eyes makes my heart ache. It's pained and sad and angry, all at the same time. "Stop, Graham." She presses harder against my chest, almost like a shove, and I step back. Augusta hops down. "You don't get to miss me anymore," she grits out.

I call after her as she walks out of the kitchen, but she doesn't stop. Although I know I'm not done—I haven't really started—trying to prove myself to her, I can't help the sting of rejection I feel. Mixed with it, though, is pride. The fact that she can still put up a fight tells me she's still my feisty girl. And as long as she's willing to fight with me, I'll consider that a positive.

As I climb the steps, I'm unsure what I'll find when I get to the bedroom. When I get closer, I hear the shower running in the bathroom and I stop to listen, hoping to hear her singing, but with as stressed as she is, it's not likely. I miss waking up and hearing her singing from my shower. I miss getting out of bed and following the sound of her voice to join her. I miss watching the water sluice over her generous dips and curves and following the path of the drops with my mouth and tongue. I miss tasting her and watching and feeling her fall apart, her fingers fisted in my hair as she'd grind herself against my face, seeking her pleasure until she'd moan my name. That sound alone was nearly enough to make me come.

The water shuts off and I still can't make myself move from the spot with my hands braced on the doorframe. Just thinking about her being naked on the other side of this flimsy piece of wood has me harder than I can recall in longer than I can remember. The shower curtain scraping against the rod has my skin humming with awareness as my heart pounds against my ribcage. I should move, but I can't.

The sink faucet comes on and I visualize her washing her face, stripping away all that makeup that I know she hates, but has been wearing in the hopes it will make her acceptable to her family. I hate them all for making her feel the need to change her appearance when exactly how she is should be more than enough. I hate them all for not loving her, the easiest person on Earth to love. I hate them all for ever making her feel inferior when she is amazing and smart and beautiful, both inside and out. I hate myself for taking her for granted when all she wanted to do was love me—even as she broke her own heart doing it. I hate myself for not being what she needed when she needed me the most. It's this thought that finally makes me step back and retreat to the bedroom.

She doesn't need me to pursue her right now. She needs me to support her and help her endure this hell. As long as she's single, I still have a chance. If it takes me the rest of my life, I will prove my love to her. But for now, I will be patient. I will bide my time and if I'm lucky enough that someday, she grants me the privilege of having access to her heart again, I will treat it like the precious and sacred thing it is.

I'm standing at the bedroom window looking out to where snow has begun falling again and I groan inwardly. I wanted so badly to take Augusta away from this place. I want to convince her to never come back. Fuck her spite and fuck all of them. I want to convince her to take me back and—.

And what? Finally be a good friend, lover, and partner to her? Finally live that dream she wanted that I shit all over? Finally let myself think about what a tiny version of us might look like? Hope she can forgive me for not immediately stepping up last time? God, I was such an idiot. To think that any amount of career success or money could be better than what I could've had with her.

Even thinking about that day makes me ache and feel sick. I'd give any amount of money to be able to turn back time and choose the correct path. The selfless one. Not the one I ultimately chose. The selfish one. The childish one. The one that cost me both of them.

"I'm guessing you won't be out shoveling until the wee hours? Since it's coming down again and all."

I turn and she blanches when she sees my face. I'm sure I look as anguished as I feel and I don't even attempt to hide it. I'm finally done being anything but real with her. "Say the word and I will. I will go out there in my underwear and barefoot and shovel us right out of here with my bare hands."

She crosses the room, her brow furrowed in concern. "What's wrong?"

"You said you don't want to talk about your family and all the shit Carrie's done to you. I can't talk about this right now because my focus needs to be on you. If we're going to talk about what I want to talk about, I'm going to do it away from this place. When you've had time to recover and hopefully be of a mind to listen and not immediately slam the door in my face if I show up at your apartment."

I thumb away a tear that's started sliding down my cheek and clear my throat. Augusta takes a hesitant step forward and my heart rate ratchets up. I don't dare move from this spot. I don't dare breathe or flinch or blink. Not with her still coming my way.

When she's close enough that if I leaned six inches toward her, my body would be against hers, she reaches a tentative hand up to my chest, placing it over my heart. There's no way she can miss how it's thundering.

She releases a pent-up breath. "You miss me?"

I shut my eyes, willing the pain to go away, and nod. "Every day."

Her hand travels up my chest and the side of my neck and I let out a shuddery breath with her touch. She slips her hand around to the back of my neck and pulls my face down nearly to hers. My eyes pop open in shock. "Even Scrooge got a visit from his past on Christmas Eve. Just for tonight, Graham. Since I didn't get you anything for Christmas, you can have me."

My chest heaves, and even as I'm moving us toward the bed, I shake my head. "I don't only want tonight, Augusta. I want forever."

She stops and I nearly collide with her. "Tonight is all I can promise you. You want to talk and drag all that shit back up sometime in the near future? You will give me this and not ask for anything else from me after tonight. I can't do more than this right now and I'm not sure I can again. Let me have this."

When it's a chance to make love to the only woman I've ever really loved for what could be the last time or not at all? It's a no-brainer. "For tonight only?"

She nods. "I'm yours until the sun comes up."

"Deal." I slam my mouth to hers and waste no time wrapping my arms around her, shuffling us toward the bed again. Kissing Augusta feels like coming home. She tastes the same, her lips and tongue move the same way they used to. She takes when she kisses; demands space and pushes the pace and I fucking love it.

Her fingers nimbly work my belt and button and fly of my jeans, shoving them down my hips at the same time I'm letting my hands roam down her back and over her ass. I groan when I'm able to tug up the hem of her gown and dig my fingers into the soft flesh of her bare ass. I'm short of breath and hard as a rock after less than ten seconds. I clumsily step out of my jeans and break our kiss, taking the opportunity to drag my shirt over my head. I toss it on the floor and sit on the bed, pulling her down with me.

Augusta comes willingly, straddling my lap. A beat later, she grabs my face, claiming my mouth again. She rolls her hips, a soft moan working its way up her throat. Sweet Jesus, it's nearly enough to end me. Running my hands up her thighs and hips, I try to memorize this moment. It may very well be the last time I have her like this, and I'll be damned if I don't savor it.

I intentionally slow our kisses, needing more time to enjoy this, and bring one of my hands up to the back of her neck to thread my fingers into her hair. I give the strands a gentle tug as I tilt her head back and she lets out a soft gasp, her fingernails digging into my traps. Kissing my way down her jaw, I can't help but smile against her skin as I breathe her in. Lavender and rosemary, same as always. "Fuck, you're perfect, babe."

She grips my hair as I lick and nip my way down her neck as she moans my name.

I can't begin to tell you the number of times I've heard countless women say my name during sex. Augusta doing it was the only one that's ever made me feel something to hear it. She's the only one I ever cared to hear it from. The rest were just nameless, faceless, and empty.

With Augusta, it's never been empty. Not even once.

How I didn't know I was gone for her that first time, I'll never know. God knows if I could go back, I would've followed Gemma and Brewster's lead and dragged her to the nearest wedding chapel. I would've locked that shit down the next morning.

Hopefully someday, that can be a reality. Tonight, though, I'll relish every single second I get to have her. Tonight, she's mine again.

Needing to feel her under me, I wrap my arms around her and flip us on the bed. Like she always does, she lets out a squeak of surprise that makes us both laugh. I allow myself a moment to simply take her in as I brush a damp strand of hair off her forehead. "God, you're gorgeous, Augusta."

She blows out a breath, color rising in her cheeks, as she lifts her hand to my face. "So are you. Thank you for always making me feel beautiful."

"Never doubt that you are, Tesoro."

She huffs a laugh. "Damn you and your Italian."

I chuckle. "I only know Tesoro and the swear words."

"It's still very sexy. I bet you use it on all the girls."

I shake my head as I run my hand down her body. "Only you. You were the only one I ever considered actually learning it for. So that someday, when I took you to Italy, you'd be impressed with my fluency and want to give me all the sex."

She grins. "I'm pretty sure the Italian wine would've been enough to have me doing that."

"I'll remember that," I say, lowering my mouth to hers as I inch my fingers up her inner thigh.

She rolls her hips, grinding herself against me and I can't bite back a groan at feeling her, our bodies only separated by the thin fabric of my underwear. I slide my hand under the hem of her gown and—.

The bedroom door crashes open and I'm appalled and shocked and fucking enraged. Augusta shrieks as both our heads snap to the entrance to see Carrie and Mason about to enter.

"What the hell? Y'all don't knock?" I yell, and for some reason, they're still standing there. Mason's mouth is hanging open, his face beet red, and Carrie's expression is more malicious. Fuck, I really want to murder this woman. "Get out."

Mason stammers an apology, retreating down the hall, but

Carrie just strides her happy ass right on into the room. "This will only take a second; we need to get the gifts for under the tree."

I jump up, very aware I'm only in my underwear and could give a fuck as I bar her entry. "What part of 'get out' don't you understand? You should've picked a better hiding spot. Come back in the morning." I grip her arm, guiding her a few feet back and slam the door, locking it before she has a chance to try the knob again.

After I allow myself a few deep breaths to calm down, I turn around to return to the bed. Augusta has pulled herself up to sitting and is under the covers, her knees pulled up to her chest. Her expression is one of mortification and anger as tears stream down her face. I drop onto the bed next to her, pulling her into my arms. "I'm so sorry, babe."

Shrugging, she sniffles. "What's one more humiliation, right? Not like I haven't endured it my whole life. Makes sense this would get ruined, too."

I take her face in my hands, not willing to let this time I have with her go to waste. "Nothing is ruined. It's probably no worse than the time we got caught in that carwash. The guy drying my car got an eyeful of your ass, remember?"

She snorts a watery laugh. "Jesus, that was awful."

"I'm sure he enjoyed it, though. You were so caught up, you didn't even stop until you were finished. I, on the other hand, had blue balls."

She scoffs. "Yeah, until we got out of there and you pulled out onto the road. Then you got excellent road head, if I do say so myself."

I drop a kiss onto her lips. "Your road head was always excellent." Tugging the covers down and shifting on the bed until I'm between her legs, I hook my arms under her knees to yank her down the mattress. "I'm guessing your sister no longer needs photographic proof that I find you wildly irresistible. Pretty sure my raging hard on was enough evidence."

"It's not weird now?" she asks, hesitant.

I give her a slow shake of my head as I bend to brush a kiss across her lips. "No. If anything, it gives me incentive to make you scream even louder."

She swats me playfully. "Graham, it's not funny."

I capture her hand in mine, turning it over to press a kiss to her palm. "You see me laughing? I haven't had you in five years; you think I'm not going to pull out all the stops?"

A flush travels from her cheeks to her chest, and I need to see where it ends. Trailing my eyes down her body, my gaze stops at the hem of her gown where it's risen to mid-thigh. "I've missed all your cute nightgowns. The gnomes are a nice touch."

She bites her bottom lip, offering me a shy smile. "They're comfy."

"I like you comfy. But I like you even better naked."

And as she drags her nightgown over her head, it's almost as if the last five years fall away as well.

CHAPTER ELEVEN

GRAHAM — APRIL, FIVE YEARS AGO

"Can I get another gin and tonic?" I ask after returning to the bar following a conversation with Brewster about his and Gemma's sleazy producer. My head is pounding from the loud music blaring through the reception hall. I don't do big parties. I don't like heavily crowded spaces. I don't like loud noises. I get overstimulated and cranky and turn into an asshole. Okay, I take that back. I'm almost always an asshole.

But I suppose attending your baby sister's wedding reception is a reason to brave all the things you hate, right? Especially when there's an open bar and your room has been paid for by the people sponsoring this glorified ad circus. At least, that's what I'm going to tell myself. Plus, I don't have to be sober since there aren't any speeches and I don't have to dance. So, another G&T it is.

Accepting my drink and turning my body to take in the room, I let my eyes find her like they do every time we're in the same room. I can't help myself. Augusta Parsons. My sister's best friend. For twelve years, she's been a near-constant presence at all of our family gatherings. My parents have practically adopted her and everyone adores her. It's easy to do.

Augusta has this easy grace and amazing laugh and enviable self-confidence. She also gives me shit. Endless amounts of shit. For everything. Whether it's about my expensive suits or the fact that I'm a money-hungry lawyer (her words) or that I wear a perpetual scowl. But the shit she gives doesn't come across as mean or condescending, and as I've gotten to know Augusta little by little over the years, I've come to realize she's only like that with people she's comfortable with. So, I've learned to enjoy her ribbing and will occasionally give it back to her.

But now, as I stand watching her and Gemma sing and laugh, dancing along to some old Britney Spears song, I can't help but smile. Sometime in the last several months, she's gotten her septum pierced. It glints in the light of the crystal chandeliers of the opulent space. This, combined with her shoulder-length, sandy blonde hair that's curled with some bright purple streaks peeking out, her knee-length, red satin dress that shows off her lush curves to aching perfection, and her ever-present Docs—I swear, someday, she'll probably be buried in those—she's like this mix of punk and princess.

I'm not sure she's ever looked better.

Okay, I take that back. Currently, her makeup is super heavy—smoky eye, dark red lip, tons of blush—and isn't *her*. Of course, neither is the dress, since she typically favors long, flowy skirts or shredded jeans, but the makeup is super jarring. I've never known her to wear more than just a swipe of mascara, eyeliner, and lip balm. Not that she doesn't look stunning, because like I said, I really can't take my eyes off of her, but her looks need no adornment. I think she knows it and is comfortable enough with herself to tell society and their beauty standards to fuck off. I like that about her.

Truth be told, I like a lot of things about Augusta Parsons; not the least of which are her considerable curves. She's also smart and driven and not afraid to speak her mind. She's fiercely loyal to Gemma and has had no issues telling me off on her behalf on more than one occasion over the years.

If she weren't Gemma's best friend, I would've already tried my luck with her. As it is, there's some sort of unwritten rule about not fucking your sibling's best friend, right? No harm in looking, though.

Except, as my eyes come back up her body for about the tenth time in as many minutes, my gaze locks with hers and my pulse instantly begins to hammer. I think for a second that either of us will look away, but even as the music changes to something with a more sensual rhythm and Gemma is pulled away by another partygoer, Augusta simply shimmies her hips and dances like no one is watching. No one but me, anyway. And still, our stares stay locked.

Surely, everyone can feel this, right? There must be some palpable change in the room's temperature, or maybe the lights have gotten brighter. All I know is, there's something here. I down my drink and order water. No need to get sloppy if I can convince myself to at least go ask her to dance. Maybe I can get her number? Maybe I can buy her a drink sometime? Maybe I —. The song ends, and as she leaves the dance floor, I still can't take my eyes off of her. She returns to her table and picks up her purse.

My heart gives this unexpected lurch.

She's leaving? Shit.

There's no way, after tonight, either of us will probably look at the other like this again. God knows we wouldn't be able to get away with it at a family gathering. This is the first time the crowd's been big enough where something like that wouldn't be noticed.

I'm about to pull my wallet out to tip the bartender and go after her, when she surprises me by walking up to the bar. I don't hear what she says to the bartender, but she doesn't spare me a glance. I'm not sure if maybe the moment is already broken or if I imagined the whole thing.

The bartender slides a martini glass across to her and she stirs her drink with the skewered olives before she lifts them to her mouth. She wraps her full lips around the garnish and slowly pulls the toothpick away. Surely she knows how fucking sexy that was, right?

Holy shit.

I'm hard for her.

Not that I haven't been hard for her in the past, because *fuck*.

Memories of her flash through my mind. Augusta and Gemma sacking out in the living room during college while I tried to study for the bar exam. Augusta always wearing those adorable—and short—nightgowns that perfectly showcased her thick thighs and big, perfect ass. Augusta laughing easily at some inside joke she and Gemma shared. Augusta singing beautifully at the top of her lungs to the radio in the car. Augusta, with her sassy demeanor; always so quick to be playful and give me shit.

It was definitely no easy task staying focused.

Not when she was always so *there*. Not when she is always like a ray of fucking sunshine after so many days of rain.

I should look away so I don't creep her out. She doesn't need me leering at her. Just because she looks like some sex goddess incarnate doesn't mean she's inviting me to stare at her like some lecherous creep. It probably wouldn't matter anyway. There's no way she'd ever even consider letting me buy her a drink; let alone do anything more than that. She barely tolerates my grumpy ass.

I mentally shake myself to stop the spiral before it starts.

Why the fuck am I spazzing out? I don't have trouble with women. I'm a good-looking guy and I have game. As surly as I can be, women seem to be able to overlook it long enough for me to get them naked. Maybe it's the fact that I inherited my mother's olive complexion, my father's tall height and stocky build, and Nonna's jet black hair. Maybe they think I'm mysterious. Or hell, maybe it's just the fact that I'm a lawyer; I don't know. Whatever it is that does it for a lot of women, I apparently project it. I've never had any qualms about leaning into it.

But the fact of the matter is, I don't know any of the women I leave with for the night. We don't exchange more than first names, possibly occupations, and a lot of times, ages. No jail bait for me, thanks.

I know Augusta, though. I don't think it would stop me from sleeping with her, but I think she's one of those gushy romantic types and it could get messy fast if she thought I wanted more than one night. I don't do more than one night.

Blowing out a breath, I glance down into my glass before hazarding another look to see if she's still at the bar. She is, and her body is turned toward me, even though she's ten feet away. She leans against the bar, her hip popped slightly, and she wears a sexy smile that has my dick straining against the fly of my pants.

Her eyes drop to her clutch purse and she flips the latch, letting it fall open as she reaches inside. Bringing her eyes back to mine, she lifts a brow in what seems like some sort of challenge as she slips something under her napkin. She jerks her chin in its direction before tapping the bar and stepping away.

Confused, intrigued, and maybe even a bit terrified, I give myself three seconds to hesitate before I'm standing in the space she just vacated. I lift the napkin, expecting to possibly find her business card. Maybe I got lucky and won't even have to ask for her number. Although, my reaction time must be slow from the shock and the gin, because I don't immediately pick up the room key envelope. The bartender walks over a beat later to lift away her empty glass. "If you don't take her up on her offer, I will," he says with a grin.

Possessive jealousy slams into me and I blink. I don't get to be jealous. She's not mine.

She could be for tonight, apparently.

"I don't think so, man," I reply, snatching the small envelope off the bar.

Making my way up to her floor, I'm uncharacteristically nervous. I don't get nervous. I am a badass litigator. Or I will be. The badass part, anyway. As someone who recently landed their dream job with their dream law firm, I should be riding the adrenaline high. I shouldn't be fidgeting outside a hotel room, trying to psych myself up to swipe the key.

Augusta's apparently a sure thing. And God knows I want her; have wanted her for years. I never knew she might want me, though. I always assumed she merely put up with my grouchy ass for the sake of her friendship with Gemma. Who knows; maybe before tonight, she hadn't noticed me. Maybe she's just tipsy and horny and I'm convenient.

Good enough for me.

Steeling myself, I swipe the key and push down on the handle, entering the room. It's dim, with only the light from a lamp on the desk on the other side of the room to illuminate the space. Even without seeing her, I know it's her room. Not only because her boots sit inside the small closet nook, but also because it smells like her. I'm pretty sure I could identify her by that rosemary-lavender scent alone. I can't even count the number of times I've passed by her in all the years I've known her, only for that soft aroma to flood my nostrils. After tonight, I might have a whole different appreciation for that scent, as well as memories to associate with it.

Augusta stands from where she'd been sitting on the bed and walks to meet me at the end of it. Up close, she's even more beautiful than she was downstairs and I—more tentatively than a man with all my years of experience should—reach up to run the knuckle of my index finger along her jaw. Goosebumps scatter over her arms and chest, and I can't help but smile as her breath catches.

"Were you dancing like that for my benefit?" I ask as I grip the back of her neck.

She offers me a slow, sexy smile. "Why? Were you watching?"

"And what if I was?"

"Then I would say I liked that you were watching and yes, it was for your benefit."

Electricity shoots up my spine with her admission. "Do you like to be watched?"

"Apparently, I do."

Dragging my thumb down the side of her neck, I don't miss the way her pulse thunders under her skin and it makes me feel a bit better about my own nerves. "Are you drunk, Augusta?"

"No. Definitely buzzed, but I'm not without my faculties. I could probably even spell some really big words or recite poetry from memory if I needed to."

I take a step closer, our bodies nearly touching, and her breath hitches again. "I don't need poetry. I don't want poetry. You know what this is, right?" I'm not sure if I've said the last sentence for her benefit or mine, but I need to make sure we're on the same page.

Her tongue darts out to wet her lips and she lifts her chin, her eyes drilling into mine. "You don't want poetry. I don't need promises. I know who you are, Graham. I'm a big girl." She chuckles. "Literally and figuratively. You don't need to worry about me. And there's no reason for Gemma to find out."

"Good." I bend to claim her mouth, just a soft kiss to test the waters, but Augusta's soft gasp and her fingers curling into the lapels of my suit jacket, dragging me closer to deepen the connection has my skin heating in an instant.

Not breaking my mouth from hers—holy fuck, this woman kisses like she means to claim me—I toe off my shoes and slide my fingers into her hair in an attempt to regain some control of the kiss. But damn, if I don't like that she doesn't give it up easily. With my free hand, I savor the feel of her bare back under my fingers. I drag my fingertips over the softness of her waist and roundness of her hips and ass before giving it a possessive squeeze.

Augusta pulls her lips from mine, nipping at my bottom one before letting out a soft, husky laugh. "Find something you like back there?"

"Hell yeah, I did. Damn, woman."

A blush creeps into her cheeks as a shy smile pulls at the corners of her mouth. She swallows, looking up at me. "Are we really doing this?"

I move my hand back up to her waist. "We don't have to. Not if you've changed your mind."

She shakes her head. "No, it's not that. I just never thought this could ever happen. I know I invited you up here and I don't expect more than tonight because I know you don't do more than that, but this isn't something I do. Like, ever. I mean, you're really hot and I was feeling brave, but I honestly didn't expect you to show up."

I open my mouth and she presses forward. "That's not to say that I don't think I can pull someone as hot as you, because I know how good I look." I can't help but smile at her confidence, and her blush deepens. "And even though it isn't society's ideal standard, I actually like my body. But I never thought that you might."

Sliding my hand to the small of her back, I yank her flush against me and shift my hips. I'm rewarded with her sharp inhale when the evidence of exactly how much I want her presses into her stomach. I lean in to whisper in her ear. "Does that feel like I don't like your body? Jesus Christ, Augusta; you are quite possibly the sexiest fucking thing I've ever seen. I've been hard for you for years."

Her head snaps up, her big green eyes wide with surprise. "What?"

As I bend to slowly kiss my way up her jaw and down her neck, her breath hitches. Honestly, I'm not sure I've ever been more aware of a woman's reaction to me in my life. "The first time I saw you, you had on a pair of cutoff shorts and a Deadpool tank top. You were bent over to get your bag out of Gemma's trunk and your ass was like something out of a dream. Then, you stood up straight and these fucking tits were even more perfect. If you only knew how many times in the last twelve years I've gotten myself off imagining what they look like."

"You like my ass and tits?" Her voice has gone husky with lust and I don't miss the way her hips shift against me.

"Why don't you take this dress off and I'll show you exactly how much."

CHAPTER TWELVE

GRAHAM

She releases a shuddery breath as she turns away from me. "Why don't you unzip me and you can find out if reality is as good as your imagination."

Both floored and buoyed by her confidence, I drag my knuckle down her spine, reveling in the way she shivers at my touch. I slowly pull the zipper, revealing inch after beautiful inch of her soft skin. More of her body is exposed as she lets the straps of her dress fall off her shoulders and as the slinky fabric drops to the floor, it's not lost on me that I'm still entirely clothed except for my shoes.

As I take in her back and yes, her glorious ass and hips covered in red lace, I can't stifle the small sound of appreciation that works its way up my throat. I also can't stop myself from bending to brush a kiss across her bare shoulder. "Well, how does the ass stack up?" she asks, her tone playful.

"Definitely stacked, that's for sure," I reply and she chuckles, turning to face me once again. My eyes immediately fall to the matching red lace bra she wears and my dick, already throbbing, begins to ache. "Fuck." The word comes out barely above a whisper and in truth, it feels more like a prayer. Because Augusta Parsons's body was made to fucking worship.

I lift my hand to drag my fingertips down her sternum and she gives me a smug smile. "Nice, right?"

"Damn, Augusta."

Planting her hands on her hips, she lifts a brow. "Fair's fair. You don't think I want to know if reality matches my fantasies?" Her eyes roam greedily down my front and I nearly blush.

What the fuck is this, high school? Get it together, man.

"Fantasies?" I ask, shucking my jacket to drape over the back of the desk chair.

"What, you think you're the only one who's imagined things? What did you say, 'hard for years'? Pretty much."

"I didn't think you liked me," I admit, loosening my tie, my eyes never leaving hers.

"I don't have to like you to want to fuck you, Graham."

"Touché." I make quick work of the buttons of my shirt, as well as the belt and fastenings of my slacks. Since I already know I'm not spending the night, I don't want to leave here looking like that was my intention, so I neatly lay my clothes over the chair for later. Fishing out my wallet after shedding my undershirt, I retrieve a condom and return to stand in front of Augusta. I toss it on the nightstand and as I turn to face her again, she grabs my face for another deep, scorching kiss. As her lips part and she slides her tongue against mine, I waste no time letting my hands explore her bare skin, pulling her closer. "Fuck, your skin is so soft," I comment when she moves her mouth down my jaw.

She runs her hands down my torso, her fingers setting my skin on fire, before she slides them over my hips and down to my ass. "Damn, you're one to talk about asses. What did you do, rob a bakery truck to get these buns?"

A bark of laughter falls from my mouth. I've always known Augusta was funny; she and Gemma laugh all the time. But I wasn't expecting her to be playful during sex. Granted, prior to an hour ago, I was never thinking that sex with her would ever be a possibility.

"Sorry, that was cheesy," she mumbles.

Shaking my head, I pull back to look at her. "Nah, it's all gouda."

She blinks, huffing out a shocked laugh. "Did you just make a joke? Holy shit. You mean you actually have a sense of humor? And here I thought 'broody asshole' was your only personality trait."

I could feel stung by her words, but all I usually am is an asshole, so the fact that we're half-naked and she's still willing to call me out is refreshing, honestly. I like that she doesn't pretend to be someone she's not. I like that she's real.

"I am a broody asshole," I warn, tugging her with me as I shuffle us to the bed. "But that doesn't mean I'm a selfish one." Sitting, I pull her down into my lap.

She comes willingly, straddling me. Draping her arms over my shoulders, she runs her fingers up the back of my neck and into my hair. "And just how unselfish are we talking?"

Pressing a kiss to her lips, I reach up to unhook her bra. She releases me just long enough to let it slide off her arms and to the floor and I nearly groan at the sight of her perfect, full tits. Rosy pink nipples hardened to stiff peaks brush against my chest as she loops her arms around my neck again and I can't resist running my fingers up her side to cup the generous hand-ful. "So much better than I imagined. Fucking hell, Augusta." I sweep my thumb over her nipple and she huffs a breath as she rocks her hips.

As I continue teasing her nipple, I grip the back of her neck with my free hand and drag her mouth to mine, but I don't kiss her. "You going to grind all over me and get yourself off before I've even touched you?" I flick her nipple with my thumbnail and she whimpers. "Fuck, I bet it wouldn't take much, would it? Is that pussy needy? Need my fat cock to fill you up and make you feel good?"

"Oh God, Graham."

Her breathing is so shallow as her heart pounds in her chest so hard I can feel it under my hand. "You're close, aren't you, beautiful girl?" I shift my hips and groan as she continues to grind down against me, the heat of her pussy radiating through the lace of her panties making me want to flip her onto the bed and drive into her. But I like the idea of making her come just like this too much to do that just yet. "I bet you're so wet for me already, aren't you? I bet you've soaked through these panties, haven't you?"

She breathes a moan against my lips and I capture her bottom one between both of mine and gently suck it before claiming her mouth fully. Her moan turns into a whine as she grips my hair almost painfully.

"Please, Graham. Fuck." Damn if I'm not even harder hearing her plead, my name on her lips. Wrapping my arms around her, I stand just enough that I can turn to lay her on her back. She lets out a squeak of surprise, color rising to her cheeks. "Holy shit."

I grin down at her as I run my hand up her thigh. "Save that for later. I haven't even done anything yet."

She huffs a laugh and her mouth begins to form a word when I push the crotch of her panties to the side and sweep my thumb up her pussy to work her clit. She gasps and I lower my mouth to hers for a deep kiss. "Just like I thought; fucking soaked for me. Now, are you going to come for me? Or," I slide two fingers inside her and her hips buck, "do you need more?"

"Oh, fuck," she chokes out, dragging my mouth to hers as

she rocks her hips as I fuck her with my hand. She feels so fucking good coming apart around my fingers and I know she's got to be close, so I want to watch her come. Scratch that, *have* to watch her come. I need to see her facial expressions and find out exactly what she looks like the moment she orgasms.

"Jesus, Augusta; you're so fucking perfect. Come for me, beautiful girl. I can't wait to be inside you. You're going to feel so fucking good."

Her eyebrows scrunch together as her mouth falls open on a low moan, her pussy clenching down around me so tight, I almost can't move. Her head falls back against the pillows, the tendons in her neck going rigid as she tenses. A flush travels from her cheeks to her neck and chest and fuck, if it's not the most beautiful thing I've ever witnessed.

I gentle my movements, even as my body screams for me to seek my own pleasure. But like I told her, I'm not selfish. As I withdraw my hand, I lift my fingers to my mouth and draw them between my lips, savoring her taste with a groan. Fuck, she tastes perfect, too.

Augusta shoves her panties down her hips and I shake my head as I let my eyes roam over her face. "I swear, if I didn't need to be inside you so bad I'm about to die, I'd bury my face in your pussy until you begged for mercy. Fuck, you taste good."

She smirks, reaching over to the nightstand to pick up the condom. "Why don't you see if you can do that with your cock?" I reach for it, and she snatches it back. "Lose the undies."

"What, need to examine the merchandise?"

Augusta huffs a laugh. "That's exactly what I need to do. I've had this image of you in my head for years; I need to see if I'm anywhere close."

Rising from the bed, I hook my thumbs in the waistband of

my boxer briefs and push them over my hips. I nearly groan with relief when my cock pops free, but I blow out a breath instead. Her eyes drag down my entire body and I nearly blush under her scrutiny. One of her brows lifts when her gaze lands on my dick and I stifle the urge to smile. I'm a big guy and I'm... proportional. I'm never going to beat any records, but I have nothing to be ashamed of either.

"Well, damn," Augusta says, impressed, and extends the condom my direction. "Definitely as good as I imagined. Now show me what you can do with it."

It shouldn't surprise me she's as take charge in the bedroom as she is in her daily life. I can't say I hate it. I rip the foil and hurriedly roll the latex over my dick, all the while, Augusta's gaze takes in the scene. "My eyes are up here, lady."

She chuckles, blushing at being caught staring. "Sorry."

Returning to the bed, I settle myself between her thighs and grin. "Eh, I'm pretty sure I was looking at you like that with your clothes still on, so it's probably fair." I take her in fully before I brace my left hand beside her shoulder. I grip my cock to slide the tip up and down her pussy, making her huff out a breath and dig her nails into my shoulders. "I must say, though, I prefer you exactly like this. Jesus. You're so fucking wet."

"Graham, stop teasing me. Please."

I give her a smug smile. "So needy." Slamming my hips forward, I'm pretty sure I die for a split second. She gasps my name, making me need to take some deep breaths as my head swims with endorphins. "Fuck, Augusta," I groan.

She rocks her hips and I definitely die, trying with all my might not to blow like some teenager. But fuck, she's perfect. For several minutes, we simply move together, feeling our way over one another's bodies. Although we've never done this before, it's as if we had a choreographed plan ahead of time, because I'm not sure it's ever been this good with anyone else.

Between soft touches, sweet kisses, playful words, and muttered curses and praises, we've soon worked ourselves into a frenzy of moans and gasps and we're both covered in a sheen of sweat. Toward the end, all I'm able to focus on is the sound of our bodies slapping together in this mindless pursuit of pleasure.

Augusta arches her back, her movements becoming frantic, and I'm so close, I'm not sure how much longer I can last. As if reading my mind, she reaches between us to work her clit and I shift to brace the backs of her knees against my biceps to drive myself deeper, causing her to cry out. And the fact that it's my name she screams? Fucking hell.

"Holy fuck," I gasp, bending my head to suck her nipple into my mouth, flicking my tongue over the stiff peak. Her pussy clamps down so tight on my cock, I can barely move or think or breathe. It's all I can do to hold out the few more seconds until she finally lets go, her entire body quaking with the force as she chokes out a sob. With one last buck of my hips and electric jolts of pleasure shooting up my spine, I come so hard I see spots. I'm almost positive my heart is about to explode from the exertion as a low grunt falls from my mouth.

My arms are jello as I try to hold myself up and not crush her under me. I drag in lungfuls of air, sweat pouring down my face. Augusta blinks, her own chest heaving as she stares up at me. "Holy shit."

I cough out a laugh, grinning down at her as I pull out with a groan. "Told ya you should've saved it for later."

She cackles, grabbing my face for a quick, playful kiss. "You were right."

CHAPTER THIRTEEN

AUGUSTA

When I wake, my muscles languid and tired, I roll over to find the other side of the bed empty. I suspected it would be, and I could be disappointed, but when last night was what I got? Hell no. I could happily die right now and feel like I got everything I ever needed to out of life.

My phone blares from the nightstand and I don't remember plugging it up. Surely Graham wasn't that considerate. I don't have time to think about that before I blindly grope for it, not bothering to look at the screen.

"Hello?" I croak out, and clear my throat.

"Auggie?"

"Gem? Hey. What's up? Shouldn't you still be in bed with your husband?"

Gemma laughs down the line. "Believe me, I was. But did you forget you rode over with me yesterday? You were supposed to be downstairs ten minutes ago. I was just checking on you."

I blink and sit up, nearly groaning when the delicious ache

between my thighs reminds me exactly what I did last night. "Okay. Five minutes. Sorry. Overslept. Coffee?"

"Already got yours. A double shot, extra foam."

"Bless you." I hang up and scramble from the bed, dragging on the jeans and T-shirt I had on before the party. When I catch a glimpse of myself in the mirror over the dresser, I nearly flinch. My makeup is smeared down my cheeks, my hair looks like a rat's nest and I have—I step closer to the mirror to get a better look—fucking hickeys on my neck. I don't even remember that.

Jesus, Graham.

I shove my dress and all my other belongings in my bag as I scrub a makeup remover wipe over my face to remove the worst of it. I shove my feet into my Docs and don't bother lacing them until I get on the elevator.

When I step off as I'm tossing my hair into a haphazard ponytail, I immediately see Gemma checking her phone for probably the fifteenth time since she called me. She blanches when she catches sight of me and hands over my coffee. I take a long drink and hold up my free hand. "Not a word."

She mimes zipping her lips and we walk out to her car after I drop off my room key with the front desk. I lift my bag into her open trunk and slide into the passenger seat. Gemma eyes me as she gets behind the wheel. "I have questions."

"Nope."

"Oh, come on. Was it good, at least? Because, um, those are some impressive hickeys, my friend. Do I know him? Are you seeing him again?"

I pinch the bridge of my nose, knowing I'm going to need so much Gatorade and bacon to combat this hangover. Except, this hangover isn't from alcohol. This is a sex hangover. Never had one of those before.

Damn, Graham.

"Yes. It was random. No." It's not exactly a lie. Sex with Graham was completely random. A one-off that will never be repeated.

"Wow. You actually had a one-night stand?" she asks, shock clear in her tone. "You don't do one-night stands."

I shrug. "He was hot. I was tipsy and horny. It worked out. He was gone when I got up. We did not exchange numbers."

Not a single lie detected.

"Well. Good for you, I guess. But it was good?"

"Best night of my life."

Also no lies detected.

"Damn. Alright. Well, hopefully you'll run into him again. Make sure you get his number if there's a repeat performance because I don't think I've ever seen you this...well serviced."

I know she would never say any of what she just did if she knew it was Graham who'd done the *servicing*. Three times. And the only reason there was no fourth was because we ran out of condoms. Not bad for a guy who's thirty-five. I slip my sunglasses onto my face. "I'll take it under advisement."

For almost four weeks following what must've been a fever dream, I seriously consider reaching out to Graham via social media, but his words from that night play over in my mind. *You know what this is, right?* I did know what it was. Graham didn't make me promises, and I told him I didn't need any.

It's not like I *miss* him. I might miss how good the sex was. I might have taken my vibrator on multiple outings since that night. I might've dreamed about how good it was. I don't miss him. So why can't I get that night off my fucking mind?

Hoping to do exactly that, I matched with this handsome engineer on a dating app Gemma and Brewster mentioned during one of their recent shows. They were looking for guinea pigs to provide testimonials and I volunteered. Okay, that's not entirely true. Gemma was bossy, and I caved.

But as I sit across from a perfectly nice man named Garrison, I can't help but draw comparisons between Graham and him, even as we simply have drinks. He's polite and asks questions and doesn't talk too much about himself. He's only looked at my boobs a few times in the hour we've been sitting at this bar and he hasn't tried to put his hand on my thigh or suggest we get out of here.

He's tall, but not as tall as Graham. He wears a nice suit that's still not as nice as the ones Graham wears. His hair is dark, but not the glossy jet black Graham's is.

Stop it, Augusta.

"So, there's this great Italian place around the corner. Would you want to grab a bite to eat?"

Graham is part Italian. I wonder if he speaks any Italian. Gemma knows a little, but does he? I mean, more than swear words.

For fuck's sake, Augusta, knock it off.

I mentally shake the thoughts away. "Sure. Give me a moment to go freshen up?"

Garrison smiles and all I can think of are the easy smiles that Graham had during sex. I'm not sure I'd ever seen him smile that much in the twelve years I'd known him up to that point.

Now my mind must be conjuring up visions of Graham, because he's sitting at the end of the bar when I look toward the bathrooms. I blink, trying to clear my vision and my heart lurches.

Graham is *here*.

Why is Graham here? And why is he looking at me like he either wants to commit murder or is extremely constipated? Our eyes lock and my breath catches, but I manage to cover it with a cough. I turn my attention back to my date, hoping I don't look as beet red as I feel with the way heat climbs up my neck. "I'll be back and then we can go to supper, okay?"

Garrison nods. "Sure. I'll just take care of the tab and wait for you."

I stand, my knees a bit wobbly under the flowy black skirt I wear, and I take a deep breath before walking past Graham toward the bathrooms. A stool scrapes across the floor and I don't even have to look to know it's him.

It shouldn't be, but I know it is.

And what does it say about me that I leave the door unlocked as I enter the bathroom or that I'm not the least bit surprised when he walks in a few seconds later, locking it behind himself.

"Who's the suit?"

I fold my arms. "I came in here to pee, not be interrogated."

Graham gestures to the toilet. "So, pee. I'm not stopping you."

My cheeks flame. "I'm not going to pee in front of you."

He takes a step closer to me and my heart rate ratchets up as he gives me a slow smile. "Oh, so you'll lick your cum off the head of my cock and let me put my finger in your ass, but you won't pee in front of me?"

My mouth falls open in shock, but heat instantly floods my middle. "I'm on a date."

"So you won't pee in front of me because you're on a date?" he asks, confused.

"No. I mean, yes," I reply, suddenly flustered. "What I mean is, you shouldn't be talking to me like this when I'm on a date." I fidget my watchband and shift my hips—Graham notices. I sigh, hating how off kilter I feel with him so close. But

I really do have to pee, so I finally roll my eyes and make a shooing motion at him. "At least turn around."

He chuckles but still obeys as I hurriedly pee, trying not to groan with relief. "What are you even doing here?" I ask as I stand and flush, moving over to the sink to wash my hands.

"Deposition. I'm just in town until tomorrow afternoon. I go back to Atlanta after that." He steps up behind me at the sink and drags his knuckle down my back, his eyes locking with mine in the mirror. Even through the fabric of my tank top, the contact sends goosebumps scattering up my torso. "I have a hotel room. Come with me."

I turn to face him, ignoring the throbbing that's suddenly settled between my thighs. "Like I said, I'm on a date," I remind him, gripping the edge of the sink.

He plants his hands on either side of my hips, leaning in to whisper in my ear, "I don't want to date you, Augusta. I want to fuck you."

"You don't do more than one night. That would be breaking your rules." Somehow, I sound completely unaffected by his words, although my nipples pebble under my bra as I grip the sink so hard, my fingers cramp.

He nudges my knees apart with his own and grinds himself against me. He's already hard and my breath hitches with how good his body feels pressed to mine. "There's probably some rule about fucking your baby sister's best friend so hard she nearly blacks out, but we did that, too. You don't want to see if it was a fluke? You can't tell me you're going to go sleep with that guy. Not when all you can think about is that thing I did with my tongue. And besides, if you don't wake up together, technically, it was never a whole night."

"What, no other willing, young co-ed here for you to take back to your room?" I'm shocked I'm still able to form words, let alone still muster up some snark, when all I want to do is let him do that thing with his tongue again.

"I wouldn't know. I haven't been able to take my eyes off you since you walked in with that tool."

Inwardly, I love that he might be jealous, even if I never knew jealousy was something Graham was even capable of feeling. "Garrison is a very nice guy."

He scoffs, his mouth skimming along my jaw. "You don't want a nice guy, Augusta. You want me."

"Wow, you must have a pretty high opinion of yourself."

"I do, but that doesn't mean I'm not telling the truth. Because I guarantee, if I slid my hand between your legs right now, I'd find you soaked. And not for the 'very nice guy' out there. For me."

As if to prove his point, he slowly begins gathering the fabric of my skirt until it's bunched in his hand above my knee. He runs his fingertips up my inner thigh, his eyes on mine, daring me to stop him. But I don't, even though I am on a date and he's very nice and waiting at the bar to take me to dinner. Graham won't take me to dinner. Graham only wants to fuck me. He already said so. And I don't just fuck.

So why am I not stopping him? Why am I letting my head fall back on a moan as his fingertips graze the crotch of my panties? Why am I yanking his mouth to mine for a frantic kiss and working the belt of his pants? Why am I gasping as he plunges his fingers inside me? And why am I shoving his slacks and underwear over his hips and pumping my fist over his cock so hard he grunts?

I could protest when he drags the front of my tank top down to suck my nipple into his mouth. Instead, I'm hopping up onto the sink as he fishes a condom out of his wallet. An instant later, he slams inside me and I nearly scream with the perfect fullness of him. He pounds into me, covering my mouth with his hand to muffle the sound of my moans as he guides his free hand between our bodies to work my clit. What feels like seconds later, I'm coming so hard I see stars and my throat aches from the strain. A beat later, Graham's hips buck a final time, his entire body going rigid as he grunts through gritted teeth, his forehead falling to mine.

He mutters something and I pull back to look at him. My ears must be playing tricks on me, because I'm pretty sure he's just asked me to come back to his hotel room.

"Huh?" I ask, breathless.

He pulls out, dropping the condom in the trash before righting his clothes, his eyes never leaving mine. "I said, ditch your date and come with me to my hotel."

"Why?" The question is out of my mouth before I can bite it back. But seriously, he's gotten exactly what he wanted, so why would he ask me to go back to his room?

He huffs a laugh as he pulls the hem of my skirt down, slides my bra strap back up my arm, and fixes the front of my shirt. "Because you and I both know you want to."

It's a testament to how dazed I am that I barely hesitate before nodding.

He gives me a slow smile. "Good girl," he offers, leaning in to press a soft kiss to my lips before tugging me off of the sink to send me back out to the bar.

What the hell am I doing?

I guess when the fuck is that good, you'll do things you didn't think you would.

I'm shocked to find Graham still in bed when I wake up. Granted, it's his alarm that wakes me, so I shouldn't be surprised, but I assumed he had some sort of internal alarm that kept him from waking up next to the women he sleeps with. He reaches over me to pick up his phone to turn off the alarm, brushing a kiss across my cheek after he does.

"You're still here?" I ask, my voice gravelly from sleep.

He chuckles. "It is my room."

"Still, I thought you'd be gone. Like before."

"Like I said, it's my room. Plus, it's not like I got a lot of sleep," he says with a smug grin. "The deposition isn't until ten, so I slept in. Want me to order some breakfast?"

I must still be asleep. Graham is offering me breakfast?

"Breakfast?"

"We didn't eat dinner, so I'm starving. I have to eat. Are you hungry?"

I blink. "I mean, I could eat."

"Okay."

"You're still here," I say again.

He laughs. "Yeah." He calls down to the front desk to order coffee, an omelet, and toast for us both. When he sets his phone back on the nightstand, he runs his hand down my bare back and nuzzles my neck. "It'll be a half hour before the food comes. Want to join me in the shower?"

I do. I definitely do. God, just his fingers brushing over my skin and his lips on my neck are enough to set me on fire. But this is the morning after. I never thought I'd have a second time with him, let alone a morning after. Forget about breakfast.

He rolls me onto my back as he kisses a path down my chest. "Or, is this better?"

My body moves of its own accord, arching into him while my mind races. This still can't mean anything, right?

I don't want to date you. I want to fuck you.

That's right. That's all he wants.

Don't forget it, Augusta.

As if he's flipped a switch, my brain goes completely blank

when his hand skims down my stomach and between my thighs. He chuckles. "So wet already. Fuck, that's hot." I moan as his fingers sweep over my clit. He draws my nipple between his lips, giving it a gentle tug with his teeth, making me hiss as I thread my fingers into his hair.

He swirls his tongue around the stiff peak, soothing the sting as his thumb replaces his fingers and he slides them inside me. "God, I love the way you feel, Augusta. So fucking perfect."

"You're not so bad yourself," I say with a moan. He crooks his fingers against my g-spot and I gasp, rocking my hips.

He braces himself on his free hand as he stares down at me. "That's it. Come for me. I want to be able to remember how hard I made you come when I'm supposed to be asking questions later. If I could, I'd go in there with you still on my fingers so I could smell you later."

"Fuck, Graham."

He gives me a slow smile, lifting a brow. "Oh, I will. And when you're still feeling it tomorrow, you'll remember it was me."

Not sure I'd be able to forget, even if I wanted to. I wasn't able to forget after almost a month last time. What's this time likely to do to me? I still don't like have to like him. But I sure like the things he can do.

He bends to capture my mouth with his and the fact that he's so far gone that stuffy, polished Graham Hopkins doesn't care about morning breath is incredibly sexy. It's enough to send thoughts out of my mind about who he might have brought back to his room if we hadn't run into each other.

But he did. And he brought you here.

I push those thoughts away, too, as he rolls the condom down and presses my knees back as he slides inside me with a groan. I gasp at the filling pressure and perfectness of him. Seriously, his cock is a masterpiece. He drags out almost to the tip before slamming back in, his pace deliciously torturous. "Fucking hell, beautiful girl; this pussy is perfect."

I let my head fall back on a deep moan. I don't want to think about how good this is. I don't want to admit that it's never been this good with anyone else and the first—or second or third—time definitely wasn't a fluke because this time has been just as good. I don't want to think about the command this man has over my body and the reactions he's able to effortlessly coax from it. I don't want to think about how I left a perfectly good date that might have turned into an actual relationship and love and a future for someone who will never be able to offer me any of those things.

I don't want to date you. I want to fuck you.

My body doesn't care that my heart wants things like love and marriage and family; despite the fact no one has truly ever loved me and my example of family dynamics is totally fucked up. I still want those things for myself. That won't be with Graham, though. And I don't give a shit.

Maybe no-strings fun is exactly what I've been missing. Sure seems like something's been missing up to this point. I can do a non-commitment thing, right? Well, duh. That's what this is. And fuck, it's good.

So good, that after we actually eat and shower—where it's *good* again—and I'm about to leave, Graham asks for my number. When he says, "Maybe we can do this again. You know, if we're ever in the same place at the same time," I don't hesitate to say yes.

CHAPTER FOURTEEN

GRAHAM

Augusta: I'll be in your neck of the woods this weekend. We're in Athens, so I know it's not exactly Atlanta, but are you in town? Maybe we can meet up after the game.

I stare down at my phone. In the past two months since I saw Augusta on her date and brought her back to my hotel room, we've hooked up several times. I've had to make some trips in and around Knoxville and reached out to her when I was there. This is the first time she's reached out to me.

Even though I'm actually scheduled to go to Miami for the weekend with my best friend, Kyle, I'm already shooting him a text to let him know I got called into work and won't be able to make the trip. What the hell is wrong with me? I don't do shit like this. I don't lie to my best friend and give up weekend guys' trips where there will be beautiful, tan women in bikinis and lots of easy sex.

But, Augusta...

Augusta is...different. She's bossy and sassy and sexy as fuck. She's like some drug I can't get enough of and I don't know what to think about it. I don't know what this thing is between us and I'm not sure if the fact that I'm even wondering what this thing is even means anything. All I know is, I just canceled on Kyle without a second thought because a woman— okay, not just any woman, but still—asked if I wanted to meet up.

> Graham: I am in town. And I'm free. When do you get in?

> Augusta: Friday evening. Team will go through a practice, but I'm free after until the game on Saturday. We leave Sunday morning. I know it's a hike, so if you didn't feel like driving back home, you can stay with me.

> Graham: Like I said, when do you get in? Send me the info. I'll be there.

> Augusta: And like I said, Friday evening. You want to come then? It'll be late.

Sometimes I hate texting since you can't convey tone. I don't know if her question means she doesn't want me to come until Saturday or if she's just confirming I do. I finally just hit the FaceTime option next to her name so I can actually talk to her.

For several seconds, she doesn't answer, but then her face fills the screen and I blink. "Are you in the bathtub?"

She rolls her eyes. "Yeah. That's why it took me so long to answer, I had a mask on. I had to wash it off."

I huff a laugh. "Oh, so you'll let me do unspeakably filthy things to you, but I can't see you in a beauty mask?"

"A girl needs *some* mystery," she quips and I can't help but smile.

"Okay, so this weekend. What's the deal? You don't want me to come until Saturday or what?"

She shakes her head as she sips a glass of wine. "No, it's not that. This is just the first time either of us will have been somewhere for more than a single night. I wasn't sure what the rules were."

"I didn't know we had hard and fast rules. I figured we were kinda making things up as we go along."

Augusta nods, thoughtful. "Okay. So, do you want to come on Friday?"

I shrug. "Sure. Will you show up in your uniform and be all 'bossy athletic trainer?'"

She rolls her eyes. "Why? You want me to make you hurt?"

"Ooh, pain. You don't know, I might get off on that sort of thing."

She snorts. "No you don't. You whine like a little bitch when I dig my nails into your back."

"True. Okay. Yeah, no pain. So, if I came in on Friday, what time would I need to be there?"

"Like I said, the team has a practice, but I'm free after that. Probably around eight, I guess?"

"Do you want to grab a late supper, or will you be eating with the team?"

She frowns, her brows drawn down in confusion. "Dinner?"

"We have to eat, right? I'll be working until at least six and with traffic and stuff, it'll put me getting to Athens probably just before eight. Like I said, if you've already got dinner plans or you're eating with the team, I get it. I'm just wanting to plan accordingly."

"Oh. Okay. No, we all do our own things usually. The team all eats together, but the sports medicine team does their own thing."

"Alright, so we'll go eat."

"We don't normally do that," she says, her tone hesitant.

"So you don't want to? I mean, we have breakfast together."

She lifts a brow. "Room service breakfast after spending the night together is different than actually going out to dinner."

"You make it sound like it's some kind of payment for services rendered. Do you think that's what I view it as?" My tone comes out more affronted than I plan, but I'm not sure why. Augusta and I are casual. But the way she said it makes me feel like all I see her as is sex.

Isn't it, though?

Her cheeks flame. "No. I don't feel like some kind of sex worker or anything and I don't feel used, so don't get all indignant. You were the one who said you didn't want to date me; only fuck me. I'm just trying to keep my expectations managed correctly, Graham. Dinner is a 'date' thing."

I don't want to date you. I want to fuck you.

I did say that to her. "It's just dinner, Augusta; not a declaration." I sound snarky and I don't like it. I also don't miss the way Augusta blinks before looking away from the phone.

What am I doing?

After a beat, she nods. "Okay. So, dinner?"

"Sure. Want me to just pick you up at the hotel and we can come back after?"

"Alright. Do you want to stay until Sunday?"

"You mean two nights of great sex as opposed to one? It's a no-brainer, beautiful girl."

She tucks her hair behind her ear as she drags her top teeth over her bottom lip. "Sounds good to me," she finally says with a smile. "I'll send you the hotel information and add your name to my room reservation."

Her smile seems a bit forced and I frown. "Are you mad?"

She shakes her head, taking another sip of her wine. "No. Why would I be mad?"

I huff a laugh. "Well, for one, you sound mad. Or at the very least, annoyed. Are you?"

"No, Graham; I'm not. Like I said, I'm just keeping everything straight."

"What's that supposed to mean?"

"Exactly what I said. Nothing has changed. Us going to dinner and you calling me pet names and us spending two nights together instead of just one doesn't mean they have. Like I said, I'm just keeping things straight. We're not dating. We're just fucking."

"Yeah," I reply, but I don't like the way I feel when she says the words. It's like she thinks I'd never want more from her than that and has to remind herself. That does make me feel like I'm using her; even though we talk and text and I'd consider us friends at this point. Her thinking I wouldn't date her makes me feel like shit. Because Augusta's amazing. She's beautiful and smart and hilarious and confident. She's someone any man would be lucky to have as their partner.

I open my mouth to tell her all this, when the screen flickers and she sighs. "Gemma's calling me. I'll send you the info. See you Friday." She disconnects the call before I have a chance to even tell her goodbye, and I'm left feeling out of sorts. I might be an asshole, but I'm not a shitty person and I'd like to think I don't mistreat people.

Just because Augusta and I aren't in a committed relationship doesn't mean we can't have dinner or go out when we are together, right? I'd never want her to think I'm ashamed to be seen with her or anything, not that I think she does. She doesn't have self-image issues. I love how confident she is. But I also don't want her to feel as though all I see her as is a hookup.

I mean, that's essentially what I implied the first night we were together and the night at the bar. *I don't want to date you. I want to fuck you.* Maybe if she hadn't stayed with me that night and I didn't see exactly how beautiful she is in the mornings with her skin all warm and her hair all wild, it might not bother me. But now it does.

What the fuck does it all mean? I don't do relationships. I do sex. Period. That's it. Even if the only person I'm sleeping with currently is Augusta, it doesn't mean anything, right? Is she sleeping with other people? We don't talk about stuff like that, but I know if she had an actual boyfriend, she wouldn't still be sleeping with me. The thought of someone else taking her out or her going home with someone else makes jealousy slither through my chest and bile rise up in my throat. The idea that someone else gets to see her in the mornings or watch her face when she comes? I loathe it.

Fuck.

But I'm not a hypocrite. I'm not going to ask her to not sleep with other people if I'm not willing to do the same. Is that something I can actually agree to, though? I will admit, it's been easy to turn down other women when I don't go out and I'm getting amazing sex on a pretty regular basis. Especially when it's with someone I genuinely like; someone I can carry on a conversation with and actually know.

Is that a *relationship?* I'm thirty-five. I should know what one looks like, right? I've had a fantastic model for one in my parents' relationship. But it's never been something I wanted for myself. All I wanted was the job and the money. Sex was sex and relationships were unnecessary to achieve that. But what does it mean if I want more than just sex from Augusta?

I'm still mulling all those thoughts over a few days later when Augusta walks out of her hotel dressed in a pair of shorts and a tank top after the team's practice. She climbs into the passenger seat and as it's been a couple of weeks since I've seen her, I can't help but kiss her. So I lean over the console and pull her to me to give her a deep kiss. God, I've missed her and I almost tell her that, but bite it back. I'm not sure why, but since I still don't know what I want, it seems like I'd be leading her on to say something like that, so I don't.

When she leans back, she blinks in surprise. "Hello to you, too," she says with a smile. "So, where to?"

"Pizza? I passed a place on the way here. Decent crowd, so it should be pretty good."

She nods. "Perfect." She takes in my clothes. "You're not in a suit."

I huff a laugh. "Did you expect me to be? I changed before I left the office."

"I'm not sure I've seen you not in a suit since law school. I wasn't even sure you still owned a pair of jeans."

"Well, I do."

She grins. "I can see that."

A few minutes later, we pull up to the restaurant and as we walk inside, I fight the urge to take Augusta's hand in mine. *Seriously, am I twelve?* But when the host leads us to a U-shaped corner booth, I don't hesitate to scoot right next to her and drape my arm over the back of the booth.

After we've received our beers and have placed our order for pizza, I lean over to skim my fingertips down her bare arm. I brush a kiss under her ear before resting my forehead against the side of her head. "I'm glad I get to see you this weekend."

She smiles, but it's tentative, as if my statement weirds her out. To further prove my suspicion, she tucks her hair behind her ear and fidgets with her watchband.

Frowning, I pull back. "Why does what I said make you uncomfortable?"

She neutralizes her expression and shakes her head, folding her hands in her lap. "It doesn't."

"Bullshit."

Another one of her tells—dragging her teeth over her bottom lip—shows itself. All I can say is, it's good Augusta's not a poker player because she'd lose every hand. I like that I know this about her. I'm not sure I'm allowed to know this or if she likes that I know it—or, hell if she even *knows* that I know it. But I do.

She takes a long drink of her beer. "You shouldn't say stuff like that. That's all."

I frown even more, surprised by her response. "I'm not allowed to tell you I'm happy to see you?"

She shrugs, even more uncomfortable, and wiggles her septum ring with the tip of her thumb before dropping her hand. "Yeah, of course. I'm just not used to hearing you say it."

I mean, she's not wrong. We give each other shit and have really hot sex, but we're not sentimental. I nod. "I know. But I am happy to see you and I wanted you to know it."

"I'm happy to see you, too," she says after a beat. We're quiet for a few minutes until Augusta's phone rings. "Shit, it's Gemma. I'm going to go see what she needs. I just talked to her this morning, so I'm not sure what it could be."

"Sure." She steps away and as I drink my beer, I notice hers is low. A moment later, our pizza is delivered and I order some ranch dressing for Augusta and refills of our beers.

She comes back right after the server stops by to drop off the items and she frowns, eyeing the pizza. "Damn. I forgot to order ranch." She makes to signal the server and because I'm mid bite, I tap her arm and point to the cup that sits next to her fresh beer. "Oh," she replies, surprised.

I swallow my bite. "What?"

"You ordered me ranch?"

I shrug. "And a refill on your beer."

"How did you know I like ranch?"

I offer her an incredulous frown. "I've known you for twelve years, Augusta. I know you dip your pizza in ranch and that you get headaches when you drink red wine. You have tells when you're uncomfortable or weirded out. I know you don't like to wear foundation or heavy makeup because you have super sensitive skin and it makes you break out. I know you always sleep with one foot out of the covers because otherwise, you feel smothered. You hate chocolate unless you're on your period and then it's only something like chocolate-covered pretzels. I know you." I drop my slice of pizza back on its plate. "I get the feeling that all you think I see you as is a warm body and, to be honest, it's a bit insulting. I like you as a person and I know you; probably better than you think."

Her cheeks flame as she takes an angry bite of her pizza, but she doesn't say anything.

Kicking myself for word vomiting all over her, I blow out a breath and sip my beer. "What did Gemma want? Or is it something just between the two of you?"

She shakes her head, relaxing.

Probably glad I didn't keep talking about how I "know" her.

"She just said the Feds picked Curtis up today since they finally had enough evidence to charge him for all the stuff he did to Gem and Brewster."

"That's good. I'm sure they'll be glad to have that sorted. They'll probably still have to testify, but at least he won't be a problem for them anymore."

"No, and they got some offers from some bigger markets for syndication, too, so they're feeling pretty good today."

"I'd say so," I reply with a nod.

CHAPTER FIFTEEN

AUGUSTA

The entire way back to the hotel is tense and I can't figure out why. Okay, I do know why. It's because Graham said all that stuff and alarm bells went off in my head. My heart wanted to go all ooey-gooey, and that's not what Graham and I have.

I remind myself every time I see him, it's only sex. It's only physical. There are NO feelings. N-O, nada, zip, zilch, zero feelings involved. But try as I might, this heart of mine is attempting to beat down the door I've locked it behind where Graham's concerned. Because he doesn't do love. He doesn't do dating. He only does fucking.

Except now, he's wanting to spend a weekend together. He's ordered me ranch and he *knows* me. Plus, he feels insulted that all I think he sees me as is a fucking warm body.

Well, excuse the hell out of me.

Thankfully, he doesn't push me to talk as we make the drive to the hotel. Or when he grabs his bag from the trunk of his car. Or as we walk to the elevator to ride up to the room. It's not until we get to the room, I've gone through my entire night-time routine, and I start getting naked while he stands there fully clothed that he actually says anything.

"What are you doing?" he asks with a frown.

I drop my hands from where I'm about to unhook my bra and peer at him, confused. "What do you mean? I'm getting naked. Isn't that what we do?"

His cheeks flame. "I figured we'd hang out; maybe watch some TV or something."

I blink. "You don't want to have sex?"

Graham pinches the bridge of his nose. "Fuck yes, I want to have sex. With you, in case you were about to ask. But I'm also happy to just spend time with you, Augusta."

"That's not what we do, Graham." I fold my arms and almost laugh when his eyes fall to my cleavage for a split second before returning to my face. "That's what *couples* do. Last I checked, that's not us."

"Are you sleeping with other people?"

I recoil, shocked by his question. "What?"

"It's not a complex question, Augusta. Are you currently sleeping with other people?"

I clench my jaw. "I understood the question perfectly, so no need to be a condescending asshole. It surprised me, is all. What does it matter if I am?"

I'm not and haven't been. I haven't slept with anyone since him and for a while before the wedding, but he doesn't need to know that.

"Because I don't want you to sleep with other people."

Anger, hot and instant, floods my chest and my mouth falls open. "You don't get to tell me who I can sleep with. Like I said, we're not a couple. We're not dating. You've made it very clear that you don't date. You only fuck, Graham."

He licks his lips and his throat rolls with a swallow. "I'm not sleeping with anyone else. I haven't since the wedding." My mouth falls open again, this time in disbelief. Graham closes the distance between us as he rakes his fingers through his hair and clears his throat. My heart lurches because I realize he's nervous. I've never seen him nervous. Ever. "I don't want you to sleep with other people because I want to be the only one you're sleeping with. And I want you to be the only one I'm sleeping with."

"What?" is all I can say because I'm too stunned to say much else.

He opens his mouth and closes it again until he finds the words he's looking for. "Look, I don't know how to do this, but all I know is, the thought of anyone else touching you or kissing you makes me want to commit murder. And I'm not a hypocrite. I can't expect you to not see other people if I'm not willing to also not see other people. I still think we need to keep Gemma out of it—at least for a while longer—because I don't know what kind of boyfriend I would be and I don't want to make things weird if I fuck up.

"I've been on her shit list for a while with how I was after she broke up with Kyle since he and I are still friends, but I don't want her to hate me. You're her best friend and honestly, I think she loves you more than she does me. So even though I don't know how to do this sort of thing, I think I want more than what we've been doing. I don't know what that looks like with our work schedules or anything, but I want more than just sex with you, Augusta. I like you."

"Boyfriend?" I ask, still trying to process everything he just said.

Color creeps into his cheeks as he takes another step closer. "Yeah. So, are you sleeping with anyone else? Can't have my girlfriend sleeping with other people."

I huff a laugh. "No. I'm not. I've been on some dates, but haven't slept with anyone. Also not since the wedding."

He gives me a smug grin and lifts a brow. "It's because I'm the best, right?"

I roll my eyes. "I could ask you the same thing."

Graham takes my face in his hands. "And I would say yes." Warmth floods my chest as he bends to press a kiss to my lips. "So, is that a yes? To being exclusive?"

I wrap my arms around his waist and give him a playful smile. "Are you asking me to go steady, Graham?"

He laughs. "If that's what it will take for you to give me the answer I want."

I bite my lip. "I don't know; I might need some convincing."

He leans in, kissing a trail down the side of my neck. "Would this need to be done verbally, or..."

Reaching behind my back, I unhook my bra. "I'm more of an actions-over-words kind of gal."

Nodding, he shuffles me back toward the bed. "I can get behind some action."

I pull his mouth almost to mine. "I'd be happy to let you get behind *me*."

Graham drags in a deep breath. "I do enjoy watching your ass."

"Pretty sure you like to do more than just watch it."

He lifts a brow. "Pretty sure you like the things I do to it, too."

"Did you hear a complaint in any of what I said?"

"No, but it's hard to hear anything when you still have your clothes on."

I hurriedly strip off the rest of my clothes while Graham does the same. I turn the covers down and crawl into bed. Just before he joins me, he pivots and jogs, naked, over to his bag to retrieve a box of condoms. "Trojan really should pay you at this point. You've probably financed their CEO's vacation home by now."

He laughs, tossing the box on the nightstand as he lies down beside me. "Probably. Just so you know, I got tested last month and I'm clean, so if you're on the pill or whatever, and we're exclusive, I'm cool to ditch them."

I shake my head. "I'm not."

His brows lift in surprise. "You're not clean?"

"No." I hurry to clarify. "I am. I get tested at least once a year and I only had a few partners before you. I meant, I'm not on anything. I don't like artificial hormones and I'm allergic to copper, so I can't get the non-hormonal IUD. So, unless you want little Grahams walking around, suit up, my friend."

He shakes his head and chuckles. "Yeah, no thanks. No kids for me. Like, ever."

I don't react to his words, but my heart sinks. No kids is a deal-breaker for me. I want kids. Lots of kids. "So, if you don't want kids, have you had a vasectomy?"

"No. I probably will; I just haven't gotten around to it."

I nod, trying not to think about the fact this man, who just said he wants at least a semi-serious relationship with me, doesn't want children. I try not to think about how I assumed that by the time I was thirty, I'd already have kids. I'm settled in my career, I'm debt free, I'm saving for a house. All that's missing is *the* guy. And ever since the wedding, I've been keeping my heart under lock and key because I was convinced Graham could never be *the* guy. I didn't think he'd ever want to be anyone's guy. But now he wants exclusivity. That's the foundation for a future.

Stop it, brain. You've been exclusive for thirty seconds. Just enjoy it.

He runs a knuckle along my jaw. "You okay?"

Pushing all those thoughts aside, I nod. "Yeah, still just trying to absorb everything. I wasn't expecting this."

He props himself up on an elbow, draping his arm around

my waist to tug me closer as he tangles his legs with mine. "A good surprise, I hope? After we FaceTimed the other day, I was a bit out of sorts and couldn't figure out why. Then I realized I don't want anyone else, Augusta. I've never wanted anything serious, and I don't know if I'll be any good at it, but you're pretty awesome. I'd rather no one else know how awesome you are in bed."

I laugh. "Right back at you. What will the female population of Atlanta do without you to occupy their time?"

"Find some other rich, handsome, well-dressed lawyer to give them lots of orgasms?"

Trailing my fingers down his chest and abdomen, I reach between us to stroke him and he huffs a breath. "As long as I'm the only one this rich, handsome, well-dressed lawyer gives orgasms to." He was half-hard when I wrapped my fingers around him, but within seconds, he's fully erect and I push him on his back to straddle his waist.

Graham's eyes drag down my face and torso, and his cock jerks against my ass. As he runs his hands up the outsides of my thighs, I bend to give him a deep kiss. I'm not sure I'll ever get enough of him, and now that I've been given permission to have him all to myself? It's surreal.

He grips my ass, making a sound of appreciation in the back of his throat, and I chuckle. "It's like you're obsessed with that thing."

"Not sure I'm not. It's quite the specimen."

"Yeah, yours is pretty nice, too. All of you is pretty nice." I drop kisses on his chest and shimmy down his waist, causing him to groan as my pussy slides over his dick. I nip at the skin below his belly button as I run my hand up his thigh to wrap my fingers around his cock. "I especially like this part," I say, pressing a kiss to the head. He jerks in my hand and a thick bead of pre-cum forms at the tip. I lick it away, the taste of salt hitting my tongue as he inhales sharply.

I hold his eyes, sinking my lips around him as I take him to the back of my throat, and his mouth falls open on a ragged huff. "That fucking mouth. Jesus Christ, Augusta." I chuckle and he hisses, his hips bucking as his fingers sink into my hair.

Closing my eyes, I pump my fist and work the head of his dick with my mouth, focused on the sounds of his pleasure and how much I enjoy doing this for him. I can't keep from pressing my thighs together, wanting some relief of my own.

He drags in a breath as his grip tightens in my hair. "You like sucking my cock, beautiful girl? You're so fucking good at it. But you're shifting that sweet ass like you need something. That pretty pussy getting all wet for me?"

I take him deep again and he grunts, yanking me off of him. "Fuck, woman. I think you're trying to kill me."

Laughing, I move back up his body. "What a way to go, right?"

He pulls my mouth to his as he runs his free hand down my body, stopping at my breasts to tease my nipples. They're always sensitive, but he's got some sort of magic touch, because within what feels like seconds, my breathing turns into choppy moans as he plucks, flicks, and rolls my nipple with his fingertips. Breaking our kiss, he smiles against my lips. "I love how you can get off just with me playing with your tits. Fuck, it's hot. But I bet that pussy's aching for my cock to fill it up, huh?"

"Graham," I whine.

"I know. You want it so bad, don't you? Would you beg for it?"

"Please," I reply automatically. I reach down between my thighs to work my clit, but he snatches my hand away.

"No. I'm the only one who gets to get you off tonight. You want it?"

I give him a jerky nod. "Uh-huh." The word comes out high and thin and my breaths are so shallow, I'm not sure I won't hyperventilate.

"I know you do. Get a condom and put it on me. I'm going to pound that sweet pussy from behind."

I'm so close already, when I reach over to the nightstand, my hands are trembling as I fumble with the box. I'm gasping by the time I get it open and rip off a square. I tear it open and hurriedly roll it over his length.

He gives me a final kiss. "That's my girl. Now get on your hands and knees. I want that ass up in the air for me."

I scramble to obey as Graham climbs up behind me. He skims his hand down my back and I shift my hips, feeling him hard against me. He grips my hips before sliding his hands over the curve of my butt. "This ass, I swear. Fuck."

I shift my hips back and side-to-side, hoping to encourage him to get on with things for the sake of the throbbing ache between my thighs. This results in him landing a sharp smack to my ass, making me gasp and whimper. The sensation seems to shoot straight to my pussy and I don't even have to feel myself to know that I'm even wetter than I was.

Graham rubs his hand over the area, soothing the sting, and chuckles. "You liked that."

"So did you," I say.

"Fuck yes, I did. Seeing my handprint on this pretty pale skin? Fucking sexy."

"So do it again."

He inhales a deep breath. "Is that what you want?"

I look over my shoulder at him. "What I want is for you to stop dicking around and fuck me."

He teases my clit with the tip of his cock and I gasp. "So bossy. Don't I take care of you?" Another sharp smack lands on the opposite cheek and I grunt. "Fuck, you're practically dripping. I wonder if you clench down when you get spanked." He grabs my hips and slams inside me and I cry out. "Too much?"

I huff a laugh. "I'm not fragile, sweetheart."

"My girl's mouthy, too. Let's see if I can't help you with that attitude."

I look over my shoulder at him again and lift a brow. "Have at it."

Heat flashes in his dark brown eyes and I'm smiling as he pulls out slowly and drives back in, setting a brutal rhythm that's punctuated with stinging smacks to alternating cheeks. "Fuck, Augusta," he grunts, gripping my hips as I cry out again. "You get so fucking tight when I do that. Jesus."

"Graham," I plead, so close that tears well in my eyes with how intense it feels.

"You want me to stop?"

"Fuck me. Please."

He drops a kiss onto my shoulder blade. "I've got you." Bowing his body around mine, he continues his deliciously slow thrusts as he reaches around to work my clit. "You're so fucking beautiful when you come, you know that?" I whimper, my legs nearly giving out. "You're going to come for me now, aren't you? And you're going to say my name when you do because I'm the one who fucks this cunt so good."

"Fuck," I gasp, choking out a sob.

"You're so close, beautiful girl. You going to give it to me?"

"Oh, God."

He chuckles and groans through gritted teeth. "That's not my name, Augusta."

He pinches my clit, the sharp, sudden sensation triggering my orgasm so intensely, I scream. And yeah, I totally say his name. Because, *fuck*. Graham drops his forehead to my shoulder, bucking his hips a few final times before his entire body shudders as he mutters something unintelligible. He gasps, dropping his hand to the bed to catch himself.

However, I do collapse and when he rises, asking me if I need anything, I wave him off. "Tell Gemma I died happy."

He laughs as he walks to the bathroom, but he returns a few minutes later, climbing back into bed with me to pull me into his arms. "Okay, but what am I supposed to tell your family?"

I shake my head. "You don't have to tell my family anything. Just Gemma. And then you can tell her you're the one who killed me with your cock."

He laughs, tugging the covers up around us. "Nice. I'm sure that won't be an awkward conversation or anything."

"You're a lawyer. You'll come up with some lawyerly mumbo jumbo to talk her in circles until she forgets what you were trying to tell her in the first place."

"Mumbo jumbo? We prefer gobbledygook, thanks."

I snort a laugh and look up at him. "You're really funny sometimes, you know that?"

He sweeps the hair off my face, tucking it behind my ear. "I don't think I am."

"Well, maybe I'm rubbing off on you," I say with a shrug.

He nods and presses a soft kiss to my lips. "Probably. I have fun with you."

"I have fun with you, too." I snuggle closer to him, marveling that this is a thing I get to do now. What's even more shocking is that he won't be doing it with anyone else. "I know things about you, too, you know."

His brows draw together in confusion. "What do you mean?"

"At the restaurant, you spouted off a bunch of stuff you know about me. I know stuff about you, too."

He gives me a lopsided grin. "Oh, yeah? Try me."

"Challenge accepted. You hate crowds and loud noises and

are easily overstimulated. You're not a big fan of music, but when Gemma interned for that radio station before she went to work with Brewster, you would listen to her show every day so you could give her constructive feedback, regardless of the fact that you hate country music. You still listen to her show; even now.

"You love good food. Which, that one's not hard to reconcile with the way your family cooks. And regardless of the fact that you and Gem don't always get along, you love her fiercely and worry about her. You claim to be a lawyer because the money's good, but you started in family law because you wanted to help spouses escape bad marriages and adoptive families get their happy endings. Litigators are mostly after the big bucks, but you honestly want to help the people who have been wronged."

I give him a slow smile. "Your favorite movie is *A Time to Kill* and you secretly love that your parents are proud of your accomplishments, even if you pretend you're indifferent. And despite you being a broody asshole most of the time, you're also a good man and someone I'm glad I've gotten to see that side of."

He blinks as his throat rolls with a swallow. "Wow, I was expecting you to out me for liking pumpkin spice lattes."

I laugh and press a kiss to his chest. "I was saving that blackmail material for our first fight."

CHAPTER SIXTEEN

AUGUSTA — PRESENT DAY

I've never been good at resisting him. Not since that April night at Gemma and Brewster's wedding reception when Gem and I were singing along with Britney Spears at the top of our lungs, and I made eye contact with Graham from across the room. He seemed to be undressing me with his eyes and my insides lit up like the Christmas tree at Rockefeller Center.

It's not as if I'd been blind for twelve years up to that point; Graham has always been my best friend's hot older brother. He seemed entirely indifferent to me. For years, I thought it was because I was "the chubby girl". I tried not to take it personally because I probably wasn't his type. No problem. Besides, there were plenty of hot guys who gave me the time of day, so one who didn't wasn't a big deal.

But at the reception, when Gemma and I danced and laughed and celebrated her falling in love with her best friend of ten years, something changed. His eyes locking with mine changed something in me.

And yeah, there was a shit ton of vodka responsible for my courage, but as soon as I could make my way back over to the bar, I decided to take a chance. I didn't say a word to him, just slipped my room key under a bar napkin and quirked an eyebrow at him in invitation. And maybe, in challenge.

What followed was the night that I still think of as the standard for all of my sexual experiences. Sadly, no one has lived up to it again. No one except the man himself, that is. No promises were given and none were expected and he was gone when I woke up. And I was okay with it. I assumed I had my one night and I very well could've died a happy woman at that point.

But a few weeks later, after our sneaky bar bathroom quickie and the night we spent together, numbers were exchanged. If we happened to be in the same city, we'd see if we were available. We still both agreed it was best if Gemma didn't find out because between my history of being a hopeless romantic and Graham's lack of enthusiasm about love and commitment, we knew she'd never understand.

Then casual became exclusive, since neither of us were interested in sleeping with other people, but still in secret. Then came my break during the offseason. It was a month of cohabitation and somewhere in the mix, I fell in love. Although no one knew, I didn't care, because for the first time since I'd fallen for Trey, I truly let myself love with my whole heart.

Then, everything changed, and I swore I'd never let him in again. Not into my body. Not into my heart.

For five years, I've stayed true to the promise I made myself. I've endured parties and cookouts and events where we had to be in the same place at the same time. Granted, I always made sure to keep at least ten feet between the two of us so I couldn't smell him or really hear him speak. And other than when needing to converse with him for specific matters, our interactions have been minimal and contentious.

So tell me why I'm currently tugging my Christmas gnome

nightgown over my head and watching his eyes take in my body like Tiny Tim at the Christmas feast.

Oh, right. *I miss you.* Definitely not the three words I thought it would take to get me on my back for him again, but my heart and vagina are both brazen hussies and, as I've established, I can't resist this man.

Maybe it's the way he's showed up for me since we got here yesterday—was that *just* yesterday? He has stood up for me and hasn't asked for anything in return. Maybe it's because he thinks I hate him when I could never hate him. Especially because I've never actually stopped loving him; despite everything that transpired between us and after. Maybe it's because he's said he'd do things differently and regrets how everything turned out. And maybe it's *Tesoro.* That after five years, he's pulled it out and knows what a puddle it turns me into. Or hell, maybe I just want to get laid and no one is better at it than him.

Whatever it is, I've given him this one night and, like our first night, there are no promises. But fuck, if it doesn't feel like there should be.

I lie here, naked and proud, simply letting him look his fill. My skin heats under his gaze, but he doesn't touch me after my gown has been discarded. It's as if he wants to reacquaint himself with my form by sight alone.

As he's almost always done once I'm topless, he bends to brush his lips over the freckle next to my belly button. "I've missed my freckle," he remarks as he plants soft kisses up my stomach and between the valley of my breasts, continuing higher and higher until his mouth claims mine in a deep, hungry kiss that snaps whatever thread was holding us back. I can't resist wrapping my legs around his hips to pull him against me. He's still in his underwear, but he's hard and thick and in the perfect position for me to grind myself against him.

I can't bite back a moan as he shifts his hips. He smiles

against my lips. "That pretty pussy needy, Tesoro? You going to let me have you?"

I can only let out a soft gasp as he continues to rub against me exactly how he knows I like and fuck, how has it been five years since I let this man touch me? How have I stood in the same room with him, been at the same parties, and not dragged him to a secluded spot to let him coax my body into sobs of unbelievable pleasure before now?

Graham kisses down my jaw and neck, chuckling when I continue to exhale breathy moans. "Look at you, so fucking perfect for me. Should've just kidnapped you years ago and gotten it over with. Not let you go until you remembered how good this is." His hand skims up my waist and I shiver when his thumb brushes over my nipple. "Jesus, I've missed these tits."

"Pretty sure they've missed you, too," I admit. He smiles that lazy, cocky grin of his as he trails kisses back down my chest. How I thought he didn't have an easy smile, I'll never know. When it's only us; when it was good? He never stopped smiling. To see him smile like this again is nearly too much for my heart to bear.

I roll my hips against him and he groans through gritted teeth. "Fuck. You're going to have to stop that. I can't be blowing my load in my pants like a teenager."

"You're not wearing any pants," I remind him with a playful grin. I do it again, but he pins my hips with his own. I scoff. "Dirty move."

I gasp as he bends to capture my nipple between his lips, sucking it to a stiff point. When he pulls off a beat later, it's with an audible *pop* and, try as I might, I can't keep a desperate whimper from working its way up my throat.

"Are you that needy? You need me to make you feel good?" Moving down my body, his eyes never leave mine. "I bet no one has given it to you like you need for years, have they? You want me to spread you open and remind you what you've been missing? I bet you're so wet already, aren't you?"

He nips at the soft skin of my stomach. While I used to loathe my body—thanks, Mom and Carrie—over the years, as men, and especially Graham, have treated my body as if they can't get enough of it. Having someone kiss over my stretch marks or trace them lovingly with a fingertip only helps me love my body even more. Every dimple, every roll, every crease, every jiggle.

Even now, as Graham trails his mouth over to my hip, encountering that fold of skin where there's some overlap, he simply presses his lips to it, his movements almost reverent, on his journey toward exactly where I want him. As my anticipation builds and his hands slide up my inner thighs, I let my head fall back onto the pillows. But when his thumbs sweep up my pussy to spread me wide, and his tongue follows the same path, a long, low moan falls from my mouth.

He groans against my heated, wet flesh and settles in to expertly flick, suck, and nibble my clit, the vibration hums throughout my entire core, making me gasp his name. As if by muscle memory, my fingers immediately thread through his hair and I grind my hips, needing more. In no time at all, my heart is crashing against my ribs and my breaths are beginning to grow shallow.

Again, his low groan reverberates through me and I whimper, already so close. Fuck. He's so good and no one else has ever been able to find the exact rhythm and pressure to get me from zero to sixty, probably faster than Graham's C-Class.

"Oh, God, don't stop. Please, don't stop," I plead, my voice gone husky with lust. He chuckles and I gasp with the sensation. "Fuck, Graham." My breaths coming in short, high pants, I raise my head to look at him down the length of my body and his eyes are closed as he feasts, his own hips grinding against the mattress.

It's that sight that finally pushes me over. To see him so lost in giving me pleasure he can't resist seeking his own, any way he can? I'm gone. A choked rasp falls from my mouth as my legs shake with the intensity and swiftness of my orgasm. As he always does, he gentles his movements until I've come down before kissing his way back up my body.

When his eyes find mine again, they're hooded and full of desire and affection. And because I can't think of more than simply being in lust with Graham at this moment, I drag his face to mine to claim his mouth with a desperate kiss. After only a moment, he breaks his lips from mine. "Fuck, I've missed the way you taste."

I swallow as I try to catch my breath. "I've missed your mouth."

He huffs a laugh. "The feeling is mutual."

After another quick kiss, he hops off the bed and I watch him walk over to his suitcase. I'm not sure I'll ever get used to what he looks like. Graham isn't ripped and chiseled, but he's strong and solid, and I love the feel of his muscles flexing when we move together. His thick thighs, dusted with coarse, black hairs. His chest and abdomen covered in that same coarse, black hair that I love to feel against my own smooth skin. His firm, round ass nestled like two perfect globes in his boxer briefs. I could take a bite out of it. After fishing out a strip of condoms from his bag, he turns to rejoin me on the bed. I let my gaze rake down his body and I couldn't miss the sizable bulge in the front of his underwear if I tried.

I sit up, scooting toward the edge of the bed to grip his hips as he comes closer. I pull him between my knees and as I look up his torso, I'm forced to crane my neck to see his face because he's so tall. As I dart my tongue out to wet my lips, his nostrils flare in anticipation, and even in the dim light, I don't miss how big his pupils are. When I brush kisses over his stomach, he drags in a breath, his free hand coming to settle on my jaw. I look back up at him as I let my hands roam over his ass and up and down the backs of his thighs before running my fingertips under the waistband of his underwear.

"You've missed my mouth?"

He drags his thumb over my bottom lip. "I've missed all of you, Tesoro."

"Would you like me to get you ready for me? Have you missed seeing my lips wrapped around that fat cock of yours?"

His eyes fall closed as he blows out a breath. "Jesus, woman. I forgot how dirty your mouth is."

I lift a brow. "That was not an answer to my question."

Graham chuckles. "Augusta, I've been harder than I can ever remember in my life for the past twenty minutes. I'm even harder now. Fuck yes. I always want your mouth."

"Good answer." I drag his underwear down his hips and he groans when his dick pops free. Honestly, it's all I can do to keep my own whimper of need held back at the sight of him. God, how I've missed his cock. When he's inside me, it's like he was made just for me. He's able to hit every sweet spot I never knew existed until him and he's just...perfect. "Damn, that's a sight for sore eyes."

He opens his mouth to say something, but whatever it is dies as I run my hand down the length of him before sinking my lips over the head of his cock.

"Fuck," he breathes, his hand sliding back and into my hair. I take him deep a few times the way he likes before swirling my tongue around the crown and flicking the sensitive spot on the underside of the tip. "Jesus Christ, babe." His words come out as a gasp and his hips buck just before he pulls me off of him.

"Hey, I wasn't done," I protest, offering him a smug smile.

His chest heaves as he rips off a condom and tears the foil with his teeth. I scoot back on the bed, watching him as he rolls it down before joining me. He settles between my thighs and where his expression was previously all hunger and need, it's now one that makes my heart kick over. My knees bracket his hips and it's so surreal to be with him like this again after all this time.

I close my eyes in anticipation and Graham runs his hand along my jaw. "No, I want to see your eyes when I make love to you." Slowly, I open them to find his already drilling into mine. "If I only get tonight, I get all of you. And if I only get tonight," he shifts his hips and I gasp as he enters me, taking a couple of deep breaths of his own, "then I'm going to say what I should've said five years ago."

"Graham," I protest, but it devolves into a deep moan as he drags his hips back and slams forward again, wiping my mind of everything I was about to say.

I dig my nails into his lats as I rock my pelvis, driving him deeper. He groans through gritted teeth as he grips my ass possessively with his other hand. "Fucking hell, Tesoro. So fucking perfect." The hand on my jaw slides to the back of my neck as he claims my mouth, his kiss frantic.

I let the sensation of him wash over me; the familiar perfectness of being with him. It has never been and will never be as good with anyone who's not Graham. This thought should fill me with bitterness, but all it does is make me see that there's only him for me and the last five years of still loving him weren't in vain.

Although I've only promised him tonight, I already know I'm a liar. I won't be able to give him up again and if, after all the shit I've been through, I can still feel love, shouldn't I be able to have it?

I'm brought out of my thoughts when Graham shifts to

brace the back of my knee over his bicep and the change in angle and intensity of his thrusts nearly makes me see stars. I choke out a sob as I'm seconds away from coming undone again.

His hand still gripping my jaw, he forces me to look at him when I attempt to avert my eyes, unable to hold his gaze. Even though I will never stop loving this man for as long as I live, fear of what could happen if I allow myself to be happy wraps its vine-like tendrils around my heart and grips tight. But Graham doesn't let me look away. Even as his face is pinched in concentration and beads of sweat pop on his forehead as his breathing turns ragged, he still somehow finds words. He pistons his hips in a deliciously slow, deep rhythm that has me nearly unable to breathe as he pounds into me.

"I fucking love you, Augusta. I never stopped. There is no one else for me. And you think this is only for tonight, but you're mine, Tesoro. Forever. Say it."

"Graham," I plead.

He presses my knee back farther and I cry out, but it's muffled by his lips on mine. When he breaks our kiss, he rests his forehead on mine as I gasp for breath. "Say it, Augusta."

And because I already knew I never stopped being his, I don't hesitate, even as fear continues to try to take hold. He offered to be my shield earlier tonight, so maybe he can also be strong enough for both of us, too. "Yours. Forever," I breathe. As I let go, wave after wave of acute, almost too intense, pleasure crashes over me and my head lolls back onto the pillows as a raspy sigh works its way up my throat.

Graham crashes his lips to mine again as he pumps his hips one final time, grunting through gritted teeth as his body shudders above me. His chest heaves with his labored breaths and he slowly lowers my leg back to the mattress, peppering my face with soft kisses.

A beat later, when he pulls out, my body mourns the loss and I drag his mouth back to mine, needing connection. He shifts to lie beside me, breaking our kiss to grab a tissue from the box on the nightstand to dispose of the condom in the small trashcan by my bed. After, he faces me again, tucking a stray hair behind my ear as he offers me a small, tender smile that makes my heart ache.

Tears well in my eyes and his brow furrows in confusion. He opens his mouth, but I put my finger to his lips so I can get the words out. "I love you, too."

He instantly relaxes, pulling my hand away from his mouth. "As well you should; that was some of my best work. I'm not as young as I used to be, you know."

I snort a watery laugh. "You're such an asshole."

"Yeah, but I'm your asshole."

CHAPTER SEVENTEEN

AUGUSTA

I wake from what may have been the best dream in my life. Dreams of Graham and me and several hours of mind-blowing sex. I shift my hips as I roll over and realize it was very much not a dream. Delicious soreness radiates throughout my limbs and I can't help but smile.

Graham pulls me into his arms, his body curling around mine as he brushes a kiss under my ear. "Merry Christmas, Tesoro."

"You, too." He feels around on the front of my body, groping and rubbing, but it doesn't feel sexual and I huff a laugh. "What are you doing?"

"Just making sure I'm actually awake and it wasn't a dream."

He pinches my hip and I swat his hand. "You're supposed to pinch yourself, asshole."

"I'll remember that next time. I'm going to go get a shower and then, if no one is downstairs, I'll make some coffee."

"Coffee sounds nice. What time is it?"

He checks his watch. "Seven."

"Yeah, you're good. No one should be up for at least another hour. Why don't you do coffee first and then shower?"

He nuzzles under my ear, causing goosebumps to scatter down my arms. "Oh, so you value caffeine more than my personal hygiene?"

"Absolutely."

Graham chuckles as he presses a kiss to the side of my neck. "Done. Want me to bring you some?"

I snuggle deeper under the covers. "Duh. Why do you think I said coffee and then shower? It's so much more efficient. Gah, it's like you don't even know me."

"Oh, but I do. I think I proved that last night. I know all the ways to get you off, at any rate."

"Yeah, yeah. Coffee."

"So bossy. Good thing I love you." With a final kiss, he leaves the bed and I don't bother watching him drag on clothes to head downstairs in favor of attempting to get a few more minutes of sleep.

I don't doze back off, but when the bedroom door opens again only a couple of minutes later, I smile, not even opening my eyes. "That was fast."

"God, you're disgusting."

I sit bolt upright, clutching the covers to my chest as Carrie walks into the room, still in her pajamas. "What are you doing in here? Didn't you learn your lesson last night about knocking? Jesus, Carrie."

She stops in her tracks, color rising to her cheeks. It's not until she begins walking toward the bed that I realize I said all that out loud and my heart begins to race the closer she comes to the bed. "My, my. Did my big sister finally grow some balls? You think you're some hot shit now and you can forget your place? You think just because Graham is here, he can protect you?"

Faster than I can comprehend what's coming, she slaps me across the face and snatches my hair, yanking my head back painfully. She gets in my face and bile rises in my throat, but I refuse to react to her abuse, since that's exactly what she wants.

Her eyes roam over my face, a disgusted snarl on her lips. "Have you forgotten about all the things I've taken from you, Gus? I see you still don't drive. Probably a good thing. Those brake lines can be so tricky, you know. And it'd be a shame if you happened to fall down another flight of stairs. So sad what happened last time. This time, it could be more than just a baby that you lose."

I blink rapidly, attempting to hold my tears at bay.

It's not my real life. I will survive this. Don't react. It's what she wants.

"What, nothing to say, bitch?" Carrie spits out. "Or are you not going to mouth off to me again? Trash doesn't get to talk back. Does Graham know what a sniveling little cunt you are? How desperate you are for everyone to love you? How nobody here ever wanted you and your piece-of-shit father died just so he could get away from you? You're so fucking pathetic if you think that any man—let alone a man like Graham—could ever want you for more than just a fuck. You are a waste of space, Gus, and wastes of space don't deserve nice things. You sure as hell don't deserve Graham and I did that bastard baby of yours a favor. No way we need another Parsons walking around here, taking up space they don't deserve."

When I still don't react, she lets me go, pivoting to stride over to the closet like she didn't just threaten bodily harm against me and spout all the hateful things she always has. I count to ten in my head and calmly breathe in and out in an attempt to ward off a panic attack.

A moment later, while Carrie is still gathering gifts from the closet, Graham walks back in, a cup of coffee in hand, a huge smile on his face. "Your coffee, Tesoro." He doesn't even seem to notice my sister until he sees my face and then looks around, annoyance filling his features. "Something we can help you with, Carrie?" He hands me my coffee and turns to put himself between her and me.

He has no clue what just happened, and yet he still wants to protect me from her.

"What? You told me to wait until this morning. I waited until this morning. Jeez."

Graham walks over to the closet. "Here, let me help. Don't need you in here bothering Augusta when she's trying to rest." He picks up the rest of the gifts and ferries them out into the hall. "There. Next year, don't hide them here. Otherwise, Santa might decide to dump them out in the hall a little early."

Carrie walks out and sets her packages down before planting her hands on her hips. She narrows her eyes at Graham. "You know—." She doesn't get any further, because he's already slammed and locked the door.

God, I love this man. Even as shook up as I am, I can't help but smile when I see the goofy grin on his face as he walks over to the bed. He sits next to me. "I should probably wait a few minutes before I try to go shower." He examines my face, reaching up to brush the back of his finger over my inflamed skin where Carrie slapped me. I try not to wince because it stings like a bitch. "Your cheek's all red."

I shrug and sip my coffee. "Probably just where I slept on it. It'll go away." It's definitely not the first time she's slapped me and I know by the time I go downstairs, it'll be gone. "Please tell me the weather should clear up soon. I've only got a few more days off and I don't plan on spending them here."

He pulls his phone out, navigating to his weather app. A beat later, his lips curl into a triumphant smile. "Look at this.

It'll be in the fifties by this afternoon. Hopefully, we'll be out of here by tomorrow morning."

"Praise baby Jesus." He takes my coffee from my hand and sets it on the nightstand before leaning in to trail kisses down my neck. "What happened to taking a shower?"

He tugs the blanket down my body before running his hands up my waist and over my breasts. I inhale quickly, heat and need shooting through my middle. "I'm thinking it's best if we hide out for a little while. Let your sister cool down. What better way to pass the time than by letting you get me naked again?"

I huff a laugh as I yank up the hem of his shirt. "You are so smart," I say, peppering his cheek and jaw with kisses. "I bet you could be a lawyer or something. You're very convincing."

He grins as he moves his mouth down my chest. "Oh, you have no idea how convincing I can be."

"I bet I do, but for argument's sake, *convince* away."

"With pleasure."

After breakfast and clean up, everyone open gifts. David sits in his recliner and Mom, Carrie, and Mason all take the sofa. Graham and I drag a couple of chairs in from the dining room so we don't have to sit on the floor. The kids are all surrounded by shredded wrapping paper, toys, and sporting equipment, but they have already abandoned them all and returned to their electronic devices.

I tend to go the standard gift-card-to-a-nice-restaurant route for my parents and Carrie and Mason. For the kids, I give them gift cards for the bookstore so they can pick out their own gifts. That way, I can't be accused of attempting to brainwash them or something equally asinine. As usual, Mom and Carrie seem to go all out for one another and their families. Carrie and Mason gift Mom and David with a week away at an all-inclusive resort in Jamaica and my parents give my sister and brother-in-law a week at a winery in Napa.

I learned long ago that I would never receive anything heartfelt—or even nice—from my mom or my sister. With how Carrie is raising her children, I'm not surprised that I don't receive gifts from them, either. I'd be lying if I said I wasn't nervous about opening what they got me, simply because I dread Graham's reaction. Sure enough, when my mother hands me an envelope, she smiles. "This is from us and Carrie and her family."

I nod, pasting a smile on my face, already suspecting what it will be, since every year, it's some variation of the same thing. I open the envelope and am not a bit shocked to see a year's subscription to Weight Watchers. "Thank you. I'm sure y'all put a lot of thought into this."

Graham's grip on my knee tightens when he sees my gift, but as I warned him this would probably happen and made him promise not to explode, he doesn't react any more than that. Never mind that as soon as I get home, I'll toss the envelope in the trash. Nothing against the weight-loss program, but I like my body exactly as it is. Plus, staying chunky and in charge just rubs them both the wrong way and is about the only way I can fight back against them and their fatphobia.

He leans over to me and whispers in my ear. "This is bullshit. Next year, I say we just go on a vacation. We bring Mom and Dad, Gem, Brewster, and the kids and thumb our noses at these assholes."

I huff a laugh. "Not a bad plan."

"Graham, I'm sorry we don't have anything for you. If Augusta had told us anything at all about you, we could've prepared."

He gives my mother a tight smile. "No problem, Mrs. Harvey. I have all the gift I need right here." He turns his gaze on me and his smile softens and I can't keep my grin held back.

As I glance out the window, I almost do a happy dance when I see the sun shining brightly and water pouring off the roof.

Please God, let all the snow melt. Fast.

———

By three o'clock, with the snow melting nearly faster than I can blink, we decide to take a walk toward the road to check the conditions. I know from experience, the county will have shoveled and salted the main highway, but these secondary country roads don't typically get much attention. I'm hoping with all I'm worth, the snow will have melted enough that we can make our escape today.

For the first several moments of our walk, we simply stroll hand-in-hand down the driveway. It should feel strange that only two days ago, Graham and I were still at each other's throats, and now we're blissed out and I'm thinking about the future again. "When do you have to be back in Atlanta?" I ask, dreading his answer.

"Day after New Year's." He's quiet for a beat. "I hope you'll take pity on me and let me borrow the other side of your bed until I have to go back."

I snap my head in his direction, surprised. "Really? Of course you're staying with me. That'd be amazing."

He smiles and huffs a relieved laugh. "Great. Our office shuts down until then, thank goodness. When I was still in family law, I'd get swamped with business the week after Christmas with wives who are fed up that their husband bought them a vacuum cleaner instead of the pair of earrings they wanted."

I chuckle. "Yikes. Do you really like litigation? I know you did back in the day, but do you still?"

"Parts of it. The paydays are nice, don't get me wrong, but the fact that there are things that end up requiring class-action suits is shitty, and it gets old. Businesses and corporations should be able to prevent the stuff that our firm represents. Sometimes I miss doing all the wills and stuff, too, from when I did estates. It was always interesting to read when someone gets left everything and you just know their other family members will shit a brick. Thus, the pro bono side of things."

"My parents are leaving everything to Carrie."

He frowns. "How do you know that?"

I sigh. "Last year, when I was going through their insurance EOBs, there was an envelope from a law firm. I suspected what it would be before I even opened it. I wasn't even that surprised. Part of me wonders if Mom left it in there on purpose in the hopes I'd find it."

Graham's jaw clenches and he pinches the bridge of his nose. "Babe, I love you, but we are not coming back here. If you want to come for Christmas morning, fine. But we are not spending any significant time with your family in the future. I understand you want to fight this war quietly and maintain a stiff upper lip and all that shit, but I can't watch them treat you the way they do. I won't survive it. I will have a massive heart attack or stroke from holding back all my rage. Besides, are these really the kind of people you want around when we have kids?"

My heart lurches with his unexpected words. "Who said anything about kids? We're back together for twelve hours and you're already talking about kids?"

He turns to face me, his expression sincere as he wraps his arms around my waist. "Yeah, I am."

I blow out a breath. "I don't know what to do with that answer."

His brow furrows. "Are you saying you don't want kids anymore? Or, just that you don't want them with me? I know I screwed up so bad, but I've—."

I shake my head quickly and cut him off. "No, that's not what I'm saying. Not at all. I just think this is a serious discussion. I need a few days away from my family, an intensive session with my therapist, and snuggles with my godchildren. I think we have to tell your sister that we're together and at least some version of past events, otherwise all this seems super insta-lovey. Although I think she'd believe that about me, you're a different story. As far as any of your family knows, we pretty much hate each other. They're going to need time to adjust. I have a job here; a life. You have a job and life in Atlanta. We'll figure it out, but I can't do it today, okay?"

He heaves a relieved sigh. "I can live with that. Damn, I thought I was the level-headed one. Look at you, coming at me with logic."

I offer him a sly smile. "It's probably all the orgasms. They've gone straight to your head."

He laughs. "I believe you would probably be correct." Five more minutes has us at the end of the driveway and Graham nods when he sees the mostly cleared road. "I think this will do. We'll need to head out soon so we can be on the main road before it gets dark."

"You ain't gotta tell me twice. Let's roll."

CHAPTER EIGHTEEN

GRAHAM

It takes us all of ten minutes to pack our shit once we get back to Augusta's room. "Okay, I'm ready," she says with a smile.

She heads for the bedroom door, but I block her way. "No way. You're not leaving here until you look like you. What that means is that you're going to put your Docs on, take all that shit off your face since it's been bugging you the whole time we've been here, and you're going to put your septum ring back in. I want *my* Augusta back, not some fake version who's only trying to not rock the boat."

She blows out a breath and I press forward. "What are they going to do? They don't even know we're leaving. We're going to walk down with all our shit and they'll probably be shocked you didn't run it by them. For at least the next five minutes—or, however long it takes us to get out to my car—you are going to be you.

"You are not your mom or your sister, thank God. Stop trying to make them think you care about their opinion of you. You expend way too much mental energy trying to be invisible in front of them." I take her face in my hands, marveling once again that this is now a thing I get to do. "You, my beautiful girl, are never, in a trillion years, ever going to be invisible. Stop trying."

She's thoughtful for a moment and nods. "Okay." Over the next five minutes, she transforms back into the sassy, free-spirited woman I fell in love with. Originally, she was wearing a navy, knee-length dress, almost identical to the red and black ones she's worn the other days we've been here. She trades the dress for a pair of light wash, shredded skinny jeans, a black tank top, and a chunky, tan cardigan. Gone are the pearls, the high necklines, and the shapeless fabrics. The clothes fit her sexy body exactly like they were made for her.

Damn, this woman is hot.

When she finishes tying the laces of her Docs, she stands from the bed, her septum ring glinting in the light. I nod, a giant, approving grin on my face. "There she is. Gorgeous. And all mine."

She blushes, her posture the most relaxed it's been since I picked her up at the airport. "Let's go." I take her backpack and slip it over my shoulder before picking up my suitcase to follow her down the stairs. Conversation ceases when we make it to the living room. "Well, it looks like the roads are clear, so we're going to head out so we can put in a visit with Graham's family."

April and Carrie both gape at her appearance and Amelia's eyes go wide. "Wow, you have a ring in your nose. That's so cool."

Carrie's cheeks flame with anger. "Oh, great, that's a good influence for her. What in the world are you wearing? You look like you crawled out of a Goodwill dumpster."

I expect to have to put Carrie in her place, but Augusta squares her shoulders. "Thank you so much. Considering most of my clothes come from thrift stores, that's exactly the look I was going for. Mom, David, Mason, Merry Christmas. Amelia, thanks for the compliment. Maybe when you're eighteen, I'll take you to get yours done," she says with a smirk aimed at her sister.

Carrie sputters in disbelief, so I nudge Augusta toward the door. "Thank y'all for having me. Merry Christmas."

David and Mason both wave from their seats, and we stroll out the front door and down the porch steps. I pop the trunk on my car, dropping our bags inside. Once we're inside the cab, Augusta lets out a giggle as I start the car and crank up the heat. "What, babe?"

"I told off my sister. Like big time. Well, big time for me. It was exhilarating. It was like you said; I was expending too much mental energy trying to be invisible. I've done it for thirty years. I'm done. I like myself. I love my body. If they don't, that's a them problem and I'm done trying to prove my worth to them. Fuck 'em."

A bark of surprised laughter falls from my mouth. "Well, hell yeah. There's my girl. I knew you were in there somewhere."

She worries her bottom lip. "I don't think I could've done it without you being here with me. Thank you for standing up for me and giving me the courage to stand up for myself."

I lean over the console to pull her toward me and press a kiss to her lips. "You had the courage all along. I'm just glad you found it. I'm glad I got to see it."

"Me, too. Now, take me home and get me naked again. I want my bed to smell like you before you have to go back to Atlanta."

"Yes, ma'am."

Forty minutes later, after Augusta gives me directions to her apartment in Knoxville, I'm pulling into the parking lot adjacent to her building. "Is it okay if I park here while I'm in town, or do I need to park in a public lot?"

She shakes her head. "No, I have a spot."

"Okay, but what about your car?"

"I don't have one."

Surprised by her answer, I frown. "What do you mean, you don't have one?"

She shrugs. "I sold it. I live within walking distance or bus distance of pretty much anything. I Uber when I need to go anywhere else."

"You sold your car?"

"I can always get another one if I need it, but I don't. One of my colleagues actually lives in my building, so we carpool and I split gas with him when we're working. When he has company, I let him borrow my spot. If I have to travel with one of the teams, I ride the bus. It's not a big deal."

Bothered, but unsure why, I just nod. "Okay, so I can park here?"

"Yeah. My assigned space is over there." She points to an empty spot and I guide my car into it. After we get out and retrieve our luggage from my trunk, we walk up to a door with a keypad, where she punches in a code to open the door.

I take in the building's interior as we make our way to the elevator. It's an older building, in the heart of downtown, and in close proximity to a lot of restaurants and shops. I know from visiting this neighborhood when I lived in Knoxville, it's a great location for fun activities.

The walls have exposed brick and polished stained concrete floors—it gives an almost industrial feel. We climb onto the elevator and she pushes the button for the eighth floor. "So, how long have you lived here?"

She thinks for a moment. "Almost three years. I've always loved this area, and it's close to the school. I'm sure I could get a lot more place for less money, but I honestly love it. The building has a lot to offer as far as amenities go, and it's secure, so that was a huge selling point for me. The older I get, the less I trust humans in general."

"I know what you mean." I'm about to ask how she gets groceries if she doesn't have a car when the elevator opens. I follow Augusta as she takes a right and starts down a long hallway, headed straight toward a door. She fishes out her keys and I notice she has a doorbell camera mounted to her door. "You like that thing?" I ask, pointing at it. "I keep debating on getting one, but I'm not sure. Is the subscription worth it?"

"I like it. I can see who's at my door before I answer it. I don't even have to get off my couch. I think of it as a digital peephole."

"Pretty cool."

She unlocks the door and ushers me inside. The apartment isn't overly large—only one bedroom from the looks of it. The walls are white, with patches of exposed brick and the same sealed concrete floors. Augusta immediately opens a metal sliding door to our left to reveal her bedroom.

Tossing her bag on the bed, she begins unpacking. "I'm going to start a load of laundry; do you need anything done?"

Following her lead, I lay my suitcase on the king-sized, black metal bed with gray and olive green bedding. I fish out all my dirty clothes except my suit, since I'll take it to the cleaners once I get home.

Home. That's going to require some consideration. There's no way, considering I just got her back, that I'm doing a long-distance relationship for any longer than is absolutely necessary. I will admit, we made it work before with relative ease, but I want to wake up beside her every day, not just a few weekends a month or on the off chance she has a few days off during one of the teams' seasons.

Both our schedules are packed with travel and responsibilities and one of us will have to make a career change. Definitely something to—.

"Earth to Graham." I blink, focusing my attention on Augusta, and she laughs. "Wow, you were totally spaced. I bet you didn't hear a word I said, did you?"

I shake my head. "No. Sorry. I got distracted. What were you saying?"

"I was thinking, everything will be closed today since it's Christmas, so we can have a cozy night in, unless you want to attempt to make it to your parents' house. But it's already starting to get dark and their road is almost as bad as my parents', and your car—beautiful as she is—wasn't built for treacherous road conditions. But if you want to brave it, I'm happy to go along for the adventure. Or, we make the rounds tomorrow, after more of the snow has had a chance to melt. I have stuff here to cook for tonight and there is absolutely nothing in this apartment that is diet or sugar-free."

I huff a laugh. "Oh, thank God. I think tomorrow's fine. My parents weren't expecting me today anyway, so that'll be good. I'm thinking Gem will be there, too, since Mom and Dad have Collier and Mom likes to fuss over Gemma right after she has a baby."

"I remember. Your mom is good like that." She gathers up her laundry. "Alright, laundry is in the hall behind the curtain." We trek out of the bedroom and she pulls the curtain in question aside for us to dump our clothes in. As small a thing as doing our laundry together is, it reminds me of the month we spent living together the summer after we became exclusive. Those were some of the happiest days of my life. I can only hope the days ahead are as good.

After starting the machine, she gestures to the back of the apartment, continuing the tour. Floor-to-ceiling windows that span nearly the entire width of the apartment showcase a view that overlooks the street below and you can see much of downtown. "Wow. This is some view."

"Right? I love it. At night, it's nice to just sit and watch the cars as they go by. You'd think with all the traffic it would be loud, but it's not. Even with the windows cracked, you get a bit of noise, but nothing that would be annoying. It's like this funky kind of white noise. When the weather's nice, I'll sit and read with the windows open. It's great."

The living room and kitchen are one large open room, with the kitchen area to the left. State-of-the-art stainless steel appliances fit perfectly into the space that's complimented by the dark gray stained cabinets and quartz countertops. There actually isn't much counter space, so she's added an olive green colored island with two backless stools lined up one side. A black, rectangular table sits flush against the windows and is surrounded on three sides by four chairs. I'm assuming she pulls it away from the windows if she has company.

In what could be considered the living room, she's put down an area rug with black, gray, and olive green accents and she has a dove gray twill loveseat and oversized upholstered chair for seating facing the mounted TV. Tying the space together is a black coffee table and single end table with a lamp.

A few pieces of artwork dot the walls of the apartment, but with a view like the one she has, who needs wall art? She walks past me toward the kitchen, and I reach out to pull her into my arms. I rest my forehead against the side of her head as she relaxes against me. "Your place is great. It's very you."

She wraps her arms around me and hugs me tight. "I'm glad you like it. I'd be lying if I said I ever expected to see you here, though."

Looking down at her, I bring my hand up to drag my knuckle along her jaw. "I know." I blow out a breath. "I'm so sorry for everything that happened."

She shakes her head. "I don't want to talk about any of that right now. Please? Like I said, I need space from my parents and Carrie before I even begin to unpack that."

I nod. "I know. I just want you to know that I am in this. I want you. I want us. I want all of it. Whatever 'it' looks like."

Augusta swallows. "Okay."

I believe her agreement, but her eyes and tone convey hesitancy. I can't blame her. Not after everything *before*. I'll just have to prove myself to her. Whatever that takes.

She steps back and I drop my arms as she continues walking toward the kitchen. "So, let's see what we've got here."

After a delicious supper of pasta carbonara and sugar cookies for dessert, I notice for the first time that Augusta doesn't have a tree. "Why don't you put a tree up?"

She sighs. "Because Christmas has become one of those things that just represents pain and trauma for me. Part of me would prefer to skip it all together. I show up every year simply to spite my family and show them that no matter what they do, I'm still stronger than they give me credit for. They'll probably never see it that way, but it's how I make my stand, so that's what I do.

"If they ever asked me to stop coming, I would, though. I'm fully aware my approach isn't a healthy one. My therapist has never come out and said it, but she's alluded to me cutting ties with them since they're the root of the majority of my trauma, but I'm stubborn, I guess."

"Yeah. You are. And listen, I'll support you however you

need, but your therapist would be right to suggest that. That is the most toxic environment I've ever been in and I now feel like I need to call *my* therapist."

She lifts a brow. "Do you have a therapist?"

"No, but your family makes me want to get one. Plus, aren't all millennials in therapy anymore?"

She chuckles. "Probably. And those who aren't in therapy are usually the ones the people who go to therapy talk about."

"Definitely." Sipping my water, I ask, "So, you only go to your parents' at Christmas? What about Thanksgiving?"

"I always volunteer to work. There's usually a basketball game and most people want to be with their families. My parents don't even ask anymore." She pumps her brows. "It doesn't hurt that the games are usually in some warm locale and I can spend some time on the beach." She waffles her hands like scales. "Fresh ocean breeze and fruity drinks. Mom's dry-ass turkey and stuffing. I think you know which one I'm picking."

"I don't blame you."

CHAPTER NINETEEN

GRAHAM

"Damn. This is a nice bed," I remark after we climb under the covers.

"Right? I love it. Honestly, I love everything about my place. I love that none of my family's toxic energy is here, and it's all mine."

Running my hand over her side and hip, I tug her closer. "So, they've never been here?"

She shakes her head. "They don't even know where I live."

I frown. "How is that possible? You've been here three years."

Augusta shrugs and lightly drags her nails down my chest, making my skin hum with awareness. "I didn't tell them when I moved. They don't send me birthday cards or Christmas cards. Carrie doesn't send me invites to the kids' parties and stuff. There's no reason for them to know. They live barely a half-hour away and have never once reached out to see about stopping by or anything. I only see them at Christmas. After everything I said today, I'd be surprised if I hear anything from them for months."

I shake my head. "I hate that for you."

She shrugs again before slipping her hand into my underwear. "I don't want to talk about them anymore, Graham."

Letting out a quick exhale as she strokes me, I grin at her. "I'm guessing you don't want to talk at all, do you, Tesoro?"

She leans closer, bringing her lips to mine. "Nope. Not unless it's you telling me all the dirty things you want to do to me."

"Done." I snatch her hand away and roll her on her back, settling between her thighs. I grind myself against her and her mouth falls open on a moan. "Do you know how much I love watching your face do that? Fuck, it's beautiful. I have dreams about that." Dropping a kiss on her lips, I slide my hand up her nightgown and her waist to cup her perfect tit. I lightly brush my thumb over her nipple. She inhales and huffs a breath when I pluck the stiff peak between my thumb and index finger.

"You know what else I dream about?"

"Hmm?" she asks with a moan.

"You. Sitting on my face." Her eyes fly open, her brows drawing together. She opens her mouth to protest and I shake my head, tweaking her nipple, need settling low in my abdomen as she gasps. "And if you say some shit about how you'll suffocate me, I will remind you of what I said the last time I asked you to do it: What a way to go. You're going to ride my face and then you're going to ride my cock and kiss your taste out of my mouth." She rolls her hips, letting out a soft moan. "Now get naked and put that pretty pussy on my face."

Color rises to her cheeks, but as I roll off of her and onto my back, she gets to her knees, dragging her gown over her head. I toss the pillows into the floor and scoot a few feet down the bed. She straddles my chest and I look up her body, unable to keep the hunger out of my gaze. "Look at you. Damn, you're beautiful."

She gives me a soft smile and as I hook my arms around her thighs to yank her forward, she lets out a surprised squeak. I can't help but chuckle as she rises to her knees again to travel even higher up my body. I let my eyes fall back down to my target, my mouth watering at the sight of her. She's pink and wet and fucking gorgeous.

Augusta lowers herself fully and I kiss my way up her inner thigh and I can't resist sucking a mark so I can look at it later. She inhales sharply and as I pull my mouth off, pleased with my handiwork, I glance up at her. She huffs a laugh, but when she opens her mouth to say something, I drag my tongue up her pussy to her clit and she gasps. I'm not sure I'll ever get used to how perfect she feels and tastes on my tongue; regardless of how many times I have her like this.

And fuck, do I relish this. But my favorite part is, once I get into the rhythm and pressure that she likes, she always, without fail, threads her fingers through my hair and rocks her hips. God knows Augusta has never been content to be a passive participant. I know once she does this, most of the time, she's only a few minutes from soaking my face.

But tonight, I don't want her only a few minutes out from her orgasm. I want to draw it out; make her earn it. So when she's so close, her breaths start coming in choppy pants and her grip on my hair turns painful, I change up the rhythm enough so that it pulls her back from the precipice.

She gasps, choking out a protest, and I laugh. "Such an asshole," she says, but with the vibration from my laughter, she barely gets the words out for the deep moan that follows. I slowly work her back up again, this time also running my hands over her thighs and hips, up her waist to her breasts to tease her nipples. The rocking of her hips turns frantic and again, her grip on my hair and breathing tell me she's close again. Once again, I back her down.

She lets out a cry of frustration and because I know she's probably not used to being edged—hell, the men she's been with in the last five years probably didn't even know what to do with her—I don't draw out her torture for long.

I begin to work her up a third time, swirling my tongue around her clit over and over until she's nearly yanking my hair out by the root as she rides my face, her movements almost feral. When I finally let her go over this time, she seems almost surprised. A raspy sigh falls from her mouth as her legs shake and I drink up every bit of her.

After she's able to speak again, Augusta leans forward, grabbing the metal bar of the headboard to scoot down my chest. "Such an asshole," she repeats between ragged breaths.

I laugh as I pluck a condom off the nightstand, and as I push my underwear down my hips and legs, Augusta claims my mouth with a deep kiss. I forget what I'm doing for a moment before the foil packet crinkling in my hand reminds me as I wrap my arms around her.

Letting out a reluctant groan, I break my lips from hers. "Half a second. I swear."

She snorts a soft laugh. "See, I figure you'd be able to put that on without having to see it anymore."

"I probably could, but your mouth is distracting, so I'm liable to forget how to put it on altogether."

She nods, a huge grin on her face. "Nice."

Condom rolled down, I pull her mouth back to mine as she slides her hips down my body. She doesn't even stop our kiss as she grips my cock and guides it inside her. We both moan as she sinks down my length and I have to take some deep breaths. When she rocks her hips, I grab her waist, because I'm about ten seconds from blowing already. I feel like a fucking virgin every time I get inside her. "Wait. Fuck," I say with a gasp as I try to regain control of myself.

Augusta gives me a smug smile. "Looks like that's not the only thing you're liable to forget. Although, forgetting how to last because it feels too good? That's a huge compliment, my friend. So, I don't care."

She grips my chin as she braces her other hand beside my head. "Just fuck me, Graham." She rolls her hips and I groan. Her eyes roam over my face. "You talk about my face, but damn, yours is something, too."

After dropping a kiss on my lips, she pulls herself upright and closes her eyes as she rocks her hips. Simply watching her find her rhythm and seek her own pleasure is nearly enough to get me off all on its own, but my body demands movement. Hearing her gasp as I buck up into her is pretty nice, too, though.

Now that I've pushed through that immediate rush of sensation, I know I'm good for as long as she wants this. As I continue to thrust, Augusta moans, reaching forward to hold the headboard for stability, her tits bouncing with every movement.

"Jesus Christ, Tesoro; fucking look at you. So perfect."

She lets out a long moan, her face pinched in concentration. "Shit, Graham." Still maintaining my rhythm, I run my hand up her waist to cup her tit and flick her nipple with my middle finger. She whimpers, her pussy clenching down around my dick. "Oh, God," she whines.

"You going to come for me, beautiful girl? You're so close again, aren't you?" The flush traveling down her neck and chest tells me that yes, she's very close. Her movements growing more rigid and her breathing again becoming choppy are also good indicators. Her pussy pulsing around me, making it difficult to concentrate, is a fucking dead giveaway.

I lift my head and capture her nipple between my teeth, giving it a gentle tug and she screams, her pussy clenching so hard it nearly makes me gasp. She slumps against my chest, her breathing labored. I pull out only long enough to roll us on the bed, push her thighs back, and slam myself inside her again.

She chokes out a gasp, her nails digging into my forearms. "Fuck, Graham."

I huff a laugh. "Too much?"

She shakes her head. "No. So good."

Bending to claim her mouth for a hungry kiss, my control begins to slip as beads of sweat slide down my temples. Augusta grips the back of my neck to hold me in place, and I can't sustain the kiss and breathe at the same time.

"You got one more in you?" I grit out. She whimpers but gives me a jerky nod. "That's my girl. Get there."

Augusta reaches between us and works her clit as I continue to pound into her, about to lose my mind. A few seconds later, when she lets go for a final time, I can't even hold back long enough for her orgasm to completely crest before mine hits me with a choked grunt, electricity shooting up my spine and down my limbs.

I pull out with a groan and shift to lie beside her as my breathing returns to normal. She rolls on her side to face me, a sweet smile pulling at the corners of her lips. "I like you in my bed."

Plucking a hair off her sweaty forehead, I nod. "I like me in your bed, too. And I'll make it happen as much as possible."

She sighs. "We don't have to talk about that right now."

"I know it's not exactly sexy pillow talk, but we need to talk about it. I don't want to go back to only seeing you a few times a month, Augusta. I know we made it work before, but I don't want to do that again. I'm not prepared to not wake up with you a majority of my mornings."

"We literally just got back together. We haven't told your

family and we haven't even decided how much we're going to tell Gemma."

"What's wrong with the truth? I mean, maybe not all the gory details, but the gist of things. Honestly, I'm shocked you never told her any of it."

She shakes her head. "It's like you said that night in Athens; I'm pretty sure she likes me more than you," she says with a smirk and then sobers. "I didn't want to cause a rift between the two of you or between her and me for not telling her. Gem's been my constant for almost twenty years and I'm afraid to do anything to upset that."

I nod. "Okay, well, we have to tell her at least a little of what happened, otherwise, she's not going to understand how we're so serious so quickly."

She looks away for a moment in thought as she scrapes her top teeth over her bottom lip before returning her gaze to me. "Your sister isn't stupid. She'll put the pieces together."

I swallow, knowing she's right. "And that will be my shit sandwich to endure." Pressing a kiss to her forehead, I sigh. "I can deal with it as long as her reaction doesn't change you wanting to be with me. I love you."

"I know. I love you, too. I'm sure I'll have some blowback to deal with, too. She's going to be pissed I didn't tell her. And then she'll be grossed out because she talked about how 'well serviced' I looked after her wedding reception," she says with a chuckle and I can't help but laugh.

"Probably. I'll be right back." I climb from the bed and head to the bathroom. I reach to grab a tissue and freeze. "Augusta?"

"Yeah?"

Blowing out a breath, I turn to face her. "The condom broke."

CHAPTER TWENTY

AUGUSTA — AUGUST, FIVE YEARS AGO

"Augusta?" Graham calls from the bathroom after what might be the most bittersweet sex of my life. Sweet, because duh, it's Graham and sex is always good. Bitter, because I'm heading home today after our month-long cohabitation experiment. Which I must admit, went so much more smoothly than I could've ever imagined.

Now, I'm lying in bed, my heart still racing and breathing labored, in a pile of languid muscles. "Yeah?" I reply, my tone relaxed.

"The condom broke."

My eyes fly open as I sit up. "What?"

"The fucking condom broke," he repeats, his tone panicked.

Although I'm thrown off, I do some quick mental math. "I think we're okay; I shouldn't be ovulating." He practically scrambles to put on some clothes, and I frown. "What are you doing?"

"I'm going to run to the store and get a morning-after pill. Just to be safe." I don't even have time to react before he's dropping a kiss on my cheek and sprinting out the door, leaving me alone and reeling from his reaction.

I know Graham said he doesn't want kids, but I honestly didn't expect this sort of reaction from him. I personally can think of many worse things than having a baby. And Graham's baby at that.

I'm still in the same place ten minutes later when Graham comes back into the bedroom, box and bottle of water in hand. "Here, babe."

I blink up at him. "I don't want to take that."

His brows rise. "What? Why not? The condom broke. You're not on anything. You have to, so you don't get pregnant."

"I don't like artificial hormones. You know that."

He blinks, dropping to sit next to me on the bed. "Not liking something is different than not being able to have something. It's just a precaution." He extends the items in my direction and I swallow, my chest growing tight.

"Would me getting pregnant be the worst thing?" I can't help but ask.

He chokes out a laugh. "I can literally think of nothing I want less. You know I don't want kids."

"Not even with me?" I try to hide how stung I feel by his words, but I'm not sure I'm successful since my question comes out as weak and pained.

His brows draw down in confusion. "I don't see what that has to do with it. I don't want kids. End of story." My heart sinks. Graham blinks as he sees the resigned expression on my face. "Augusta, I didn't mean I don't—."

I hold out my hand. "Just give me the pills, Graham."

He opens his mouth but shuts it again when I snatch the items from him. I pop the pills from their blister pack and shove them in my mouth with shaky hands before downing the entire bottle of water. I climb from the bed, stomping into the bathroom. I slam the door, only for Graham to walk in seconds later after I've started the shower. "Why are you so upset?"

"I'm fine, Graham. I have to get ready to leave."

He closes the distance between us and pulls me into his arm. Even though I should shrug him off, I let him hold me because I love his arms around me. Because I love him. Although I haven't told him, I do. And his words hurt. He drops his forehead to my temple. "Talk to me, Tesoro."

Tesoro.

Treasure.

He started calling me that after our night in Athens, when we decided to be exclusive. Pretty sure the moment he told me what it meant, I fell for him. Oh, who am I kidding? I was probably falling for Graham Hopkins for years.

I push him away. "You don't get to trot out the Italian when you think I'm pissed because you think it'll calm me down."

"But you are pissed."

I fold my arms across my chest. I'm naked and he's fully clothed and I'm feeling exposed. I also feel like I've just let myself get pressured into something that pushes my personal boundaries. I'm angry at myself and Graham and I don't want to explode on him.

Looking down, I nod. "Yeah. I am."

"I don't understand why. Talk to me. This isn't a big deal."

I snap my head up. "It is a big deal. To me, it's a huge deal. You don't want kids. Ever. I honestly thought I'd already have them by now. So, for me, getting pregnant would be a shock, but it wouldn't end my life. You don't feel the same way. And I get it. That's your choice."

I already know what I have to do and I'm about to break my own heart, but I'm really good at pretending to be indifferent since I've had a lifetime of practice.

"So, maybe when I go home today, we should just call

things good. It's my fault, really. You told me months ago that you don't want kids. I should've let that be a sign that there was never going to be a real future for us. And that's okay. You should have all the things you want in life—or, don't want, as the case may be."

Graham blinks. "What are you saying?"

"I'm saying that I can't be with someone who doesn't want kids. It's a deal-breaker for me. And regardless how much I—I care, I can't get more invested in a relationship that won't go anywhere." I feel the cracks beginning in my façade and while he stands there, entirely stunned, I climb into the shower.

"Augusta, don't do this."

I ignore him as silent tears roll down my face. I've become an expert at crying in quiet, so this is a piece of cake. I don't bother washing my hair and do the world's fastest shower before I shutoff the spray, reaching out to grab my towel.

Graham leans against the sink, his arms folded across his chest, his expression pained. "We can talk about this."

I shake my head as I hurriedly dry off. "There's nothing to talk about, Graham." As I walk back to the bedroom, he's hot on my heels. I hurriedly pull on clothes, cursing under my breath when I realize I'm still wet in places, but I'm too mad to care.

"Bullshit, Augusta. There's a lot to talk about. Besides, we've only been together for a few months."

"Almost five months since Gemma's party," I correct, fastening my shorts and yanking a T-shirt over my head. "We've been living together for the last month. Besides, we're not kids. You're thirty-five, Graham. I'm thirty. But regardless of how long we've been together, it won't change the fact that the things we want in our life are fundamentally different. I knew that going in, so that's on me."

"I don't want us to break up; I care about you."

Sliding my feet into my Chacos, I tighten the straps before

pulling myself to my full height. "Do you ever see yourself changing your mind about kids?"

He's quiet for a moment before he shakes his head. "No."

"Okay. And I want to be a mom. There's nothing else to do here."

Thankfully, I'm already packed, so all I have to do is grab my phone from the charger and hoist my pack onto my shoulder. "Augusta, please," Graham pleads, barring my exit.

I ignore how sad his eyes are and how his hands are cupping my face. Instead, I draw on every ounce of resolve I possess to pull his hands away from my cheeks. "Don't worry, if I do end up pregnant, you don't have to do anything. No one even has to know it's yours."

I shove past him and out the door of his apartment. My phone is ringing before I even get out of the parking lot, but I ignore it. When it doesn't stop ringing or lighting up with text notifications, I finally just turn it off. I drive the entire way back to Knoxville, tears silently rolling down my face.

I suppose I should thank my family for their treatment of me over the years, since it taught me how to act normal and compartmentalize, even as I fall apart. It's probably some kind of trauma response, honestly. But for now, it's the only fucking thing keeping me going, so I lean into it.

In the six weeks since I left Graham's apartment, he's stopped calling and I should be glad. Except the basket full of tests under my bathroom sink, along with the ultrasound, says I should call him. But he doesn't want this and I do and I already told him he wouldn't have to do anything, so what's the point?

My kid won't be the first to grow up without a dad. But they'll never have to question if they're loved or valued or worthy. They already are. As mad as I am at Graham and as mad as I am at myself for allowing myself to continue a relationship I knew was doomed from the start, my conscience won't let me not tell him. It's not like we won't see each other in the future and I'm not willing to sever ties with his entire family simply to avoid him. They're pretty much the only real family I have. So I send a text when I know I should call, but I just can't hear his voice and keep my composure.

Fucking hormones.

> Augusta: Turns out, morning-after pills aren't as effective when you're over a certain weight. I'm keeping it. Like I told you, I don't expect anything from you, but you have the right to know.

I'm not sure whether to be upset or relieved that the text goes from "delivered" to "read" and he doesn't respond. He also doesn't call. I can't deny the ache that he doesn't, though. Because try as I might not to, I still love him.

An hour later, after I've thrown up for the fourth time today, I'm brushing my teeth and trying not to puke all over again. As I'm shutting off the water, someone bangs on my front door. Tired and still sad, I blow out a breath, knowing it's probably the old man from next door who keeps accidentally turning off his wi-fi—he always asks me for help.

"Mr. Duncan, give me—." The rest of the words die in my mouth at the sight of Graham at my door. I fold my arms across my chest. "What are you doing here? How are you here?"

He doesn't wait for an invitation, but I don't protest when he steps inside, because I don't relish having whatever this conversation turns into where everyone in my apartment complex can see.

He's dressed in a suit and his hair is longer and he's got a full beard. *That's new.* "I'm in town for work. You sent me a fucking text to tell me you're pregnant? Is it true, or is it some sick joke?"

My breath hitches with his accusation. "You think I'd joke about something like that? Fuck, Graham. Yes, it's true. You want to see the ultrasound?" He physically recoils, as if I've struck him, and bile rises up my throat, but I manage to speak. "Well, if you read the text, you'll also see I said that I don't expect anything from you. But when I show up super pregnant at the next get together, I didn't want you to be surprised and Gemma or your parents find out it's yours. I meant what I said. You're absolved. I don't need you for anything."

"So you're just going to have this kid? *My* kid?"

I clench my jaw. "It's not yours. It's mine. You don't want kids; I'm not asking you to have one."

He hangs his head, taking a deep breath before his eyes come back to mine. "Okay. Well, I can still help take care of things. Whatever you need. I take care of my responsibilities."

Indignant rage floods my chest, heat filling my cheeks. "No," I spit out.

He blinks. "What do you mean, *no?*"

"You don't get to throw money at this."

"So, you'd rather struggle?"

"I'll be fine. Like I said, I don't need you. I sure as fuck don't need your money. This isn't your *responsibility.*"

He reaches for me, but I bat his hands away. He inhales a deep breath, dropping his hands to his side. "Augusta, at least let me do something."

"Have you changed your mind? You want to be a father?"

"I want you." Hope wants to claw its way up the pit I threw it down when I left Atlanta, but I refuse to give it purchase.

"Answer the fucking question, Graham. Do you want to be a father? If it were anyone besides me, would you want this?"

"Augusta, please, it's complicated. I care about you." His tone is contrite and resigned, and I already know the answer.

I swallow, chewing on my bottom lip as I wrap my arms around myself, needing to put space between us, even as I'm unable to move from where I stand. "That's not an answer. Just be honest. Please. With me; with yourself."

"I don't want to hurt you."

"I know." And I believe him. I believe he truly doesn't want to hurt me. I believe he cares about me. I also believe this isn't something he can make himself want and it not eat away at him. Because it's not something that I can make myself not want and it not eat away at me. Neither of us deserves that type of existence.

"Please, just let me help," he pleads, his eyes so sad.

"If you want to help, just forget. Forget about me. Forget about this. Forget about us. I will never ask you for anything and your family will never know. Gem was always going to be 'Aunt Gemma' regardless. I'm good with my decision, Graham. And I love you enough to let you be good with yours. You don't have to feel guilty. If, someday, you have a change of heart, that's great, but it's never going to be something I expect and I'll never resent you if you don't."

My reply is calm and I think it shocks both of us because I love this man. I love this man more than I've ever loved anyone. But I'm not willing to let someone take responsibility for some-thing they have no interest in being an active participant in. I won't let my child feel anything close to what I've felt my entire life simply to assuage his guilt. I won't let my child ever feel like a burden.

"Please believe me when I say I could never regret our time together. This will forever be the best thing that ever happened to me," I say, letting my hand fall to my nonexistent bump. "The fact that it's yours is the best part. Truly. To know that your family will be my family, even if they don't know it, it's the most wonderful gift I could ever be given.

"But I refuse to let my child ever know what it feels like to be unwanted or as though they're someone's worst mistake. You're a good man, Graham. And I believe if I asked you to do this, you would step up because you care about what your family thinks and you care about what I think about you. But I cannot let you resent me or this child because this is not a life you want. I love you too much for that.

"I would rather us end like this than for you to half-ass it and this child be the one who suffers. Kids can always tell when they're not someone's choice. I'd rather us at least be able to be around your family and them still see you as the great man you are. I don't want to be your burden. Please don't ask me to be. Like I said, just forget. I want so many wonderful things for you. Truly. Whatever you want for you life, you should have it. And so should I."

He blinks, his eyes welling with tears. "I'm so sorry, Augusta."

I shake my head. "Don't be. I'm not."

"I don't know the right thing to do here."

Nodding, I step forward and swipe a tear off his cheek. "I know. That's why I'm telling you what to do. You don't owe me anything. Ever. You don't need to feel guilty or bad or anything. I hope that you'll just look back on our time together and smile. I hope that you now know what a big heart you actually have and you find someone who wants the same things you do. But please, don't try to give me money. I don't want it. I don't need it. I just need you to live your life exactly the way you dreamed. Because that's what I'm going to do."

CHAPTER TWENTY-ONE

AUGUSTA — DECEMBER, FIVE YEARS AGO

"So, how are things?" Gemma asks and I hear Christmas music in the background of the phone call.

I sigh as I sit on the bed in my room, avoiding my family. "Exactly the same as always. I'm pretending to be invisible."

"Have you told them yet?"

"No. I know I can't hide it much longer, but it's not like I need one more thing for them to harp on me about. Let's go down the list, shall we? I have a job in sports. Oh, the horror. I'm unmarried at thirty. I'm fat. Like it's some fucking moral failing. And now, we can add pregnant. What will society say? I wonder if my mother will say something along the lines of, 'oh, our daughter—you know, the fat one—she's unmarried and got herself knocked up'."

Gemma chuckles. "I mean, you could just not tell them. You could say fuck 'em all and never see them again. That is always an option. Come spend Christmas with us. You come to everything else. You're family, Auggie. You know that, right?"

Flashes of spending Christmas with Graham and our child and us not being a family fill me with sadness. "I don't know,

Gem. It's not a bad idea, but I think if I did anything, it'd just be me and the nugget making our own traditions. Did I tell you I narrowed down names? I've been hesitant, but now that I'm this far past the twelve-week mark and I actually felt the baby kick last night, it's starting to feel even more real."

"I'm sure. Okay, lay 'em on me. What will I be calling my little niece or nephew?"

I can't help but smile at her words. "Well, if it's a girl, it'll be Georgia and if it's a boy, it'll be Wesley."

"Perfect. Now, is there any significance to these names in particular; so I know to be even more excited about them?"

I'm not about to tell her Georgia is because the baby was conceived in Georgia and it will always hold a special place in my heart. "I've just always liked the name Georgia. And Wesley was my dad's middle name, so that's all, really."

"Well, I think they're gorgeous." Shouts from the other end of the line filter through to me and I wonder what a family experience like hers is like for Christmas. I've been around them for other gatherings, but Christmas is its own unique thing and I'll never have that. Not with this bunch. Gemma comes back on the line. "Sorry, Auggie, I have to go. Graham just got here."

I try not to react to his name and paste a smile on my face, even though she can't see it. "Sure. Well, I'll talk to you in a day or two."

"Alright. Also, Brew wants to know when we're going to go on a double date with you and Wyatt again."

"Soon, I hope. He's with his parents today, but we're supposed to meet at my place tomorrow to have our own Christmas."

"Brew won't shut up about him. Pretty sure he's got a little guy crush on him."

I huff a laugh. "Well, he's pretty great, so who can blame

him? I'm sure he's just glad to finally have someone to shop for flannel and beard oils with."

My best friend laughs. "Probably. Well, try to have a good holiday, okay? Love you."

"Love you, too. See you soon."

I disconnect the call and sigh. I'm about to get up when my phone rings and I smile when I see the name on the screen. If you had asked me the week everything came to a close with Graham, I would've said I'd never be okay again. Regardless of the fact that I am at peace with my choice and his, I still loved him. I will probably always love him.

Meeting someone a week after letting Graham go wasn't something I ever saw coming. But we both happened to be at a book signing for one of our favorite authors and struck up a conversation. He was cute and sweet and funny and talked about his adorable daughter. At the end of the night, when he asked me for my number, I shocked even myself by giving it to him. When I came clean about my pregnancy on our second date—after I decided I actually liked him—he told me it wasn't a deal-breaker.

Cue the butterflies and heart flips.

"Hey, you," I say as I press the phone to my ear.

"Hey yourself. How are you feeling today?"

"It's a Christmas miracle because I did not, in fact, throw up."

He chuckles down the line. "Well, how about that. Did you tell your parents yet?"

I sigh. "No. I just had this conversation with Gemma, so I don't have the energy to have it again right now. I'm tired. I am growing another human, after all."

"I know. But you look so sexy doing it. Seriously, hottest pregnant lady ever."

I snort a laugh. "You can't even really tell I'm pregnant."

"Sure I can. Your boobs are huge."

"Spoken like a man. I'll have you know, my boobs were huge before I got pregnant, so there."

"Well, then I am a very lucky man," he replies, his tone playful.

"How are things at your parents? Did Aubrey like the Easy Bake Oven you got her?"

"Are you kidding? She's already made me four cookies. It's her favorite gift ever."

"That's great," I say with a smile and slump when Mom calls my name from downstairs. "Listen, I have to go. I'll see you tomorrow, okay?"

"Okay. Call me when you leave Loudon and I'll head to your apartment."

"Sounds good. Merry Christmas, Wyatt."

"Merry Christmas, Augusta."

Standing from the bed, I roll my shoulders, sighing as I shove my phone in the pocket of my dress before heading for the door. When it swings open, I nearly startle when I see Carrie standing on the other side, her expression neutral. "Mom called for us."

"I know," I reply, dropping my eyes to the floor as I step past her.

"You're pregnant?" she asks in a whisper.

My stomach drops. "Were you eavesdropping?"

She stands up straighter. "Not when you're talking loud enough that the whole house can hear you. That big mouth of yours could be heard all the way to my room." She folds her arms, letting her eyes fall to my stomach, her expression something akin to a grimace. "How far along?"

"Almost twenty weeks," I say finally, unsure how to feel about her calmly asking me questions and not simply hurling abuses at me.

"Wow. Is your new boyfriend the father?"

How long was she standing out here? "No."

She huffs a laugh. "So you slept with one guy and you're dating another? God, that's classy."

There she is. I shrug. "It's my reality. I haven't told Mom and David yet, so if you can wait to say anything, I'd appreciate it." I try my best not to act like any of it means a whole lot, because otherwise, it gives Carrie ammunition.

She rolls her eyes, motioning for me to go by. "Whatever. Let's go. I'm hungry."

I nod and head toward the stairs, willing myself to just announce my pregnancy at the dinner table. Next year, if I come back and bring the baby, Wyatt might also be with me. Would it make Graham jealous to see another man raise his child? Would it—. A hard shove from behind me sends me flying down the steps. It happens so fast, I don't even have time to react or grab for the railing.

It's not like in the movies when the person tumbles down a set of stairs. Out of the twelve stairs from top to bottom, I only actually touch the top one. I land facedown on the third or fourth step up and slide the rest of the way, a sharp pain radiating through my abdomen and down my legs.

I blink to awareness and Amelia screams like only a four-year-old can. Mason jumps up off the sofa, running over to drop to his knees to check on me. "Oh, God, Augusta. Are you okay?"

"She's fine," Carrie says, dismissively. "God, she's so clumsy."

I clutch my belly, praying with all I'm worth that the baby's okay. "The baby," I gasp out.

Mason lowers his face closer to mine. "What?"

"Pregnant," I rasp, not having recovered my breath yet.

His eyes widen. "You're pregnant? How far along?"

"Nineteen weeks."

He immediately pulls out his phone to call nine-one-one. Mom and David stream in from the kitchen and stare down at the floor where I still lay. I try to get up, but Mason won't let me move.

"Augusta, what are you doing in the floor? Did you take a spill?" Mom asks.

I look at my sister, who sits on the steps, her expression smug. Rage and terror floods my system and more than anything in this moment, I wish I had the ability to turn back the clock sixty seconds.

"Oh, you know her, Mom; she's so clumsy. I'm sure she's fine."

"Carrie, she's pregnant," Mason argues as soon as he hangs up with emergency services. "Augusta, they'll be here soon, okay?"

"Pregnant?" my mother repeats, her tone incredulous.

"Oh, my," David mutters.

I just close my eyes.

"I bet she's not even pregnant," Carrie says with a scoff.

A single tear rolls down my cheek, but that's all I allow myself. I can cry later—whether out of sadness and loss or relief.

I refuse to do it now. Not in front of her.

CHAPTER TWENTY-TWO

GRAHAM

"So things are going good at work, Graham?" Mom asks across the dinner table. I've only been paying attention to about a third of the conversations because none of this feels real anymore. Not without Augusta. But I blink, trying to replay the question my mother just asked.

I take another drink of my gin and tonic and offer her a smile. "Sure. Great."

Dad eyes me. "Is it a big fad for lawyers to have a beard and long hair now?"

I gesture to my brother-in-law. "Can't have Brewster showing me up. Everyone knows I've got the better hair."

Gemma scoffs. "Please. Brew's hair is immaculate. Yours is just," she scrunches up her face in confusion, "shaggy and unkempt. Not at all like someone who really cares about a beard and hair. If you're really serious about growing it out, Brew's got some great oils he's started using on his beard that he and Wyatt picked up last weekend."

I know most of Gemma and Brewster's friends from various

cookouts one or both of them have hosted over the years and I don't recognize the name. "Who's Wyatt?"

"Augusta's new boyfriend. So sweet. He's a great guy," my mother supplies.

Outwardly, I don't react, and appear mostly disinterested, even as my heart sinks and my grip tightens on my fork. "Oh? I didn't know she was seeing anyone."

Warming to her topic, Mom smiles. "He's got the sweetest little girl, too. Of course, I don't think Augusta's met her yet, but his mother and I are actually in bookclub together, so I've seen her. He's already used to kids, and he's wild about Augusta, so I look for him to stick around and raise the baby."

"Mom," Gemma warns. "Augusta doesn't need us telling everyone her business. Graham doesn't care who Augusta's boyfriend is and God knows he's not going to care that she's pregnant since he's allergic to anything related to kids."

My mother holds up her hands in surrender. "You're right; my mistake. I'm just so thrilled for her. She deserves to be happy."

"Yeah, she does. And the fact that Brew and I already love him is a huge plus," my sister says with a grin. "Sure beats awkward double dates with some of the other guys she's dated in the past."

The bite of meatball and red sauce I've just crammed in my mouth turns rancid and I force myself to choke it down. Almost four months ago, Augusta calmly laid out the reasons she didn't want my help. I'm still not sure how she wasn't a mess. God knows I am. I haven't stopped being a mess since I left her apartment.

I don't sleep. I barely eat. I only shower because my paralegal threatened to tell the partners I've got too much on my plate if I can't at least manage my personal hygiene. To be honest, I'm more scared of Janice than I of am the partners. But for the last thirteen weeks, all I've thought about is what she asked me.

If it were anyone besides me, would you want this?

I told her it was complicated. And it is. I'm still not sure I want it. But I haven't stopped wanting her. I love her. And I didn't even fucking tell her.

Now she has a boyfriend. One who already has a kid and is probably going to raise *my* baby.

It's not yours. It's mine.

She said that, too. God, she's so selfless. She said she loved me enough to give me up so I could have everything I dreamed about. What if my dreams have changed? But what if I'm too late?

I still don't know if I want to be a dad, but I want her. And they're a package deal now.

If it were anyone besides me, would you want this?

No. If it were anyone but her, I wouldn't want this. But no one else is her. Why couldn't I have said that?

Hours later, after gifts have been opened and *Die Hard* has been watched, I'm restless. So restless that when I climb into my car to head to my hotel, I don't go there. Although it's probably a mistake, I head to Augusta's. It's late—almost midnight—but her light is on, so I take it as a good sign. I can always leave if she refuses to answer the door. I finally stopped calling when she sent a text that said *don't call me unless you've changed your mind.*

Even as I knock on the door, I have no clue what I'm going to say to her. Except to tell that her I want her back. Her and the baby. Because she wants the baby and I want her.

Hushed voices come through the door, but I can't make out

what they say. The door opens, and for the second time tonight, my heart sinks. This must be the boyfriend, judging by the great beard. "Can I help you?"

I clear my throat. "I stopped by to see Augusta."

A muscle in his jaw tics, but he doesn't look offended or upset that someone is here to see her. "Now's not a good time."

"Sure," I say, resigned, and nod. "Sorry to bother you." The door begins to close, but it stills when I hear Augusta's voice. My throat immediately grows tight, but I manage to keep my emotions in check.

The guy—Will or Wayne or something—sighs and opens the door wider, motioning for me to enter. I give him a grateful nod as I step inside. I take a few steps into the room but notice Augusta doesn't have a tree up or any holiday decorations displayed.

When my eyes fall on her, she's on the couch, her lap covered in a thick quilt. She looks tired and makes no move to rise from the sofa. The guy looks at me fully, his expression unreadable. He's a couple inches shorter than me, his hair a few shades lighter than my own, but he's a stocky, good-looking white guy in his late twenties or early thirties. He extends his hand. "Wyatt Hayes."

I return his handshake. "Graham Hopkins."

Something flickers in his gaze and he looks at Augusta for a split second before dropping my hand with a nod and going to kneel next to her. I don't hear what they say, but it's clear by his body language he cares about her. Hell, he's probably already in love with her. Who could blame him?

She nods, giving him a quick kiss, the action making possessive jealousy slither through my chest. As he stands again, I try not to look like I want to murder him. He spares me a glance before heading toward the bedroom. When the door shuts, Augusta asks, "What do you want, Graham?"

I gesture to the other end of the sofa. "May I sit?"

"Yeah. But it's late and I'm tired, so can you make it fast?" She doesn't sound like herself and I want to ask her what's wrong, but the truth is, it's probably just because I'm here.

"You told me not to call unless I changed my mind. I figured a call wasn't good enough. I changed my mind."

She tucks her hair behind her ear, fidgets her watch band, and scrapes her top teeth over her bottom lip. I don't say anything. She swallows and blows out a breath. "Why now?"

I purposely don't look toward the bedroom and splay my hands. "You asked me if this were anyone else, would I want it. I wouldn't. But it's you, so that changes things."

"Why, Graham?" Her voice comes out hoarse and she clears her throat. "Because you found out I have a boyfriend? You decided to show up at midnight on Christmas to make some big declaration because you're jealous?"

"Yes, I heard, but that's not why. I haven't stopped thinking about the stuff you said the last time I was here. And like I said, this isn't something I would want with anyone else, but with you, I would."

She folds her hands in her lap as she chews her bottom lip. "So, you're saying you're ready to be a father now?"

"With you, I am."

"I'm with someone else, Graham," she says with finality. "So, I'm not on the table. Would you still want it if I wasn't part of the package?" I blink, opening my mouth to speak, but close it again. Augusta nods. "That's what I thought. You want me, and you'd take a tagalong if that's the only way I'd have you. But you don't want fatherhood. And that's okay. Like I told you, I want you to have the life you want, and I couldn't live with myself if you settled." She looks away, blinking rapidly. "It doesn't matter now anyway."

I stand up, suddenly angry. "I'm here, so yeah, I'd say it

does matter. Just because I hesitate doesn't mean I wouldn't want it. I'm allowed to have five fucking seconds to absorb information. I—."

"Graham," she cuts in, her eyes wet. I close my mouth, alarm bells clanging in my mind. "It doesn't matter because there's no baby." She looks at her lap. "Not anymore. I...fell at my parents and had a miscarriage."

"When?" I ask, my voice choked.

"Today."

"Today?" I repeat, the sudden loss of something I didn't know I wanted until just this moment hitting me with the force of a mack truck. I drop to my knees beside her. "I'm so sorry."

She nods. "Me, too." She shifts on the sofa, wincing in pain, and my heart lurches.

"Can I get you anything?"

She shakes her head. "No, Wyatt's got me."

I blow out a shaky breath. "Right. Wyatt. I hope he knows how lucky he is."

She nods again. "He does."

I stand, shoving my hands in my pockets, my heart cracking in a way I never thought it was possible for me to experience. "I probably wouldn't have been any good at it anyway. So we probably dodged a bullet here." Augusta's breath hitches with my words and I hate myself, but apparently I can't stop. "Glad you'll get a clean slate. Maybe it's for the best, huh?"

Angry tears well in her eyes and she hauls herself off the couch. I blink in surprise. She's probably supposed to be resting and now I've said all this shit and I truly wish I could take it all back. I open my mouth, but her quick slap across my face silences me. I can't even be mad because I deserved it.

"How dare you, Graham? You don't get to be upset when you didn't even fucking want this. You don't get to say *we* dodged a bullet when *you* weren't a part of it. You didn't even want this before it was a possibility. What was it you said, 'I can think of nothing I want less'? Now you don't have to worry about it.

"And fuck you for diminishing this *loss* for me. This was *my* child. I lost this baby and none of this was for the fucking best. So you might get a clean slate, but I never will. And the only reason you came here was because you got jealous. I'm guessing the next time I would've seen you if you hadn't heard about Wyatt was at the next cookout. And even then, unless I was with someone, you wouldn't have been able to even muster up a reaction. I don't doubt that you miss me or that you still want me. But I don't want you. I don't miss you. And I want you to leave."

She teeters, unsteady, and I'm afraid she's going to collapse. "Augusta, please sit down. I'm worried—."

She spits out, "You don't get to worry about me. Get out."

As if summoned by her last words, Wyatt emerges from the bedroom, his posture tense. I hold my hands up. "I'm going. I'm sorry I bothered you. Let me know if you need anything."

"I won't, Graham. Goodbye."

I nod, pivoting to walk out the door. I barely make it to my car before the torrent of sobs erupts from my chest.

CHAPTER TWENTY-THREE

AUGUSTA — PRESENT DAY

The condom broke.

I don't react to his words. Not at first. Mainly because I'm not sure how to react. Not when all I can think about was the last time he uttered that same sentence and everything that happened after. I simply draw my knees up to my chest and try to breathe.

He's back in the bed a few seconds later. "I think we should be okay. I get tested every month and I'm always careful. I'll go tomorrow to make sure."

I still don't say anything, because I don't know how I'm supposed to feel. I know I can't go back to my parents' again if I get pregnant. Not after last time. I decided that a long time ago. Guess it's good I walked out of that house one last time as myself.

Graham takes my face in his hands. "Hey, look at me. Like I said, I'm almost positive I'm clean. I'm really sorry, but I'll make sure."

I blink. "Okay. I should be good, too. Creed was the only guy I'd been with in a year and we were always careful."

"I'm sorry, Creed? What kind of name is Creed?"

"One he probably gave himself."

Graham chuckles, pressing a kiss to my forehead. "Are you okay; you look freaked out."

I chew my bottom lip. "You're a lot calmer than I thought you'd be," I admit.

He releases a breath. "That's because I am calm. If it weren't simply for the prospect of being safe for our health until we can be sure, I would ditch the condoms today." I blink, and I'm sure the look on my face is some mix of skepticism and incredulity and he nods. "I know; probably not ever something you thought you'd hear me say."

"No," I confess. "I thought you were allergic to kids." My words come out with a bit more bite than I intend, but to his credit, Graham doesn't wince.

He gives me a sheepish smile. "I deserved that." He drops his hands from my face and looks down as he collects his thoughts before returning his gaze to mine. "I've had five years to think over everything that happened; everything I said and did and how I failed."

I open my mouth to tell him he couldn't help the things he wanted and didn't want and that I never blamed him for his feelings; the same way I never regretted the choices I made. He puts his finger to my lips to silence me. "Let me finish?"

As I nod, he continues. "I didn't want it. I was terrified that day the condom broke and went into panic mode and did the only thing I could think to do. Despite the fact I was thirty-five, I was so fucking immature. I was selfish and was only thinking about myself and the plans that I had.

"You were so calm when you ended everything and knew exactly what you wanted. And regardless of how you felt about me, you were willing to do what it took to not get deeper into something you knew wasn't right for you. I was always so amazed at how self-aware you were. I've always admired that about you.

"Even after I came to your place after you found out you were pregnant, I still didn't think that was ever something I wanted. I was still selfish and only thinking about myself and how being a father would throw a wrench into every plan I had for my life. It would cut into my work, my ability to volunteer for cases, and move up in my firm.

"And you were still so calm. You were mature and selfless and refused to take my guilt money. Because, yeah, that's what it was. I knew I loved you, but I still didn't think I wanted it. Then you asked me all those questions and made your rational arguments and I let you send me away.

"I will freely admit that the night I showed at your place that Christmas, I was jealous. But I think it was also the kick in the ass I needed to make me see that I wanted it. I didn't want some other man—great as he probably was—to get to have *my* family. I wanted the packaged deal. I didn't want the baby if I couldn't have you, because you were the only reason I wanted the baby to begin with."

Tears burn behind my eyes as I remember that night. Graham clears his throat. "I would've done it simply so I could stay in your life, however I could. I would've been a dad simply because you would've been the mom. And that wouldn't have been fair to you or the baby. But I want to be honest with you about how I was feeling back then.

"Then when you told me what happened. I didn't realize until that moment that I wanted it regardless. Because it would've been *ours*. And any part of you—of *us*—would've been better than no part of us at all. I didn't get a clean slate, and it was my loss, too. I've hated myself every day for the things I said that night," he says, his voice thick with emotion as tears fill his eyes.

He clears his throat and wipes his face as he takes a beat to compose himself. My throat aches with my own impending tears and I force myself to breathe. "But if you got pregnant this time, even if you decided you didn't want me, I'd still want to be in that baby's life. Even if it was only on the weekends or whatever schedule we determined. You asked me five years ago if I would want it with anyone else, and I said it was complicated. Truth is, it's not complicated. I still wouldn't want it with anyone else. There's never been anyone else I would want it with. You are the only person I've ever loved, so to imagine having a child with anyone else is absurd to me.

"Although, if you decided you didn't want kids anymore, I'd support that, too. Whatever our life needs to look like, I want it. And yeah, I know we just got back together yesterday, but we never should've been apart for five years to begin with, so I'm just playing catch up.

"I understand that I'm going to have to prove myself. A lot. Historically, I've never been a relationship guy. You know this. You're the only one I've ever wanted it with, Augusta. In forty years, yours has been the only face I've ever wanted to see when I wake up in the mornings. I know we have shit we'll have to figure out, but the only non-negotiable item on my list is *us*. Whether us is just us, or includes five kids and three dogs and a partridge in a pear tree, that's what I want."

I can't help but laugh, even as tears roll down my cheeks. "You're so cheesy."

He presses a kiss to my lips. "Even Scrooge got a little sentimental at the end of the story."

"Okay," I say after a beat. "So, we're not freaked out about this?"

He laughs and lies down, pulling me with him. "No. Not freaking out."

I wring my hands as we make the drive over to Graham's parents' house. "They're going to know."

He snorts a laugh as he takes my hand in his. "How are they going to know?"

"I feel like Gemma's going to put everything together. I'm not sure I've been this relaxed since the morning after their wedding reception. She's got a freaky mind and makes all sorts of connections." I pull my sweater off my shoulder, displaying the prominent love bite he left this morning. "Plus, your affinity for leaving me all marked up may be the dead giveaway. You left a ton of hickeys on my neck after that first night."

"Well, okay. So what if they know?"

I sigh. "For starters, you and I haven't discussed everything. I would like to have a concrete idea of what we want before we go in guns blazing. Between Gemma and your mom, they're going to have a ton of questions and I'm still too on edge after leaving my parents and everything that's happened with us."

Disappointment flashes in Graham's expression for a split second, but he shutters it. "Okay. I get that. I know you had that big talk with your therapist today after having to deal with your family and us getting back together; it's a lot. I understand. We'll just tell them we came straight from your parents' place to here and I'm taking you home after. How's that?"

Relieved that he's on board, I smile. "You're the best. I will totally make all the cloak and dagger worth it."

He chuckles, pressing a kiss to the back of my hand. "I will hold you to that."

A few minutes later, we're pulling up at the brick ranch

house that has always felt like home to me. It's definitely the only place aside from my apartments that's felt like home. We climb out of the car and Graham grabs his gifts for everyone. I grab the one I have for Collier, as well as the pound cake I made for everyone to share.

As soon as we walk in the door, the sound of Collier's bare feet thudding against the hardwood floors hits my ears before I even see him. His eyes light up, his dark brown hair flopping as he runs right into my arms. "Auggie!" I scoop him up and breathe in his sweet little boy smell.

"Colly!" I say, matching his energy. "How is my favorite boy?"

He squirms out of my arms and I set him down. "I have a baby sister."

I smile, squatting until we're eye level. "I know. What do we think about her?"

"She cries. A lot," he says, wide-eyed. "And she poops all the time."

I can't help but laugh. "I know. You did, too." I open my purse to pull out his gift. "Merry Christmas."

His eyes light up. "Thank you, Auggie." He throws his arms around me for a quick hug that melts my insides, and then grabs his gift and takes off.

I stand up and Graham shakes his head. "I guess I'm chopped liver."

"What can I say; the kid loves me."

"With good reason," he says, his voice low.

I lower my own voice. "You can't be all nice to me, you know. People will think you've seen me—."

"There you two are," Marilyn Hopkins's voice sounds from behind me and I school my features as I turn to face her. She looks the same as she always does. She's average height with brown hair, like Gemma's, with darker features and brown eyes, where her daughter's are hazel. She's in her mid-sixties and on the plump side and I just adore her. Her hair is cut in a long pixie and she's dressed comfortably in navy leggings and a tunic-length, cream-colored sweater.

Graham greets his mother first, with a quick hug and kiss on the cheek, before turning her over to me. My hug with her is much longer, and it's like coming home. "Hey, Mrs. H. How's my favorite lady?"

She gives me a loud, sweet kiss on the cheek as we part. "Good." Taking my face in her hands, she examines me. "How were things at your parents'?"

"Same as always. I made a pound cake, so I hope you're ready to feed me. You know what kind of food those people have," I say with an exaggerated shudder and she laughs.

"You know it." She looks over her shoulder, where Graham has gone to sit with his father and Collier on the sofa. "When Graham said you were coming with him, I made a lasagna. Your favorite." Her eyes soften. "I hope my son didn't make things harder on you while you were there. I know things aren't easy for you when you're with your family, but if I need to wallop him for being his normal self, you just let me know."

I huff a laugh. "No, ma'am. He was great. Made it almost bearable, actually."

"Good to hear." She gestures to a room down the hall. "Gemma's in with the baby if you want to go visit. Brewster ran to get some stuff from their house, but he'll be back soon. Lasagna will be out in about twenty."

"Okay." She gives me a final squeeze before heading back to the kitchen. I take a deep breath and make my way to the bedroom Marilyn indicated, knocking softly on the door. When Gemma's voice comes through, telling me to enter, I step inside.

She sits in an upholstered rocker by a large window, nursing the baby. Her hair is pulled up in a messy bun and she looks tired, but happy. Her outfit consists of black leggings, a tan nursing tank and a red cardigan. My best friend of almost twenty years smiles up at me from her chair.

"Hey, Mama. How you feeling?" I ask, leaning down to give her a kiss on the cheek.

She grins. "Like I had a baby. Good thing she's cute." She sobers. "How are you? Your sister still a cunt?"

I snort a laugh, dropping onto the bed a few feet away from Gemma's rocker. "Damn, it's like you know her or something."

"Graham didn't seem too happy with the way they were treating you."

I shake my head. "He wasn't. I'm not sure I'll go back," I admit.

Her eyes widen. "Shut up. Seriously? You've finally had enough?"

"I think so. I mean, Graham and I were just pretending to be together, but Carrie didn't know that. She hit on him several times and said in front of everyone how there was no way someone like me could ever pull a guy like him."

"I really hate her."

"Me, too. But it just made me see that there's a reason I've never taken anyone home and have chosen guys who weren't actually good enough for me. Because if I lost them, it wasn't a big deal. But I can't ever bring anyone home for real because that's the kind of reception they'll get. It's mortifying."

I sigh. "I'm just so tired of trying to be invisible and make them think I matter. I'm a good person and I've tried my entire life to get them to accept me and they never will. If I'm ever going to be able to have anything good in my life, I have to be done with them. I had a call with my therapist first thing this morning. Pretty sure she wanted to pop the champagne when I said all that."

Gemma laughs. "As she should. You should only have

people in your life who know your value and love you. Because yeah, you are a good person and an excellent friend, sister, and auntie. Collier was so excited because his Auggie was coming over."

I nod. "I was excited to see him, too. That kid gives the best hugs."

She grins. "He sure does." Doing up her tank top, she shifts the baby in her arms as Julie promptly lets out a soft burp. "Want to hold your goddaughter?"

Warmth blooms in my chest, and I squeeze some sanitizer from a nearby bottle into my hands and rub them together. When they're dry, I extend my hands in a *gimme* motion and rise so she won't have to get up. "Let me see this little nugget." I take Julie in my arms and adjust her blankets, making to return to the bed.

"Here, you can have this chair. I have to pee, and I need to walk for a few minutes. You care to keep an eye on her? She shouldn't need anything, so you'll probably be bored."

I shake my head, taking the rocker once she vacates it. "Never. Get out of here and let me tell this little girl all the best stories about her mommy." A moment later, the door shuts and I lift the sweet bundle to my nose to breathe in her newborn baby smell.

After, I lay her on my lap and unwrap her to examine her fingers and toes and all the features that make her who she is. She has jet black hair like Graham and long fingers like Brewster. She reminds me a lot of Collier when he was this small, and they have the same nose that they've both inherited from Gemma and Graham's dad's side of the family. She also has the slight cleft in her chin that Brewster's brother has. I've never seen Brewster without a beard, so for all I know, he has one, too.

I take her tiny fist in my hand and although she's sleeping, it doesn't stop me from having the same conversation I had with her brother after he was born. "Hey, little girl. I'm your Aunt Auggie. You should know, this family you've got here is the best one ever. You are really lucky. Your mommy and daddy and Nonna and Grandpa and Uncle Graham all love you so, so much. And I love you, too. No matter what, that won't change. And Graham seems like a big grumpy goose, but he's really a sweetheart. You can trust me on that."

CHAPTER TWENTY-FOUR

GRAHAM

Gemma walks into the living room and I jump off the couch. "Here, Gem, take my seat."

She laughs at me. "I'd settle for a hug, thanks. I've been sitting for hours. Augusta's got Julie, so I'm taking a few minutes to walk." She looks around after we share a quick embrace. "Where's Collier and Mom and Dad?"

"They took him outside to get some wiggles out, I think they said. It's warming up pretty nice, so maybe they took him for a walk?"

"Okay. Then you can tell me how it really was at Augusta's parents'. Walk me to the kitchen. I smell the lasagna and I'm sure it probably needs to come out."

"Mom shut the oven off, so it should be fine."

She rolls her eyes. "Okay, then just walk me so I can refill my water. I can't sit anymore right now." My sister loops her arm in mine as we begin walking. "So, spill."

"Bad, Gem. On the plus side, I don't think she's going to go back."

She nods as we shuffle toward the kitchen. "That's what she said. She should just come here and be with us."

"That's what I told her. I said she should at least be with people who love her."

We're quiet for a moment and Gemma sighs. "Yeah, she should."

My ears perk up when the unmistakable sound of Augusta singing filters down the hall toward the kitchen and my heart lurches. Gemma starts to say something and I shush her. "Listen."

She tilts her head in the direction of the sound and smiles. "She always sings to the babies right after they're born. She did it with Collier, too." She reaches over on the counter and hits a button on a small screen. A few seconds later, the sound comes through more clearly, along with a video feed of Augusta holding a baby.

An ache spreads through my chest as I watch her look down at the tiny bundle with such love as she rocks and sings to her. My throat grows tight as I'm reminded all over again what we lost. Then Augusta's voice cracks while she sings. She swipes a tear off her cheek and I'm forced to take a deep breath and blink back my own tears.

Gemma shuts it off as she clears her throat. "Christmas is hard for her."

"I know."

Sighing, she looks down at her hands. "With her awful family and..."

She doesn't finish the sentence, but I already know what she was going to say. "I know," I repeat.

"I'm not sure if you remember a few years ago, the Christmas after Brew and I got married, Augusta was—."

"I know, Gem."

She frowns. "You know what?"

"What happened that Christmas. The baby. I know."

She peers up at me, intently searching my face. "Did she tell you while you were at her parents'?"

"No." I don't bother hiding my pain and guilt and anything else she might glean from my expression that will tell her exactly how I'd know what I do.

"Then how would you—." Her eyes go wide as realization dawns and she swallows. "Graham, are you saying—. I mean, were you—."

"Yeah," I mumble. My sister opens her mouth and I hold up my hand to stop her. "Whatever you're going to say, I've already said to myself about a million times and worse. Augusta and I have sorted through a lot of that. Honestly, I didn't plan for you to find out like this, but watching her with the baby is really hard knowing how bad she wanted it."

Gemma blinks, her eyes growing wet, but she's seething and I nearly take a step back. "But you didn't? Seriously?"

"Not then," I admit. "And Augusta knew that. She didn't want someone who was going to half-ass it. I would have."

"I could punch you in the face, Graham. How could you do that to her?"

I drag my hands through my hair. "I was selfish and immature and didn't know what I had until I lost it. Believe me, Gem, I've had five years to mull over exactly how much I fucked up. She was the best thing that ever happened to me."

Her brow furrows in confusion. "But Augusta said she got pregnant from a one-night stand."

I almost want to laugh. And cry. And fall on my knees and worship the ground that Augusta walks on for protecting me when that was the last thing I ever deserved. "No. It definitely was not a one-night stand. It was at the end of us living together for a month while she was on break."

She slumps back against the counter, clearly reeling. "Wait.

So how did y'all even start seeing each other? And you were living together? Jesus, I wish I could drink right now."

I scrub my hand down my face. "She's going to kill me. I wasn't supposed to tell you any of this. She wanted to tell you we were back together, but she wanted to wait until—."

"Hold up. *Back* together? You and Augusta are together. Like, for real?"

I blow out a breath. "Yeah. I know you probably think I'm not good enough for her. And in truth, I'm probably not. But I love her, Gemma. I've loved her for five years. I hurt her, and I was an asshole. I will do whatever it takes for the rest of my life to make up for all the ways I let her down, and she knows that."

My sister looks up at me, her expression softening. "I'd never think you weren't good enough for her. You're a good man, Graham, and Augusta's a big girl. I don't worry about her judgment. She's one of the best judges of character I know. If she loves you, I know it's because you deserve it. In all actuality, it was always going to take someone like her to even make you realize you wanted it. She doesn't take shit, and she's never had any problems giving yours back to you."

She lifts a brow. "I'm pissed at her and you for never telling me, but that's between y'all. I understand with both of your relationships with me, it was probably awkward. But for real, when did this all start?"

I look down at my feet. "Your wedding reception."

Gemma thinks back and blinks before her eyes go wide in horror. "Eww, that was you? Oh, God. Seriously, Graham?"

I can't help but laugh. "Yeah, pretty sure I didn't look too much better that next day."

"Oh, God," she repeats, her face scrunching up in disgust and I crack up.

Augusta walks into the kitchen. "I put Julie in her bassinet, so you'll probably want to turn on the monitor. What's so funny?"

Gemma looks at her, shaking her head in amazement as she switches the screen back on. "You are in so much trouble. My wedding reception? Really?"

Her eyes fly to mine, her mouth falling open as she chokes out, "You told her?"

"Sorry. It kinda slipped out," I say, my tone contrite.

Augusta folds her arms across her chest and raises a brow. "Slipped out, huh? And exactly how much 'slipped out'."

"Most of it," I admit.

Gemma steps over to her to wrap her in a hug. "I'm glad you get to be family for real, Auggie. And our kids will be cousins; it's awesome."

Augusta's eyes go wide again as she returns my sister's embrace, but she glares at me. "What did you tell her?"

"Nothing to make her think there would be kids or marriage."

"Not yet," Gemma sing-songs and steps back, a huge grin on her face.

Augusta closes the distance between us, poking me in the chest. "You realize you're a dead man, right? What happened to the plan?"

"Sorry, Tesoro. You were singing. To a baby. It made me feel sentimental."

Gemma scoffs. "Oh, God. There are even pet names. Gag me with a spoon." But she can't keep the smile off her face.

I run my hand down Augusta's arm to intertwine our fingers. "It'll be fine. We'll figure out the plan."

The front door opens and everyone walks in, including Brewster, and Augusta snatches her hand from mine. I nearly laugh as I take it again. "We might as well tell them."

She blows out a breath and nods. "Over supper?"

I give her hand a squeeze and drop it again. "Okay."

After dinner, Dad and Brewster are washing dishes while Augusta gives Collier a bath and reads him a story. Gemma heads to rest and I pour a glass of wine for my mother and water for myself before joining her out in the living room. She's sitting next to the gas fireplace, her feet propped up on the sofa. I lift her legs to put them over mine as I hand over her glass. "Thank you, honey."

"Sure. Did you have a good Christmas?"

Mom looks around the living room, where a large artificial tree sits next to the fireplace, decorated with all the handmade ornaments Gemma, me, and now, Collier have constructed throughout the years. Colorful lights are wrapped around the garland adorning the fireplace, where stockings for each family member are hung. "Next year, we'll need another stocking."

I nod. "Yeah, probably."

"I'm glad," she replies, her voice low.

"Me, too."

"I'm glad y'all were finally able to work things out." I frown and my mother lifts a brow. "Please. Y'all have been sick over each other for five years. Plus, I saw her leave her room key for you. For the next few months, when we'd talk, you seemed to be really happy. I hoped it was because you were still with her." She looks down into her wineglass. "I know that Christmas, you were in rough shape. I'm so sorry, son. For what you lost."

I blink. "You knew?"

"Suspected. When you started looking all shaggy around the same time she announced she was pregnant and with how upset you got when we talked about her at Christmas, I figured you were still heartbroken. I'm guessing I'm the only one who saw how affected you were when we talked about her dating that other man. You were gripping your fork like you wanted to break it in half. I know I talked about what a great guy he was, but most of that was to hopefully give you a kick in the pants. I'm sorry how every everything worked out back then."

I nod. "Yeah. Me, too. But why didn't you say anything?"

"Son, I love you, but when have you ever done something simply because someone thinks you should? Plus, I knew if you and Augusta had chosen not to raise that baby together, there was a reason."

I look down. "She knew I didn't want it back then, and she didn't want someone who'd view the privilege as a burden."

"Smart woman, that Augusta. Kids can always tell when they're not a priority. I mean, look at her own family; those awful people and how they've treated Augusta her whole life. I'm sure she didn't want that for her own child. It takes maturity to know that." She smiles. "Plus, Augusta's family. I would've still been Nonna, regardless. So I wasn't worried about not having a relationship with my grandchild."

Nodding, I sip my water, wishing it were gin. "She wanted to help me save face. She's better than I've ever deserved."

"You just remember that."

A few days later, I'm reluctantly packing to head back to Atlanta. For now, it's back to long-distance until we have a concrete plan for the future. We've coordinated our schedules so that on the weekends Augusta's off, we'll be together. So far, it's looking like two weekends a month. That's not nearly enough for my liking, but I just keep reminding myself that after we get over this hurdle, I'll get to wake up beside her every day for the rest of my life. Surely the short-term pain of

separation will be worth the long-term gain of forever, right?
Right.

What makes the most sense, and is something we're both
mulling over, would be if I went back into family and estate law
and relocated here, while Augusta attempted to adjust her
schedule to one where she's permanently on campus. I know
she doesn't want to leave Gemma and, in truth, I don't hate the
idea of being back in Knoxville.

As I'm folding my last load of clothes to pack away, I'm
organizing everything so that when I get back to my apartment,
I'll be able to simply put everything away and it won't be a
mess. I'm tucking my underwear in their designated pocket
when my hand bumps against something hard. I pull the items
out, realizing they're the cameras I'd tossed in haphazardly at
the last moment when we were packing at David and April's.

Figuring I might as well clear off the memory cards in the
event I have to go out of town again, I carry them to the kitchen.
Booting up my laptop, I remove the camera unit from the books
and plug them into my computer.

Knowing I have a timer on the cameras, I scrub through the
footage, simply to make sure there's not anything I need to be
concerned about. Other than some instances when Augusta
and I were hanging out or getting ready, there's not much.

I smile, letting the footage go when it picks up again after
our night together. And yeah, it shows me getting out of bed
naked, but it also documents us being all cute when she tells me
to go get her coffee. I watch myself leave the room and Augusta
snuggles back under the covers. I'm about to scrub it again
when Carrie walks in and I take my hand off the trackpad.

For the next five minutes, all I see is red.

CHAPTER TWENTY-FIVE

AUGUSTA

I'm singing along to my "Good Day" mix as I unlock the door to my apartment. After speaking with my supervisor and determining it would be possible for my position to be a permanent on-campus one, I'm riding high. With plans to discuss everything with Graham, I'm just getting to the end of "Walking on Sunshine" as I come through the door, bobbing my head.

At least, until I see the shards of plastic and laptop parts scattered across the floor. Graham is sitting in the floor by the window, his forearms draped over his drawn-up knees. I yank my earbuds from my ears and set my things down. He doesn't look at me; he doesn't look at anything. His face is splotchy, like he's been crying and his hair is disheveled.

"Graham?" I gingerly step around the shards of wires, electrical components, and jagged pieces of what's left of his laptop. Nervous when he doesn't answer or acknowledge me, I kneel in front of him to place a tentative hand on his arm. "Babe?"

"You said you fell."

He still doesn't look at me and I'm so far beyond confused

by his statement, I simply sit in front of him on the floor. "What?"

His eyes drill into mine, and they're so full of pain it makes my heart lurch. "You said you fell. But that's not true. And you said your cheek was red because you slept on it. But that's not true, either, is it?" I blink, not understanding what he's talking about. "Christmas morning, Augusta. Carrie fucking slapped you. You told me your cheek was red from sleep. Do I need to ask about the other stuff she said?" he asks, his eyes welling with tears. My breath catches as comprehension sets in.

"Tell me the fucking truth. Is she the reason you fell down the stairs, and that's why you miscarried?"

I slump, resigned. "I thought so. She always said she saw me about to fall and tried to grab me, so I don't know for sure. But I think she did."

He pounds his fist on the floor. "What the fuck, Augusta? And you just kept going back there? Did you report it?"

Tears burn my eyes and I nod. "She said I was clumsy. My parents backed her up. Mason said he didn't see anything. I honestly don't know exactly what happened."

"What else has she done? I want all of it, Augusta. What else has she done to you? What else did your parents let her get away with?"

I huff a watery, bitter laugh. "How far back do you want me to go?"

"I said all of it," he replies through gritted teeth.

I blow out a breath, unsure how he'll feel once he hears everything. Sending up a silent prayer that we'll be okay, I start. "You asked why there were no pictures of me when I was little. It's because I didn't live with them until I was seven. My mom got pregnant and had me right before she met David. She had a one-night stand with a guy she worked with, but she told him she didn't want me, so my dad said he'd raise me on his own.

Why keep the janitor's kid when you can have a nice, successful accountant's, right?

"My dad died when I was seven, but because my mom's name was on my birth certificate, social services brought her and David in. The walls were thin in the office. The social worker went out to get something and David said that they had to take me because I was her daughter. She said, 'No, *that's* a mistake I made when I was drunk. Carrie is the only daughter I have.'"

I swallow around the lump in my throat remembering that day. My dad had been dead for two days and I had no one. I went to that house and they introduced me to Carrie and even at five, she had this dead look in her eyes that I couldn't understand. I just remember feeling so alone. Especially with me being the only one to grieve my dad.

Mentally shaking away the thoughts, I clear my throat. "I think it was the only time David actually put his foot down where I was concerned. And I think he felt pity for me because he was nice to me. Mom pretty much ignored me, and all Carrie saw was someone stealing her father's attention.

"I made the mistake of calling David 'Dad' once when I was eight and she threw a softball at my face and broke my nose. After that, I ignored any kind of attention from David and kept to myself. He tried to be a good dad to me, but I was terrified of what she'd do if I let him, so I pushed him away. I think it's hurt him over the years and it's why he's indifferent to me now.

"When I was ten, I saw *Cinderella* and related to the character. I wanted to be Cinderella for Halloween and when I announced what I wanted to be, Carrie said that she was going to be Cinderella because she was prettier and that I could be Gus-Gus, you know, since I was fat. That's why she calls me Gus. That was the last year I dressed up for Halloween.

"I wasn't allowed to have friends over and Carrie would tell my mom and David that I was being mean when I tried to befriend any of the people she brought over. So I escaped into books. At least, until Carrie found out I enjoyed that. When I was eleven, she ripped all my books at the spine and told my parents I'd done it for attention. One of them was a book of Poe poems that belonged to my dad. It was one of the only things of his I had." I hold up my wrist. "That and my Timex."

I roll my shoulders, feeling the weight of all my years settling in again. "My mother worked at my school and would pack my lunch every day and because I've always been bigger than the other girls, she had me on a diet from the time I moved in with them. Then when I'd actually have something good in my lunch, Carrie would steal my lunch box and take out anything decent for herself.

"At home, I was served portions small enough for someone half my age and I was always hungry. You hear about those kids who don't have food at home because their parents can't afford it. You don't hear much about those parents who purposely restrict their child's food to the point the child is falling asleep in class and can't pay attention.

"I joined the school choir when I was fourteen and didn't tell anyone. The practices were all during school hours, so I didn't have to worry about trying to get a ride or anything. I got the lead in the spring cantata, but Carrie spilled paint all over my dress right before we were supposed to leave. My mom rarely bought me clothes that actually fit and because it was the only dress I had, I had to wear one of Carrie's. It was too tight and too short and the choir director said it didn't meet dress code, so I couldn't perform.

"When I was sixteen, David got a new car and gave me his old one. Carrie snuck out and drove it into a tree and said I'd been smoking pot and wrecked, so they took it away. Then

Carrie got a brand new car for her sixteenth birthday and also wrecked that one. She claimed I stole it and wrecked because I was jealous.

"You already know about Trey, so there's that. I also wasn't allowed to go to prom because of the wrecked cars. On the day of my high school graduation, she called my parents and told them she had a flat tire and they had to leave in the middle of the ceremony to go get her. Not that it matters, but I was valedictorian, so they missed my speech.

"Can't forget about the Nair incident. And then on my college graduation, she said she was mugged, so they had to miss that, too. The day I was supposed to start my new job, I mysteriously woke up with an empty gas tank. My old apartments have been broken into a few times and all my stuff was trashed. It's why I don't buy anything new and don't have anything I can't stand to lose."

"The baby." I finally let my eyes come to his and he wears a murderous expression as tears roll down his face. "I was talking with Gemma right before it happened and I told her I'd narrowed down names. I said if it was a boy, I was going to name the baby Wesley because that was my dad's middle name." I inhale a shaky breath. "A few months after I miscarried, Carrie announced she was pregnant. She named him Wesley."

Looking down at my hands, I heave a sigh. "I was in a...bad place after that. Wyatt tried to be there for me, and I know he loved me, but I ended things with him. After Carrie had Wesley, I sort of snapped. I confronted her in front of my parents and accused her of pushing me down the stairs and I attacked her. I got a few good punches in and I'm pretty sure I broke her nose.

"She called the cops and said the only way she wouldn't press charges was if I apologized and told our parents I'd been mistaken. I would've lost my job because she has friends in the DA's office and they would've probably slapped me with a felony battery charge or some shit. So I did it.

"A couple of months later, my brakes got bled, and I wrecked and broke my arm. I sold my car after that and moved into a more secure building and, to be honest, I'm paranoid a lot of the time. The kind of stuff she said at Christmas is pretty standard. She smacked me around a lot while we were growing up, too.

"Mom and David never believed me when I spoke up, so I finally stopped. And as long as I was invisible, things were pretty calm. So, like I told you, I survive on spite, because it's all I have. She's taken everything else from me. But I know I'm not a waste of space and me showing up year after year shows her I'm still standing. I might be a shell of myself when I'm there, but I'm there."

Graham's quiet for several long moments, a myriad of emotions rolling over his features. "We're never going back to your parents' house."

I nod. "I know."

"I'm sorry I made a mess," he says with a sad sigh.

"I don't care. I'm sorry you had to find out that way. I'm sorry I wasn't here with you when you did." I scoot on the floor until I'm sitting beside him. "I think it took you coming with me to see how bad it actually was. I know no matter what I do, it'll never be good enough, so why do I keep trying? They're not my family." My chest tightens as tears burn my eyes again. "I've never held my niece and nephews. I've never spent a single moment alone with them. It's like I have the plague where they're concerned. We go to your parents' house and Gemma hands me her three-day-old baby and leaves the room. Your family is my family."

He takes my hand in his, bringing it to his lips for a kiss

before clutching it to his chest. "Yeah. They are." He sighs. "Mom told me when we were over there, she knew the baby was mine."

I snap my head in his direction. "She knew? How?"

He huffs a laugh. "For starters, apparently, she saw the whole room key thing. And then, she said for months after that, I sounded happy whenever I'd talk to her on the phone. She said you announced you were pregnant about the time I started to turn into the Unabomber. Then at Christmas, they were talking about you and Wyatt and Mom said she could tell I was pretty messed up.

"She said you were family anyway, so she was going to be Nonna, regardless. She also said she knew if we'd decided not to raise the baby together, there had to be a good reason. Of course, I told her the truth, and she said that you were smart and it took real maturity to make the kind of decision you did. She said kids could always tell when they weren't someone's priority."

"They can," I agree.

He turns his gaze on me, and his expression is sad and tired. "I don't know how you survived all that and turned out to be this amazing person. You have the most spirit of anyone I've ever met before. If your sister ever comes near us, I will gladly hold her down and let you rearrange her face. And then we'll push her into oncoming traffic."

"So romantic. Can I get that in our wedding vows?"

He raises his eyebrows in amused surprise. "Are there going to be vows?"

I shrug. "I figure you're stuck with me; might as well make it official."

He grins. "Now that's my kind of proposal."

CHAPTER TWENTY-SIX

GRAHAM — THREE MONTHS LATER

I check my watch for the fourth time in as many minutes, growing more and more nervous that this isn't going to work out. My phone vibrates and I hurriedly fish it out.

> Augusta: How did the interview go?

I type out a quick response so I can turn my attention back to the parking lot.

> Graham: Great. I'll be home later. Chinese tonight?

> Augusta: Perfect. I'll grab it on my way home. Love you.

I shoot her a quick text back and shove my phone into my pocket as I watch the entrance to the preschool tumbling gym parking lot.

Come on, man. Where are you?

I know the class Mason brings Wesley to is starting in about five minutes and that while he's in his tumbling class, Mason goes to the cafe next door. It's probably the only time the guy actually gets to himself and I hate to encroach on it, but it can't be helped. My heart lurches when I see his minivan pull into the lot and park at a spot close to the building.

After he enters, I exit my car to walk over to the coffee shop. I order a drink in the hopes that I'm already sitting by the time he gets in here. Sure enough, I've just sat down when he walks in. I pretend to be on my phone until after he orders his coffee, but as he begins to go by again, I call his name.

He stops and blinks, trying to place me. "Graham Hopkins. I came to Christmas with Augusta."

"Oh. Right. How are you, man?"

"Good, care to join me or are you in a rush?"

He checks his watch before taking the seat across from mine. "I've got a little time. Wesley's in tumbling next door, so get your breaks while you can, you know?"

I huff a laugh. "I'm sure. Hey, while I've got you, I have to ask, you know, just out of curiosity. Um, and I don't mean to put you in any kind of awkward position, but I just have to know, is it always like that?"

Mason's eyes flit side to side as he rolls his shoulders. *He's nervous.* "What do you mean?"

I feign confusion. "You know, Christmas, with Augusta and Carrie? Is it always like that? With the way Augusta's sort of... ostracized?"

He flicks his eyes down and taps his phone screen as if needing to check for a message. "I mean, I don't know if I'd call it ostracized."

"Oh? And what would you call it?"

"Dysfunction, maybe?"

I sip my coffee as I pretend to contemplate what he's said. "Maybe. But it just seemed to me like things were unnecessarily harsh for Augusta. And if I'm going to fit in with the family, I'm just trying to understand things, you know? I mean, when Augusta and I get married and have kids," his eyes widen slightly when I mention kids and my stomach knots up, "I just want to make sure that's not what it'll be like every year."

He shifts in his chair. "Y'all are talking about having kids?"

"Definitely. Between you and me, Augusta and I actually dated for a while about five years ago and things were pretty serious. But I was an idiot and thought I wasn't ready to be a dad."

He blinks, his breath quickening as he absorbs my words. "Wow. I had no idea."

"Yeah, but by the time I was ready and I went to see her, it was too late. If I'd just showed up before Christmas, maybe things would've turned out differently," I say meaningfully.

Mason fidgets with his shirt cuff and runs his fingers through his hair. I take another long sip of my coffee. "Did Augusta ever tell you what she was going to name her baby back in the day?" He shakes his head and swallows thickly. "Wesley. After her dad. It was his middle name."

He recoils as if he's been struck, all the color draining from his face. "I didn't know that. That's quite the coincidence."

"If it actually were, it would be, wouldn't it? I think we both know it's not. You might not have known before just this moment, but I'm sure some cogs are starting to turn for you."

He takes the lid off his cup and looks down into the contents. "Whatever you're trying to say or ask, I can't help you."

"I know. I just want to see if you need help with anything. I'm actually leaving litigation to return to family law, so if there was ever any situation where you might find yourself in need of something like that, I'd be happy to help you or point you in the right direction. I want to believe you're a good guy, Mason. I also know you're just trying to look out for your kids. But we could make sure things wouldn't touch them. I know you don't know me, but I'm really great at what I do.

"I'm sure there's a reason you fell in love with Carrie. Hell, she might even have some redeeming feature I'm not aware of. But the thing is, she's been abusive toward Augusta their entire lives. Stuff like that rarely stays isolated to a single area; especially not with the scope and breadth of the history of incidents Augusta has endured."

He shifts in his chair again, running his fingers through his hair once more. "I don't know what sort of incidents you'd be referring to."

"I'm sure I might believe you if you were telling the truth."

"Like I said," Mason says nervously, "I don't know what you're talking about."

I pull out my phone. "Okay. Can you watch a video for me, though? Tell me if you've encountered anything like this in your own life?"

I queue up the video on my phone and for a moment, I don't think he'll watch it, but then he does, his face losing what little color it still had. He releases a shuddery breath as he pushes the phone back across the table to me. "I'm not sure what you're hoping to accomplish here, Graham."

"Children who witness or experience abuse—even non-violent abuse—are three times more likely to engage in it themselves. They're also at higher risk for thinking that violence is the only way to resolve situations. They're at higher risk for anxiety, depression, and substance abuse.

"I understand you're in a delicate position since Carrie is the breadwinner. If it's about not having money to get out, I am happy to do the case pro-bono or call in a favor from a colleague. With that video alone, Carrie could be charged with assault since it's clear she's threatening bodily harm. She can't be brought to justice for what she did to Augusta and our baby because the statute of limitations has passed for that.

"And I realize everything I'm about to say or have said, you might run and tell Carrie. But I think you're a good man who's simply in a bad situation. Augusta said when she...fell down the stairs," I blow out a breath and try to stay calm, "you rushed over and called for an ambulance. You stood up for her at Christmas before y'all went over for the party. I'm sure that was something that cost you personally."

Mason swallows, looking down into his cup again. "What is it you think I can do for you?" He taps the screen of his phone and fidgets with his shirt cuff. "If she found out I was even talking to you—since you're connected to Augusta—I don't know what she'd do. I don't think I can help you, Graham."

I nod. "Okay. Well, I will be here next week, this same time, having coffee. Maybe we'll happen to run into each other again. My law office is actually right down the street, so I think this is a great place for me to get some work done outside of the office. Maybe I'll see you around." I offer him a smile as I ready myself to stand. "If, by chance, you need to get in touch with me before then," I pull out a card from my jacket pocket, "you can call WXOR, and talk to Gemma or Brewster. They'll get you in touch with me."

He blinks. "The radio talk show hosts?"

"Yeah. Gemma is my sister. But the card is just for the station, so nothing identifiable. If it's found, just say they were doing a remote at the grocery store and were handing out snacks or something." I leave the card on the table and tap it. "See you around, Mason."

I'm yawning as I walk in the door at home, but the sound of
Augusta singing perks me right up. I drop my messenger bag by
the door and walk toward the kitchen where I find her singing
into a broom handle. She doesn't see me at first, so I just lean
against the end of the hall and watch her belt it out and dance
along with a Green Day song blasting from the bluetooth
speaker on the counter.

Over the past several weeks, with talking more about the
abuse she endured at Carrie's hand over the years and coming
to terms with cutting ties with her family, she has become even
more herself than she's ever been. Without the constant cloud
of thinking about what it might be like the next time she visits
her parents, she's relaxed and carefree in a way I've never seen
before. It's a good thing, to be sure. I would assume the addi-
tional sessions she's had with her therapist have helped, too.

She startles when she finally catches sight of me and I push
off the wall to walk over to give her a kiss. "I expect that kind of
enthusiasm come bedtime," I say with a grin.

She scoff-laughs. "When have I ever not given it a hundred
percent in bed?"

I take the broom from her and lean it against the counter
before pulling her in for a hug. She squeezes me tight as she
lowers the music so we don't have to raise our voices to be
heard. Leaning back a few inches, I look into her eyes. "Hi."

"Hi," she replies, her voice soft. She gives me a quick kiss
before stepping back to open a cabinet to pull down a couple of
plates. "So, you said the interview went good in your text, but
you didn't elaborate."

"Yeah, Mason showed up to take Wesley to tumbling. But I
got the job."

She freezes, her hand poised to rake out a portion of veggie
lo mein, her eyes going wide. "You did?"

I nod. "Yep. I start in four weeks. Standard benefits, my

own office and paralegal, flex hours where I can work from home some. Diverse office and the senior partner used to work for NASA, speaks five languages fluently, and is a mother of four. You'd love her."

She feigns relief. "Well, I'm just so glad you are no longer going to be a bum."

"Right? But that now means you can no longer extort me for sexual favors since I will be a contributing member of this household again."

She snorts in amusement. "Please. I think you've rather enjoyed being a kept man for a couple of months."

"Not going to lie, it has been nice to just play spy games for a while. The covert stuff is pretty fun."

Augusta finishes dishing out our food while I fix us each a glass of water. When I sit, she asks, "So, how did it go with Mason? Did you actually talk to him?"

Chewing on my current bite of egg roll, I nod as I swallow. "He was fidgety and nervous. My guess is, Carrie is abusive at home. Maybe not physically, but chances are, with the way she's always been with you, she's like that with him, too. I told him about the Wesley thing and he had no idea. You could see it in his face. And after he watched the video, he was extra squirrelly."

"You think he'll help?"

"Who knows? He was spooked, that's for sure. I'm sure he's just thinking about the kids and money. He probably feels pretty helpless. I've seen it in abused women a lot. It's more rare in men, but not unheard of, obviously. He's practically powerless. Especially if your sister has held all the financial cards for years. Do you know what he did before he became a stay-at-home dad?"

Augusta thinks for a moment. "I think he worked in finance. Although, she always made more money and with the cost of daycare, it just made sense for him to stay home. Plus, he loves being a dad. You can tell he loves those kids. Carrie pretends. It's convincing, but I've seen it enough to know."

I nod. "I bet, if she got analyzed, she'd probably exhibit a lot of psychopathic tendencies. Maybe we'll get to find out."

"At this point, I think I'd settle for watching Mason leave her and take the kids."

"I mean, you could always go ahead and file the report. That way, there's a record of behavior."

Eyes focused on some fixed point across the room, she shakes her head as she rolls her engagement ring on her finger. "Not yet. I want to stick to the plan."

I turn on my stool to face her, putting my hand on her thigh to give it a squeeze. "You know you don't have to do any of this, right? We can just forget it. We'll still be married and happy and we can forget all about them."

She offers me her full attention, her expression stony. "No. I fully recognize that it's a pretty drastic and dramatic plan, but the longer I'm away from them and the more I think about it, the more I want to go through with it. She's taken so much more from me than I even thought. It's not just that she pushed me down the stairs when I was pregnant and then got pregnant and stole the name I was going to use just to rub it in my face.

"It's not just that she bled my brakes and trashed my place and slept with my high school boyfriend simply to make a point. It's not even that she's belittled me and body shamed me my entire life or physically abused me and mentally tormented me.

"She's robbed me of my personal safety, my dignity, and my peace of mind. Most of the time, I don't feel secure in my own home. And the fact that my parents ignored and even enabled her abuse at times is so fucking infuriating I want to scream. I

refuse to live in fear anymore. I refuse to put my future children in danger because she is a psycho.

"You wanted me to buck up and kick her ass, that's exactly
what I'm going to do. And yes, it will be public and sweet and I
hope with everything I'm worth that she tries to pull the same
old shit so that everyone will see what a fraud and monster she
is. Hopefully, that will help Mason and those kids get out and
have a good, happy, safe life. Because honestly, his life has probably been no better than mine and he's a victim, too. He
deserves this as much as I do."

CHAPTER TWENTY-SEVEN

AUGUSTA

"You think they'll actually show up?" Gemma asks a few days later as she sips a glass of champagne. "They're already ten minutes late."

"They'll be here. They wouldn't miss an opportunity to pass judgment. Probably just wanting to make an entrance and hoping that I'll be in the middle of trying on a dress or something and ruin the reveal," I say, rolling my eyes.

Marilyn shakes her head. "I think I'm going to need something stronger than champagne if they're as nasty as you've always told us they are."

"They will be," Gemma and I say in unison and share a laugh.

"You realize, though, if she says anything negative at all, I will punch her right in the tits, right?"

I take Gemma's glass with a chuckle. "Okay, Rocky. I think that's enough champagne for you." I blow out a breath as a wave of nausea rolls over me.

"How are you feeling? You're looking a little green this

morning," she mutters with a raised brow as she and Marilyn share a glance. "Anything you feel like telling us?"

"Nothing to tell. Well, nothing except that Graham and I must both be freakishly fertile. The two times we had a broken condom, I got knocked up," I add with feigned exasperation.

"I knew it," she squeals in delight. She and her mother both wrap their arms around me as I laugh, my chest flooding with warmth. As if I needed further proof that they're my family, getting to share our good news with people who only want to celebrate with Graham and me just makes me even more glad to have them in my life.

The bell over the door dings and we all sober. "I don't want them to know," I whisper, anxiety driving out my excitement.

Gemma pats my hand and Marilyn nods. "We've got you, honey. I've also got a gun if we need it."

I choke on my sparkling cider. "Mrs. H.!"

"Just in case."

My mother and Carrie walk around a partition and enter the main salon area of the bridal boutique. They're dressed in nearly identical black dresses, as if they're attending a funeral.

How festive.

I stand and greet them both with our standard nanosecond hug and barely-there cheek peck. "Mom, Carrie, this is Graham's sister, Gemma, and their mother, Marilyn."

They all shake hands and Carrie eyes Gemma. "Have we met before?"

Gemma smiles sweetly. "We have actually. During our freshman year of college, I spent one night at your house. I believe you had a little sleepover or something going on."

Carrie grins and it's actually genuine. No doubt, she's recalling putting the Nair in my shampoo. "Right. How have you been?"

"Great. You?"

"Perfect," she says and sits. "So, I'm guessing we should get on with things, right? Gus, I hope you're going to pick something that kinda," she scrunches up her face and mimes cinching in a waist, "whittles everything in."

Gemma scoffs, color coming to her cheeks. "I'm just hoping she picks something that shows off her great tits and ass. You know, those things my brother can't get enough of. If you got it, flaunt it. Lord knows, Auggie's got it," she says and shoots me a wink.

Marilyn snorts in amusement, choking on her drink, and I have to bite back my own laugh.

Carrie looks incensed by Gemma's quip and my mother grabs a glass of champagne and downs it, her expression disgusted. I'm so glad I brought Gemma and Marilyn and I don't have to face my mom and sister alone today. The truth is, I already have my dress, but this production is needed for the big plan, so I'm happy to put on the show.

"Mom, I've already picked out a few dresses; do you want to come help me with the zipper on this first one?"

She blinks in surprise. "Oh. Alright." She follows me into the room and since I'd already changed into a robe when I arrived, it takes only seconds to slip into the first dress, a cream satin, off-the-shoulder, A-line gown. I turn to allow my mother to zip it. "A little plain, don't you think?"

Ignoring her dig, I say, "Just a place to start. But I like the silhouette."

"And you really want to get married? You think Graham will be satisfied with you? He's so handsome and successful."

I turn as soon as she's finished zipping up the dress, trying my best to keep my anger in check. "Actually, yes. Believe it or not, it is possible to find love, even when you're fat. I've known Graham for almost twenty years. We dated for several months five years ago. He was the father of my baby." The color drains from her face and I continue. "All those things about me that you find fault in, he loves. And for the record, *I* am successful and beautiful and *he* is lucky to have *me*."

I step past her and out toward the main room to step up on the pedestal and inspect the dress. Gemma and Marilyn immediately clap and hoot with excitement like this is the best dress they've ever seen in their lives, playing their roles to a tee. Carrie stares at them in open-mouthed horror. "God, this is a bridal boutique, not a truck pull. Plus, that dress is hideous."

Marilyn's mouth falls open at my sister's barbed comment, but Gemma just smiles sweetly at her. When she speaks a beat later, her voice is low, but not so low I can't hear her. "Bitch, I will cut you." Her smile stays in place and her tone turns syrupy. "You can either be a positive influence in this experience or you can keep your mouth shut. You might think you run things, but I'm not afraid of you. I could break you like a twig and not think twice. So, the next thing that comes out of your mouth will be something uplifting or nothing at all. Got it?"

Carrie works her jaw, folding her arms as she sits back, crosses her legs, and does her best to look bored. Gem shoots me a wink and blows me a kiss. "Spin and let me see the back." I do and she lets out a low whistle. "Look at that ass. Damn, sis."

I breathe a laugh and Carrie huffs. My mother examines me, but keeps her mouth shut. I give it a final look, pretending to consider it. "I'm not sure this one is *the* dress."

Two hours later and twenty dresses that are all beautiful but not *it*, I pull out the final contender for today and as it's a white version of the actual dress I've chosen, I know it's perfect. The skirt is flowy and made of tulle and because it's two separate pieces, it's so much more comfortable. The top is lace, with thin shoulder straps and a deep v-neck.

When I step out of the dressing room, my mother actually blinks in surprise. "I suppose you saved the best for last."

I step up onto the pedestal and smile. "Mom, I'm going to choose to take that as a compliment. But yes, I think we have a dress."

"Hallelujah," Carrie says with a sigh.

Even though Gemma's already seen my real dress, she still tears up. "Auggie, it's beautiful and so are you."

Marilyn nods, her own eyes misty. "Just lovely, honey."

"So, where is this wedding going to be?" my sister asks with a dismissive glance at my dress.

"Actually, it's at the home of one partner from Graham's law firm. She lives on this gorgeous farm and has offered us the use of the property. It's going to be super low-key." I shoot Marilyn a grateful smile. "Marilyn is doing all the food, and it's really only close family and friends, so it'll be more like a dinner party. We're doing pie instead of cake and it'll be really intimate."

"Sounds," when Carrie starts speaking, Gemma glares at her, and my sister rolls her eyes, "quaint."

"It sounds perfect, is what I think you were going for, Carrie," Gemma counters.

"And we're doing it really soon, so you should get your invitation sometime this week."

"What's the rush?" Mom asks, starting on her third glass of champagne.

"We're just ready to start our lives together. This is what we should've been doing five years ago, but I suppose better late than never, right?"

Carrie quirks her head, latching onto the number. "Five years ago?"

Gemma nods. "Yeah, so get this; they hooked up at my wedding and had this whole secret affair for months. When they finally told me, I was so pissed. But I suppose since Graham's going to go and make her my sister all legal-like and everything, I can't be too mad."

"I know I'm not disappointed in the least to have Augusta as another daughter. Lord knows she's been family for years, so this is just a formality if you ask me," Marilyn interjects, and I offer her a small smile.

My sister lifts a brow and sips her own champagne. "So, what happened five years ago? Was it because you lost the baby?"

My eyes go wide and honestly, this is the first time I've ever actually wanted to murder her. The fact that she has the absolute gall to even let the words past her lips make me see red. But knowing I still want to follow through with the plan, I simply blow out a deep breath as I attempt to maintain my composure. Gemma chokes on her drink and Marilyn blinks in shock, color rising to her cheeks. They both open their mouths, identical murderous expressions on their faces, but I get there first. "No. We broke up before that. I was with actually dating Wyatt at that time."

I step off the pedestal and into the dressing room to redress in my street clothes. When I step out after placing the order with the clerk, my mother and sister are nowhere to be seen. "I told them they could go," Gemma explains. "I think Carrie knew it was in her best interest after what she said. I was ready to break the stem off my champagne flute and shiv the bitch."

"Here, here," Marilyn agrees, her expression still full of rage. "Although I'm not sure I would've put it quite that way."

I blow out a breath. "Well, let's just hope they even show

up at this thing. Maybe I'm giving them too much credit, though. They might not even care."

Gemma shrugs. "Either way, you'll have lasagna and some cherry pie."

I nod as we head to her car. "Silver linings, I suppose."

"Oh God, that's good," I say with a moan.

Graham laughs from the other end of the couch where he's massaging the arch of my foot. "You sound like you're enjoying this more than what we did last night."

"Never, but my feet are killing me from trying on heels all day. Your sister is trying to kill me."

"She does like her shoes. I'm glad I don't have to buy any new ones." He moves his thumbs up toward the ball of my foot and I let my head fall back in pleasure. "Damn, babe. Never knew feet were such a huge turn-on for you."

"They're not," I whine. "I'm just on them all day and I swear, this kid is already draining my entire life force."

He chuckles. "Sure, but it'll be such a cute parasite. Don't you remember how adorable Julie was?"

"Says the man who refuses to even hold a baby before it's three months old."

"They can't hold their heads up. It's creepy and they're all fragile and stuff."

I snort a laugh. "They're not that fragile. And they have to have bones that aren't fully formed just so they can be born. You will hold this baby as soon as it's born. It will be covered in all sorts of goo and blood and stuff and you will still hold it. I don't care if you're wearing a five-thousand-dollar suit. You will hold this baby; bobble head or no."

He holds up his hands in surrender. "Yes, of course I will

hold *our* baby. And it'll be covered in your goo and stuff; I can deal with that."

I roll my eyes. "Such a romantic."

He's still laughing when he pulls his phone out a moment later and blinks at the screen as it buzzes in his hand. Clearing his throat, he swipes at the screen. "Graham Hopkins...Yeah, go ahead."

He continues to rub my feet for a moment as he listens, but then stops, his brow furrowing as he sets my feet on the couch. He stands, moving toward the bedroom, returning a moment later, changed out of his previous gym shorts and into jeans and a T-shirt. The phone is still pressed to his ear as he shoves his feet into his shoes. "Alright. I'll be there in a half-hour. Send me the address." He listens for a beat. "Okay. See you in a few."

He hangs up, dropping his phone into his pocket. "What's going on?" I ask, getting to my feet.

"Mason called me."

I blink. "Seriously?"

"Yeah. Apparently, your sister got the wedding invitation in the mail. I'm guessing seeing it triggered her. Sounds like he's finally ready to make a move."

I walk over to grab his keys from the basket and extend them his direction. "Probably. I'm sure, with her having to mostly be on her best behavior at the bridal shop, then finding out where the wedding is going to be held, she's probably spinning out."

CHAPTER TWENTY-EIGHT

GRAHAM

Pulling up at Carrie and Mason's gorgeous, sprawling cape cod-style house reminds me that even though something looks beautiful on the outside, the inside might be trashed. Much like Augusta's sister herself. Mason must have been watching for me, because he opens the door before I've even hit the porch. "Hurry. I don't know how long she'll be gone." His eyes flit over my shoulder.

I take in his appearance as I ascend the steps. His cheeks are flushed, his blonde hair is disheveled, and his eyes are wild with fear.

"Sure. Do you know where she went?"

He shakes his head. "No, but probably her boyfriend's place, if was going to guess."

My eyebrows climb up my forehead as I enter the home. It looks like something out of a Pottery Barn catalog; all beige and white and traditional; not a thing out of place. No personality, either.

"Boyfriend, huh?"

He nods. "Yeah. Some guy she works with, I think."

"Okay. And where are the kids?"

He blows out a breath, raking his fingers through his hair. A beat later, he winces, dropping his hand to his side. I almost want to ask if she's hit him or something but he opens his mouth to speak and I think better of it. "Amelia's at softball practice and a friend is bringing her home. Wade's at the neighbor's. April took Wesley for the day. She does that sometimes."

"Alright, so you want to sit and tell me what happened? If Carrie comes back, I'm here asking you for some financial advice since you used to be in banking, right?"

He frowns. "Yeah. How'd you know that?"

"Augusta said she thought that's what you did before y'all had kids."

Mason gestures to an island bar in the kitchen and I don't miss how shaky his hands are. "We can sit in there, if that's okay."

"Sure." I give him a friendly smile as I take a seat at the bar. He pulls a bottle of tequila from the freezer and a shot glass from a nearby cabinet. He holds one up for me, but I shake my head. "I'm sober."

"Sorry, do I need to—."

I hold up my hand, stopping him. "No, it's fine. You go ahead."

He brings the bottle and glass over and downs a couple of shots in quick succession. "She's always had a temper. Never around the kids. Well, not really. She's a stickler for perfection, so ballgames and recitals and stuff tend to set her on edge if one of the kids is having an off day.

"And to be honest, I've never understood what her deal is with Augusta. It's as if she faults her for simply existing. I know she's always been terrible to her and I'm ashamed to admit, Christmas is sort of like a reprieve for me since she focuses her anger on her sister instead of me. I tried to stand up for Augusta that first Christmas I was with their family, but she accused me of cheating on her and said she'd ruin me at work if I ever did.

"When I quit working, anytime I'd encourage her to try to get along with Augusta, she'd remind me who paid the bills and put food on the table. She'd say that if she wanted my opinion, she'd tell me what it was since I wasn't smart enough to develop one on my own. I graduated cum laude from Dartmouth, for Christ's sake," he spits out angrily. "It was never supposed to be like this."

"I know," I agree. "It never starts off as what it ends up escalating to. It's always small things. Little slights and gaslighting and then it becomes more and more toxic and you're questioning your memory of what it was like before. At least, that's what Augusta, as well as some of my past clients, have said."

"I used to be somebody, man. I was the head of my department and I drove fancy cars and had lots of beautiful women falling all over themselves to come home with me for the night. I was active and had a ton of friends. Now I'm terrified every time the door opens since I don't know which version of Carrie I'm going to get."

He downs another shot as his eyes well with tears. "The truth is, I only married her because she was pregnant." Frowning, I do some mental math and he shakes his head. "Turns out it was a false alarm." He considers. "Although, now I'm questioning everything. But I take care of my responsibilities. That's what I thought I was doing."

My brows rise in surprise as he pours himself another shot. "You ever think about the one that got away and how different things would be if you had them? I think about the life I could've had if I hadn't thrown that one party; if I'd never met her. Don't get me wrong, I wouldn't trade my kids for anything, but I had an entirely different plan for my life; a different person I was supposed to spend the rest of my life with."

"I get that. Augusta was my one that got away. But thankfully, I got her back."

He tosses back the shot, wincing as he swallows. "Even before she was ever this...this *thing* she's become, she was highstrung and everything had to be her way or else. I honestly never thought she'd sink so low that she'd push a pregnant woman down the stairs. And I don't know anything about Augusta's brakes. I'm so sorry. We always..." He looks away, his eyes becoming unfocused as he remembers something and I just stay quiet.

He tips the shot glass back and forth in his hand and clenches his jaw. "We'd always said we were going to have two kids. After the pregnancy scare—if it even was that and not just some ploy. I mean, who even knows now? Anyway, that's what *we* decided; two kids. I would've been happy to have more because I was an only child and both my parents were gone, so I wanted a big family, but she said she only wanted two. Then, a few months after that Christmas, she got pregnant. She was supposed to be on the pill, so I just thought it was a happy accident. I'm guessing now that it wasn't."

Tears roll down his face and he wipes them away with the ball of his hand. "Who the fuck does that out of simple spite? To take something away from someone and then rub it in their face like that? And if she's capable of that, I can't continue to let this be my life. I need out. Can you help me? Me and the kids? She'll want them just to say she has them and poison them against me. I'm not sure she actually cares about them other than appearances. I'm sure that sounds awful, but more and more things are starting to fall into place in my mind and there's something wrong with her."

"We'll do whatever we have to do to get you and your kids out of this situation. Do you need a place to go? Do you fear for your safety or the kids'?"

He shakes his head. "No. She's not all that violent. She doesn't even leave a mark. She's never touched the kids."

I stand. "Okay. Well, if anything changes, you call the police and then call me. Listen, I've probably already stayed longer than I should've. I'll meet you at the cafe the next time you have to take Wesley for tumbling, okay? We'll go over some next steps and brainstorm a plan. Does that work for you?"

He nods. "Yeah. I think I can do that."

"Good. In the meantime, here's what I want you to do."

Augusta's already in bed by the time I get home and although it's still early, I'm tired. My heart goes out to Mason and his kids for their situation. It's probably easy to say a man could never be abused, but it just doesn't get reported as often as it actually happens.

After a quick shower, I climb into bed beside the woman I love, pulling her into my arms. She's not really showing yet, but when I put my hand on her stomach, it's beginning to feel different. In truth, I can't wait to feel the kicks and sensations of her belly, all big with this baby.

Even though I grew up catholic, I'm lapsed at best. When Nonna was alive, we'd go on Christmas and Easter, and she was devout. But there are times I find myself hoping and praying for a smooth, healthy pregnancy and delivery for Augusta and the baby. That the trauma from the past doesn't repeat itself.

We're keeping the pregnancy a secret from everyone except my immediate family until things are more sorted with Carrie. Although I don't think she'd be unhinged enough to pull the same stunt twice, we're not taking any chances. It doesn't stop me from being nervous about the wedding, though.

Augusta is confident everything will work out, but I'm less

optimistic. I have no reason to be; just nervous, I suppose. The plan is actually an extremely good one; complete with contingencies and fallback plans. That doesn't stop me from worrying. This is the life of the woman I love, after all. I don't put anything past Carrie at this point.

I adjust my cufflinks as I stand at the front of the tent in the backyard of the mayor's estate. It's a beautiful, sprawling farm, complete with picturesque pastures of horses and a gorgeous white barn. We're setup about a hundred yards behind the lovely and huge century-old farmhouse and fifty yards behind the pool house, where Augusta is scheduled to exit in only a few minutes.

Soft music drifts from speakers scattered around the tent and a large screen is set up, showing photos of us from over the years, as well as our engagement pictures. Rows of white chairs flank a makeshift aisle and a simple dark wood arbor dripping in wisteria stands as the only adornment for the space, allowing the backdrop of the pastures and the giant weeping willow to my right to shine.

The small group of our immediate families and a few close friends sit and speak in hushed voices as we wait for Augusta. Those in attendance include April, David, Carrie, Mason, their kids, my parents, Gemma, Brewster, their kids, the mayor, his wife, Sandra—the senior partner from my firm—as well as Kyle and a couple of Augusta's work colleagues. Brewster leans over from his post as officiant and mutters, "She sure knows how to crank up the anticipation, huh?"

I laugh and a beat later, Collier jumps down from his chair next to Gemma and jogs over to me, tugging on my suit jacket. I squat down to give him my attention. "Where's Auggie? I'm ready for pie." He tries to whisper, but he's only three, so it comes out more like a loud hiss and Gemma chides him.

I can't help but laugh as I wave off my sister. I point up at the pool house. "She's in there getting ready. She'll be out soon. Then, as soon as your dad says I can kiss the bride, we'll go have pie, okay? They'll bring all the food out of the pool house and we'll eat after, alright?"

He sighs. "Okay. But this is boring, Ham."

I roll my eyes. "I know. But the pie will be really good, okay?"

He returns to his seat and I stand up, readjusting my jacket and sleeves as motion toward the back of the tent catches my attention.

"No, Carrie; just stay here," Mason says, his voice hushed.

"I have to pee," she hisses. "It's not like I'll actually miss anything."

I try not to react as she heads toward the pool house and passes the hair stylist, who she speaks with for a brief moment. The stylist points her in the direction from which she just came. Even as my heart rate ratchets up watching her walk into the small building, instinct tells me Augusta will be fine and she can take care of herself.

It's showtime, I guess.

I nod to Kyle, who is still not Gemma's favorite person but can be relied upon to do an important job. He taps his phone screen and an earbud and gives me a thumbs up, not taking his eyes off his screen. His jaw clenches as he taps another button and a live feed of the interior of the pool house starts playing on a screen to my left. Conversations still as Carrie's voice streams through the speakers.

"I still don't know how you were able to swing all this. Like you have any kind of real connections," Carrie says, her arms folded as she paces behind Augusta as she puts the final touches on her makeup. Augusta caps the tube of lip gloss she's just used and tucks it into its pouch, storing it under the table.

"What is this?" April asks in confusion, pointing at the screen.

"Sorry, ma'am, I'm just having some issues with the slideshow. Must be some signals crossed feeding from the pool house," Kyle says, feigning uncertainty.

"Carrie, I'm trying to finish getting ready. You really should be down with the rest of the guests," Augusta offers with forced civility as she stands, hands on hips.

Her sister eyes her with barely concealed contempt. "You know he doesn't really love you, right? No one could love you. I mean, look at you."

"Yes, look at me," Augusta says with a smile. "I'm about to marry the love of my life at a beautiful farm, and there's nothing you can do about it." She sobers, her expression turning more wistful. "And when I was little, I dreamed about having you by my side to support me. I don't know why you hate me so much. Why you've tortured me and tormented me all these years when all I wanted was to be your sister."

"You're not my sister. You're a mistake. And anything I've ever done to you was so you'd see exactly how little you matter. Not to me. Not to *my* parents. Nobody wanted you there."

"But I was there, Carrie. And that just ate you up inside, didn't it? That I—a waste of space—got to share your oxygen. That I didn't have to steal other people's boyfriends to make myself feel good. That people liked me, fat and all, while you were obsessed with your looks and had to put other people down to feel like somebody. That no matter what you did, I still stood there as a reminder of everything you hate."

"You don't deserve any of this," Carrie spits out, color rising to her cheeks.

"Yet, I have it. And again, there's nothing you can do about it. There aren't any brakes for you to tamper with." Her hands come to her belly. "There aren't any stairs for you to push me down this time," she says through gritted teeth and blinks back tears. Bile rises in my throat as hushed whispers sound from around the small group.

Augusta lifts her chin in defiance. "And I don't need to keep trying to prove myself to you or Mom anymore. I'm happy. I'm getting married and you won't be able to touch *this* baby. Because after today, you'll never see me again."

"Thank God. You'll finally be gone? I can't wait." Carrie's gaze falls to Augusta's hands and her expression turns to one of disgust. "What, you didn't learn your lesson last time? Last I checked, there's nowhere you're safe from me. I can get to you anywhere I want, anytime I want. And I don't need stairs. Babies die all the time, Gus. You just remember that. Might be more fun, actually, if you got to see this one before it died. I must admit, it wasn't quite as satisfying last time."

An audible gasp rises from the chairs behind me as I blink back tears of rage, balling my hands into fists at my side.

Augusta's voice is calm when she speaks. "Like I said, you won't be able to touch this baby. If you come near me or my family, it'll be the last thing you ever do."

Carrie steps closer to her and my heart lurches, but Augusta doesn't flinch. "You think I'm afraid of you, bitch? You think, because this is your wedding, I can't make your day hell? There might not be a set of stairs for me to push you down this time, but I can sure as shit make sure you remember your place."

Without warning, she grabs a pie from a nearby table and smashes it into the front of Augusta's immaculate white dress. Augusta gasps in shock before narrowing her eyes. "You just can't let me have one nice thing, can you?" She shoves her sister back, but only hard enough to put space between the two women and wipes bright red cherry pie filling off the front of her dress.

"You don't deserve anything nice. Least of all this," Carrie shouts and runs at Augusta, who sidesteps her easily and backs up. Carrie stumbles into the table containing all the deserts and when she stands again, she's holding a knife, a murderous glint in her eye. "Everyone knows how clumsy you are. I mean, I only came in here to pee. Be a shame if, when you got up to leave, you tripped over your own feet and fell into the pie table and right into this knife. So sad. On your wedding day, no less."

I'd already turned to run up the hill when I saw the knife and I don't stop, even as I hear Gemma say something over my shoulder. By the time I make it to the pool house and bust through the door, Carrie's on the floor, out cold, Gemma standing over her, hands balled into fists. I kick the knife away and cross the room to Augusta, yanking her to me. "Your suit," she objects.

"Fuck the suit. Jesus Christ. I didn't know there was going to be a knife in here."

Gemma walks up to us, while still keeping her gaze fixed on Carrie. "We had it covered, right, Auggie?"

She pulls out of my arms, heaving a breath. "At least tell me Kyle got it all?"

"Yeah. And everyone saw it, so plenty of witnesses, too."

Mason comes in, his face a mask of terror and apology. "I'm so sorry, guys. I called the police; they should be here soon." Carrie groans and he walks over to peer down at her. "Guess what, Carrie? I'm divorcing you and you get nothing. Remember that prenup you signed? I had Graham look it over. Turns out there's a fidelity clause you must've overlooked. Guess I should thank you for cheating on me. You only had to last another year, but I guess you just had to have some variety, huh?"

"Oh, shut up, Mason." She attempts to get up and Gemma clocks her again. Carrie grunts, collapsing to the floor again.

"No one gave you permission to get up, bitch," my sister says as she shakes out her fist.

Augusta frowns at me. "What fidelity clause?"

I huff a laugh. "Mason's family insisted on the prenup because he gains access to a trust at thirty-five. Your sister got cocky, and I guess didn't read the fine print since she always knew she'd be the one earning all the money. If she cheated within the first ten years, she'd lose everything that they'd accrued during the marriage. Houses, cars, money, everything."

Mason nods. "But she had me so under her thumb and browbeaten, I didn't have it in me to leave until now. I should really be thanking you."

"Just be happy, Mason; that'll be thanks enough," Augusta says with a smile. "And let those kids eat some damn carbs. Shit."

He chuckles. "Will do."

CHAPTER TWENTY-NINE

AUGUSTA

I look down at my pie-splattered dress and back up at Graham. "I guess it's good the actual wedding isn't until tomorrow, huh?"

"What?" Carrie screeches from her place on the floor.

I grin down at her, expecting her to try to get up again, but Gemma stands ready to wallop her again. "Oh, yeah. Didn't I mention that? Tonight was only the rehearsal dinner. Do you really think I don't know you, Carrie? I knew you wouldn't be able to resist pulling your same old shit. Guess that's what you get for being predictable and giving me nearly thirty years of behavior to catalog."

Sirens sound, and I tilt my head. "Sounds like your ride's here, sis. And I hate to say it, but orange is definitely the wrong color for you."

"It's your word against mine, bitch," she spits out with a sneer.

I snort a laugh. "Oh, is that what you think? That I wouldn't be prepared? I'm marrying a lawyer, so I know there has to be evidence. In fact, the entire party saw everything." I point up to a clock by the door. "Smile for the camera. Looks like you got your big debut, sis. And you played your part perfectly. I, for one, couldn't be prouder."

She opens her mouth and Graham pipes up. "As a lawyer—although not your lawyer—Carrie, I advise you to keep your mouth shut. Threats of bodily harm are grounds for an assault charge and *oof*," he says with a wince, "between today and what you said on Christmas morning, if I were a prosecutor, I'd have a field day. Not to mention, the testimony of your own husband. Yikes. I really don't envy your attorney."

"Spouses can't testify against each other."

I snort, squatting down to put myself in her direct line of sight. "Oh, let's leave the law to the smart people, huh? What the law says is that someone cannot be *forced* to testify against their spouse, not that they can't freely give their testimony." I glance up at Graham. "Do I have that right, honey?" I ask with a sweet smile.

"Sure do, babe. Carrie, looks like you're up shit creek and the paddle just got eaten by piranhas. Sucks for ya."

Sparkly, deathtrap stilettos in hand, I climb off the elevator on our floor. Graham chuckles when I yawn for what seems like the tenth time in half as many minutes. "Tired, Tesoro?"

"Uh-huh," I say with a nod.

He unlocks the door and ushers me inside, still covered in pie and white tulle. "Want me to run you a shower and then I can rub your feet?" I stand up straighter as I enter the bedroom and try to undo the zipper of my shirt. He steps up behind me, batting away my hands so he can do it for me. "You've had an exciting day."

I yawn again and nod as the lace top slides down my arms.

"Yeah, but too bad I wasn't the one who got to punch Carrie. I was really looking forward to that."

"So was I." He unzips my skirt and it falls off my hips. He turns me to face him, taking my face in his hands. "Hopefully it's all over."

"Amen to that. Do you really think so, though? She can't, like, plead temporary insanity or anything, right?"

"Nah. With everything she said today and at Christmas and the evidence Mason collected, there's no way. She might be a psychopath, but she's not clinically insane. She may try to get a deal, but I wouldn't think the DA's office would be inclined to make it, regardless of her connections there. She attacked you at the mayor's estate and threatened to kill you. The presence of a weapon constitutes aggravated assault, if not attempted second-degree murder. It'll all just depend on the prosecutor." He drops a kiss onto my lips. "But we're not going to worry about that tonight. Tonight, you're going to get cleaned up and go to bed."

"And after tomorrow, you're stuck with me."

"Gladly," he says with a grin.

I run my hand down his tie. "What if I'd rather you clean me up? You do like cherries, don't you?" I ask with a slow smile.

He raises a brow. "It is one of the more superior pies."

I bite my lip as I tug him toward the shower. "Then it seems a shame to waste it."

He bends his head to my chest to lick a path through the sticky cherry filling stuck to my skin. "That it does."

"Okay, Auggie, you're all good."

I make a final adjustment to my skirt and blow out a breath.

"Thank God this is happening today. I'm not sure this skirt would've fit me much longer."

"I can't wait to see you get all big and round," Gemma says with a near squeal.

Laughing, I roll my eyes. "Gem, I'm already big and round."

"Whatever." She takes my hands in hers as tears well in her eyes. "I'm so happy for you. I mean, if you're sure you want to marry Graham and all. I've got pictures from his awkward bowl-cut phase if it will deter you."

I snort a laugh. "Not a chance. Trust me, I don't want him doing that thing with his tongue to anyone else."

My best friend makes a gagging noise. "I'm going to choose to believe that has something to do with envelops or ice cream cones."

We dissolve into giggles like small girls and I wrap her in a big hug. "Thank you for being my best friend and my sister and for letting me be auntie to your beautiful babies. I love you so much."

"Stop, you're going to make me cry and unlike you, I can't get by with only eyeliner and mascara."

"You stop; you're gorgeous. And now we're going to be family for real."

"Auggie, we were already family for real. This just makes it legally binding." She steps back, dabbing the corner of her eye with a tissue. "Okay, spin and let me see."

I do as instructed, and she smiles. "The wine color suits you so much better than the white. And the black dip on the edges of the skirt? Perfect."

I shrug. "Had to have something I could wear with my Docs, you know that. They're my something old."

The door to the pool house opens and Mason walks in, a tentative smile on his face. "I think they're ready for you,

Augusta." Gemma gives me a kiss on the cheek and heads out to join the congregants. I blow out a breath, picking up my bouquet of cream-colored roses to step up next to Mason. "Are you sure you want me to be the one to walk you down the aisle? Surely Graham's dad or someone else would be better suited? I really don't feel worthy of this."

I shake my head. "You're family, Mason. You're the only person in that house who's ever actually been kind to me. We were both her victims, but she doesn't get to win. We're still going to be family and I'd love to have a relationship with your kids. You have no idea how much something like that would mean to me. We'd also love for you to be Uncle Mason to our baby. Us orphans have to stick together."

He nods, his expression sad. "Yeah, we do. I'm really sorry your parents didn't show up today."

I shrug. "I should be surprised, but I'm not. I'm glad you and the kids are here, though."

He smiles, gesturing to the door. "Shall we?"

"Yes, please; take me to my man."

"Yes, ma'am."

As we make our way across the lawn, the opening chords of "You are the Reason" begin to stream from the tent. Mason keeps his eyes facing forward, but says, "I'm so happy you still allowed yourself to be happy despite her."

I huff a laugh. "Believe it or not, spite was about all I survived on for years."

"I do believe it. Hopefully, someday, I'll find what you have."

I give his arm a squeeze. "I'm sure you will. It won't be easy with everything Carrie did to you and put you through, but you deserve love, Mason. I hope when you're ready, you'll let yourself be open to it."

"Fingers crossed." We make it to the beginning of the aisle

and my eyes find Graham's. His are wet and he wears the sappiest smile I've ever seen in my life. Mason and I both laugh. "Okay, I guess I better get you down to your groom."

What feels like both no time at all and a millennia later, Mason is pressing a kiss to my cheek as he hands me off to Graham. My husband-to-be beams as we turn to face one another once we walk the few steps to the makeshift altar.

Brewster stands in front of us, looking dashing with his long, light brown hair down and wavy, his full beard neatly trimmed. I'm sure if it were up to him, he'd be here in flannel and jeans and a pair of sneakers as he married us off. Thankfully, he's a good sport and looks great in a simple black suit and white dress shirt.

Graham, on the other hand, looks entirely sexy in his favorite charcoal suit. He's paired it with a black shirt, his tie a few shades darker than my dress. His hair is its standard glossy, wavy, purposely messy mop that I can't wait to sink my fingers into. As usual, his face is covered in deliberate scruff, making him look just the least bit roguish and entirely delicious.

Brewster holds a small leather notebook, but as he speaks, he doesn't bother to open it. And like the radio host he is, his voice is buttery smooth. "Hopefully, after the events of yesterday, there will be no more drama. I mean, really, think of the pies, people." A collective chuckle travels up from the congregants, and Graham and I share an amused glance. "If you had asked me when I met Graham and Augusta almost fifteen years ago if this was something I would ever consider happening, I would've said hell no."

I scoff and my mouth falls open, but Brewster is still smiling. "But having gotten to know them both over the last decade-and-a-half, I would have to say there are no two people better suited to one another. Graham has a tendency to be a little," he lifts a brow and bobs his head from side-to-side as if in thought, "uptight and Augusta is a free spirit. Graham likes his labels and Augusta couldn't care less where the clothes come from as long as they have pockets and she got them for a great deal." I huff a laugh and shrug because he's not wrong.

"Graham can't carry a tune in a bucket and Augusta makes beautiful music. Graham is sour at times and Augusta can be too sweet. But with each other," our dear friend says with a warm smile, "they are the perfect mix of opposites, and it works. Truthfully, I think they are the only two people suited to handle one another's shit."

We all laugh softly as he continues to smile at us. "Graham, I guess we'll start with you."

Graham blows out a breath and squeezes my hand. "Tesoro, I think we both know this is five years later than we should've done it, but better late than never, right?" I huff a laugh and he smiles. "But it took me five years, three hours in the car with you, two days in literal hell, and one night with you in my arms to realize that you will always be the only one for me. I'm too serious and stuffy most of the time, but you make me want to be playful and goofy when no one else can.

"You are the only one I'd ever want to have on my life journey," he quips with a wink and I snort-laugh, "and I promise to always be your shield when you need one and your sidekick when you need that, too. I promise that my family is your family and, in truth, I think we all know they love you more than me. I promise you'll never have to worry if you have someone in your corner, because I'm there; no matter what.

"I vow to you to be the best husband and father I know how to be and I'm sure if I need improvements, you will provide detailed instructions," he says with a chuckle and I laugh. "Thank you for being the person who showed me all the things I never knew I ever wanted." He slips a simple white gold band on my finger and presses a kiss to it before glancing at Brewster, who nods approvingly before he turns his gaze on me.

"Augusta, take it away."

"I'm not sure I can follow all that, but I will definitely try," I reply with a grin. "Graham, for years, you were this...enigma to me. All serious and stuck up and you're still obsessed with clothes, but I guess it's okay, because you're really hot."

Graham laughs, shaking his head, and I squeeze his hand. "But you are so much more than that. Regardless of our messy past, you stepped up for me without a second thought and were everything I needed. And despite my best efforts to once again keep you locked out of my heart, you knocked down my defenses and claimed me as your own. You are complex and stubborn and one of the most honorable men I know.

"Falling in love with you has always been the biggest risk I ever took, but it's had the biggest reward I could've never imagined. I can't wait to do life with you for the next hundred years and watch you be the amazing husband and father you were meant to be.

"Thank you for standing up for me when I couldn't stand up for myself and never doubting that I was worth the effort. I can't imagine, with how much I love you right now, what that love will feel like twenty years in the future, but I can't wait to find out." I slip his matching white gold band onto his finger and press a kiss to the ring before turning my attention to our officiant.

"Well, then," Brewster says, slapping the notebook against his opposite palm. "Let's make this all official-like so we can all go get some food. Yada, yada, power vested and all that shit. Kiss your woman, Graham."

Graham's mouth falls open at his brother-in-law's words. "Remind me to be that sentimental when you need someone to—."

I cut him off by grabbing the lapels of his jacket, yanking him to me for a kiss. He's surprised for only a split second before he's kissing me back, his arms wrapping around me, as cheers and applause sound from the group gathered to help us celebrate today.

When he breaks the kiss, he wears a big goofy grin, and we turn to face our friends and family as Brewster announces us. We make our way down the aisle to the sound of applause from all the people who love us.

There's no dancing, and the reception is sedate. It's truly more like a family dinner, with lots of laughter, dirty jokes, and good food. Graham leans over with a bite of pie on his fork and extends it in my direction. I wrap my lips around the tines of the fork as he slides it out of my mouth. "Well, you're stuck with me." He digs into his jacket pocket and extends an envelope to me. "I hope a wedding gift will cushion the blow that you're never getting away from me again."

I offer him a thoughtful frown as I take it. "I didn't know we were doing gifts. I didn't get you anything."

The smile he returns mine with is sweet and makes my heart ache. "You gave me everything I could ever want. Now, if you don't like it, we can do something else, but just know, it will probably be a pain in the ass. But I am a lawyer, so we'd figure it out."

I open the envelop with a confused chuckle and blink at the papers as I unfold them. When it registers, my eyes go wide. "You bought an apartment?"

He nods. "In the same building. The layout is the same as that guy you work with except this one is four bedrooms instead of three. I figured, that way I could have a dedicated office and a room for the baby and if by some chance you let me knock you up again after this, that kid will also have their own room too."

I open my mouth to tell him it's too much because I know the ballpark of what a one-bedroom in my building costs, so I can only imagine the price of a four-bedroom, but he holds up his hand. "Don't even start. You love the building and the neighborhood. It's close to both of our offices." He leans a bit closer. "I don't know if you know this, but I'm a rich, handsome lawyer."

I snort. "And so humble, too."

"Nah. You're the only one who's ever been able to humble me."

Looking down at the pages again, I shake my head. "I can't believe you did this."

He puts his hand on my belly. "I told you I was all in. I meant it. I want to make a home with you. One that we fill with things that we both love. I want to make memories with our family there. I want you to feel safe and I know you feel safe there."

I bring my hand to his face as I look into his eyes. "I feel safe when I'm with you. I don't think it would've mattered if it was in a cardboard box."

He feigns annoyance. "Oh, now you tell me. I could've saved so much money."

"Too late now," I quip with a grin. "You've gone and given me my dream space. You can't take it back now."

He drops his forehead to mine. "Wouldn't think of it."

CHAPTER THIRTY

AUGUSTA

"Okay, so you'll want to make sure you're keeping up with those stretches I showed you. And if, after the next practice or game, you feel like that hamstring is tightening up again, you can also do a soak, alright?"

One of the kickers for the football team, a junior, nods. "Thanks, Augusta."

As he climbs off the table, the receptionist, Parker, sticks her head in the trainers' room. "Augusta, you have a visitor."

Knowing I don't have anyone scheduled for the rest of the day since I'm taking off after this, I frown. "Who is it?"

"She says she's your mother."

I blink. I haven't seen or heard from my mother since they hauled Carrie away in handcuffs almost five months ago. As if sensing my unease, the baby kicks up into my ribs and I inhale a sharp breath. Seeing the look of shock on my face, Parker frowns. "You want me to send her away? I know you're getting ready to leave. I can tell her you're already gone."

I'm shaking my head before she's even done speaking. "No. That's okay. I'll talk to her. Is there an exam room empty?"

"Uh, yeah. Room two is open. Want me to stick her in there?"

"Please. I'll be with her soon." She nods, flitting off, and I take a deep breath. I head to my locker to gather my things and make myself take longer than I actually need since I no longer rush to do anything she wants. I only do that for family, and she's proven she's no family of mine.

When I enter the room a few minutes later, I don't bother setting my things down. No way she gets the courtesy of thinking I'm happy to sit around and shoot the shit with her. I close the door behind me, leaning against the wall beside it, ready to make a hasty getaway if needed. Resting my hands on my almost eight months pregnant belly, I level her with an indifferent gaze. "What can I do for you? I was actually on my way out."

My mother, who looks as put together as always, sits perched on the edge of a chair in the corner, her legs crossed demurely at the ankles, not a dark hair out of place in her chignon. Despite the August heat, she's wearing dressy black slacks and a cream-colored, long-sleeved silk blouse and low heels with a strand of pearls around her neck.

I no longer own pearls.

"I came to ask you to have the charges dropped against Carrie."

A sharp bark of shocked laughter falls from my mouth and my heart rate ratchets up. "No."

Her expression hardens. "After everything I've done for you? I've never asked you for anything. You can do this. I know you have connections to have her released. She belongs with her children."

"She belongs exactly where she is. And if it's up to me, she'll spend years there. It still won't give me back everything she's taken from me, but I'll at least feel safe. Mason will be safe. His children and mine will be safe."

She opens her mouth and I shake my head. "No. You came here to talk? Let's talk, *Mom*. You want to talk about everything you've done for me? Are you talking about how you said I was a drunken mistake and Carrie was the only daughter you had? Are you talking about how you body shamed me my entire life? Are you talking about how you turned a blind eye to the abuse I suffered because of Carrie? You wanted only one daughter; you have one. And it sure as shit isn't me. You and I are not family.

"Despite the fact you saw the same thing everyone else did the night before my wedding, you refuse to believe it. Carrie threatened to kill me and she would've done it, too. She pushed me down the stairs when I was pregnant last time and you didn't even doubt her when she said otherwise. You're not stupid and you're not blind or deaf. You didn't even check on me after."

She doesn't react to my accusations or the venom in my tone, but merely fingers her pearls as she lifts an eyebrow. "You've always been so dramatic, Augusta. You setting up those cameras in an elaborate ruse to frame Carrie proves it. Did you know she's not even allowed to see her children? Mason has abandoned her and won't allow us to see the children. Do you know how that feels?"

"You expect me to feel sorry for you? You've brought this on yourself. Maybe if you acknowledged how dangerous Carrie is and took responsibility for your part in her turning out the way she has, things might be different. You coming here to fight for Carrie without even contacting me for the last five months just proves you don't care about anyone but her and yourself."

I turn to grab the handle and she speaks, her words stopping me. "Then why did you keep coming back all those years? If we were so terrible to you, why come back at all? If you knew you weren't wanted, why torture yourself trying to force a relationship with all of us?"

I blow out a breath and face her again, blinking back tears of rage. "Truthfully? Spite. Mostly to spite her, but you, too. To prove to you all that no matter what you did, how you'd try to knock me down, I'd get back up. But don't worry, I won't be back. You don't have to see me ever again. In fact, I don't want to see you ever again. You will never see any member of my family. You wanted me to disappear from your life and not be an embarrassment to you simply because my father was a janitor and I occupy a bigger body? That's fine.

"I knew a long time ago there was nothing I could ever do that would make me acceptable to you. It didn't matter how talented or smart or successful I was, I was never going to be good enough for you. But I no longer give a shit what you deem acceptable or good enough. And I'll be damned if my child ever feels an ounce of the ridicule I felt my entire life."

She stands, her eyes cold. "You know, if it weren't for David, you would've been put in foster care. At least I put a roof over your head. You had clothes on your back and shoes on your feet and food on the table. You ought to be thanking me that I took you in."

"With you as mother, foster care probably would've been a kindness. I probably would've needed less therapy. If you're done, I have plans I can't be late for."

Her jaw clenches but she doesn't say anything else and I wrench open the door. I leave the room, not bothering to look over my shoulder as I exit the building. I don't run—I couldn't if I wanted to—but I walk as quickly as I can to my car. Knowing Carrie is behind bars, I'm no longer afraid to drive, even if I did have a few panic attacks after Graham helped me pick it out.

When I pull up at the curb at our building fifteen minutes later, Graham is waiting and wastes no time jumping into the passenger seat. After a quick kiss hello, I take off. "Sorry I'm late. My mother stopped by just before I was supposed to leave."

He's in the middle of pulling the seatbelt across his chest, and freezes for a beat as he absorbs my words. "What?"

"Yeah."

"It's been five months. What could she want? Are you okay?"

I nod. "I'm fine. I finally said everything I've wanted to say to her for years, so I feel great. But she came by to ask me to have the charges dropped against Carrie."

"The fuck? Is she delusional?"

I sigh. "Must be. She was all torn up because Carrie hasn't seen the kids and Mason's abandoned her and won't let my parents see the kids anymore."

"Does she not realize it's her fault they don't see them?"

"That's what I told her. I don't think I'll ever see her again."

Even out of the corner of my eye, I see his brow furrow in concern. "And you're sure you're okay? Do you need me to drive?"

I give him a smile. "No. I am perfect. I'm excited about going to Gemma and Brewster's and can't wait to see the kids. Plus, Mason and his kids will be there, too, so I think it'll be really good for all of them. Maybe he'll loosen up a little and we can all get the kids to stop calling me Gus. That would be amazing."

He chuckles. "Okay. If you say so."

"I do. Did you happen to get the crib put together today?"

Graham nods. "Yeah. And you were right, it looks better against that other wall. There's just better flow with the other furniture."

"Told ya."

"Yeah, yeah. We know. You're always right."

"Not always, but enough that there is precedent."

He takes my hand across the console. "You know, we still have to name this kid."

"The kid in question is a *she*, remember? We have to name our daughter."

"I know. I'm still shocked you wanted to find out. What was your dad's name? I know you said his middle name was Wesley, but what was his first name?"

"Shane."

He nods. "That's a cool name. Let's go with that. Shane Hopkins. I like it."

"Really?" I ask, unable to hide my surprise. We've been back and forth about baby names for months, but this one he automatically loves?

"Yeah. It's badass. Girls that have guy names are automatically cooler when they get older."

I snort. "Yeah, because I'm worried about the cool factor."

"You should be. We can't choose a name that's going to get her ostracized. I mean, why do you think names like Bertha and Bessie and Martha don't get chosen for girls much anymore? They're old lady names. Shane, on the other hand, is infinitely cool. We'd just need a middle name to go with it."

"Marilyn," I reply without hesitation.

He blinks. "Mom? I figured you'd want to use Gemma's name."

I give him a soft smile. "Maybe for the next one?"

He nods. "Deal. Mom's going to die."

"She can't die. I need her lasagna recipe."

He laughs. "That's probably the only way you'll get it, I'm afraid."

EPILOGUE

GRAHAM — FIVE YEARS LATER

"Auggie, will you read this? You do all the voices the best," six-year-old Julie asks when Augusta returns from her third trip to the bathroom in an hour. Our niece holds up a weathered copy of *The Polar Express*, a hopeful smile on her face. I glance up from where I'm helping our daughters—five-year-old Shane and three-year-old Reese—decorate Christmas cookies, along with eight-year-old Collier and nine-year-old Wesley. Fourteen-year-old Amelia sits in the upholstered chair in the corner scrolling through her phone while eleven-year-old Wade sits on the sofa with Mason and my parents watching *White Christmas*.

Augusta smiles and takes the book from her. "I'm only the best because your dad's not here. But I'll take the win."

She walks over to the sofa and slowly lowers herself, supporting her large belly. She blows out a breath and Dad chuckles. "Augusta, you think you're going to make it three more weeks? I'm thinking that baby might have other plans."

She shrugs. "We'll just have to see, Thomas. My money's on Gemma going before me."

As if summoned, Brewster walk into the apartment holding a sleeping two-year-old Lanny as he trails a heavily pregnant Gemma. Mason rises from the sofa and rushes over to take the gifts from my sister's arms. She offers him a warm smile and friendly kiss on the cheek as she hands them off.

"Mommy, Auggie's going to read Polar 'Spress. Want to come sit?" Julie asks, patting the sofa next to her.

"Sorry, peanut. I think if I sit, I won't be able to get back up for a while. I'm sure Daddy will come sit, though, as soon as he puts Lanny down for his nap. I'm going to see what kinds of goodies Uncle Graham's got going over here."

She makes her way over to the kitchen island and Reese holds out a cookie that might actually be more frosting and sprinkles than cookie itself. "Here, Auntie Gem. I made this one just for you."

Gemma's smile is wide when she accepts it. "Oh, Reesey, it's beautiful. Thank you so much."

"Welcome," she replies, jumping off the stool she's been kneeling on to join her mother and cousin on the couch.

Shane eyes the crowd on the sofa before returning her attention to the cookie. She's methodical and calculating and shares my aversion to large groups. Gemma drops a kiss on the top of her dark head then closes the distance between us to gives me a warm hug. "Holding down the fort, I see."

"For now. At least until the sugar kicks in for the heathens. How was the party?"

"Good," she says, stretching her back. "We all got a Christmas bonus, so that'll put a dent in the addition to the house."

I snort a laugh. "Oh, please. We both know you're still flush from all that money you won at the casino all those years ago. You've invested well and from what Brewster said, you've hardly touched it."

She rolls her eyes. "Listen, I like to have a plan. I like to keep everything in line. Plus, I've got to have somewhere to put all these kids my husband insists we have."

Brewster looks up from the couch, a smirk on his face. "Last I checked, you don't object to making 'em, Pearl." He pumps his eyebrows and my mother tosses a pillow at his face.

Gemma levels narrowed eyes at her husband. "This is the last one, Brewster Lincoln."

"That's what you said last time," Augusta reminds her.

"So did you," she quips.

"Touché," my wife says with a smile.

I nudge her with my elbow. "Oh, come on. You love it. I mean, just look at Christmas alone. We're going to need to rent an event space just to hold all of us."

She laughs. "Probably. But this one really is the last one. Two boys and two girls are plenty for me."

"Yeah, dad to three girls sounds pretty good to me, too."

She leans her elbows on the counter and sways, attempting to take some of the strain off her back. "If you had asked me twenty years ago when Brew and I met if I ever saw anything like this, I would've said you were insane."

"Right? I never would've imagined anything like this."

My baby sister peers up at me. "And now look at us. It's a pretty sweet life we lead, big brother."

"Don't I know it. Thanks for being roommates with Augusta during freshman year of college. Otherwise, I wouldn't have my family."

She chuckles. "Don't sell yourself short. Someone would've eventually wanted your grumpy butt."

I stare out toward our enormous family—that now includes Mason and the kids—and shake my head. "Yeah, but it wouldn't have been this family, and this is the only one I'd ever want."

"Daddy, you think my cookie looks okay?" Shane asks, her big brown eyes searching mine.

I round the counter and bend down until we're shoulder to shoulder. "I think that might be the most perfect cookie on the planet, sweetie."

"You do one now."

"Ooh, me, too," Brewster says as he jogs over. "Can I do one, Shane?"

"Everyone can do one, Uncle Brew."

He grins. "Sounds good to me. Can you show me how to do the sprinkles to make them look like ornaments like you did?"

"Sure."

Gemma stands up straight with a groan. "I think I'm finally ready to sit." She pats Brewster on the arm. "Want to bring me a cookie once you get it decorated?"

He drops a kiss onto her lips. "You got it. Go rest. You need to put your feet up."

She rolls her eyes. "And you need to stop getting me pregnant."

He laughs. "I don't remember you complaining about what got you there."

Shane lasts about thirty more seconds before she finally gets bored and then it's just my brother-in-law and me decorating cookies. "You got your appointment scheduled yet?" I ask.

"Yeah, for about two weeks after Gemma's due date. You?"

"Three weeks after. Think you'll change your mind before that?"

"Nah. Four is plenty. If we were younger, I might say we'd have more, but I think Gemma's tired of being called 'geriatric' when she goes in for her appointments."

I laugh. "Augusta, too. She gets so offended. Like forty is old."

"Tell me about it. Most days, I still feel twenty-five." He considers. "Well, I take that back. When I get on the trampoline with the kids, I definitely feel all of my forty-three years."

"Yeah. I don't remember things being so loud when we were younger. After we took the kids to *Disney on Ice*, were your ears ringing after?"

"No, but ask me when I'm your age and I might say yes."

"I'm only two years older than you," I remind him.

"Yeah, but all that lawyering is so hard on your system. It's gotta put, what, five, ten extra years on you?"

I snort. "Oh, excuse me. We can't all be carefree radio talk show hosts. See if I offer to look over your contracts ever again."

He laughs, nudging me like the brother he's become over the two decades he's been in Gemma's life. "You've turned out to not be such a pretentious prick, you know that?"

I can't help the bark of laughter that works its way up my throat. "And you've turned out to not be such a pain in the ass, either. You make cute kids, at least."

He nods. "Thank God for that. I'm just glad they look more like your sister."

"Yeah, I don't think they'd look good with beards." We both crack up as contentment washes over me. Brewster reaches into his pocket to check his phone, his smile faltering. "Everything okay?"

He shrugs. "It's just Lawson."

I nod, understanding dawning. "Gotcha. How's he holding up?"

He's quiet for a long moment as he chooses his words. "Eh, some days are better than others. I'm sure none of the days are a picnic, but the holidays are even harder. My parents are, no doubt, trying to distract him, but I can't imagine going through what he did."

I let my eyes drift to Augusta and our girls. "Yeah," I agree. "Makes you want to hold your family closer, for sure."

"Definitely. Listen, I'm going to step away to give him a call back. Holler for me if one of the girls goes into labor?" he asks with a grin.

Gemma and Augusta both whip their heads in our direction, nearly identical murderous glares on their faces. I stand up straighter, pointing at Brewster. "Brewster said it."

He scoffs, eyes wide. "Thanks for the solidarity, bro."

"Yeah, no. They're a helluva lot scarier than you." I offer my wife and sister a wide, placating smile. "Ladies, can I get you anything?"

ALSO BY RACHAEL OGLE

Until Duet

Until August and onto Forever (Until Books 1 & 2)

Summer Lovin' Series

Fake it to Forever (Summer Lovin' Books 1 & 2)

Knox County Series

My Ada Mae (Knox County Book 1)

Not Your Girl (Knox County Book 2)

Change My Life (Knox County Book 3)

Crash Into Me (Knox County Book 4)

Talk of the Town Series

Talk of the Town (Talk of the Town Book 1)

ABOUT THE AUTHOR

For as long as she can remember, Rachael has been a voracious reader. At the age of eleven, she discovered her grandmother's stash of clench-cover romance novels and she was forever changed. A lover of many, many fictional men and one very non-fictional one, she strives to write real and emotional characters who always get their happily ever after. Rachael lives in East Tennessee with her husband and two sons on their family farm. When she's not tackling her endless TBR, she can be found drinking all the coffee in existence.

www.ingramcontent.com/pod-product-compliance
Lightning Source LLC
Chambersburg PA
CBHW050146120726
47903CB00002B/509